# SOMETHING about YOU

## J. NATHAN

Edited by Stephanie Elliot

Proofread by Gem's Precise Proofreads

Cover Design by Y'all. That Graphic.

Cover Photo by Michelle Lancaster @Lanefotograf

Cover Model Anthony Patamisi

First Edition June 2021

For my son.<br>
May hard work and dedication make<br>
all of your dreams come true.

## 1

## SHAY

I hurried down the third-floor hallway, pulling a large plastic storage bin behind me while balancing a cardboard box in my arm. I could've left the box outside the dorm where my Uber dropped me off. But, where I came from, you didn't leave your things unattended or someone would've claimed them as their own.

"Ummmph," I cried as the box in my hand flew up in the air and unceremoniously crashed to the floor sending my belongings scattering all over.

"Watch it," the girl I'd collided with said as she continued down the hall without even stopping to help me retrieve my things.

I glared at her retreating form, making a mental note of the swaying hips, too short cutoffs, and perfectly curled blonde hair cascading down to her butt. I needed to know who I should avoid at all costs at Cranmore University.

As if reading my thoughts, she glanced over her shoulder for a split second. Of course, she had to be beautiful. Why did the mean ones always get good genes? "Loser," she mumbled as she disappeared into a room on the right.

I shoved my glasses up my nose, only to have them slip back down as I dropped to my knees in the middle of the hallway. I glanced around me, but despite all the open doors lining the hallway and the music drifting through them, the hallway was empty. I grabbed the framed photo of me and my mom that had landed in front of me, careful not to look at it for too long. Today was supposed to be a good day. A new start. No need to let in the sad memories. I stuffed it into the box then scooped up my trophies for academic decathlon that lay on opposite sides of me. I quickly shoved them into the box, embarrassed two trophies brought me such pride.

"Excuse me."

I glanced up to find a pretty brunette with her parents trying to get by me with boxes in their arms.

"Sorry," I mumbled as I pushed my things to the side so they could pass by.

"Need some help?" the father asked with pity in his eyes.

I lowered my head and mumbled, "I've got it."

They didn't force their assistance on me and moved to the girl's room as I stuffed a few of my notebooks, the refurbished laptop I saved enough money to buy (praying it hadn't been destroyed), and some small trinkets into the box.

I pushed myself to my feet with the box in my arm and searched the room numbers, spotting room 333 ahead on the right. I grabbed hold of my bin and moved to it. I halted in the doorway. The family who'd just passed me hurried around the room unpacking and decorating.

"Hey," the dad said with a smile when he noticed me standing there. "We know you."

I forced a smile before glancing to the brunette who I

now realized was my roommate Kendall. Her social media account didn't do her justice. She looked like she could be a model. Maybe she was. Given her wide eyes taking in my long brown braids and five-foot-two, ninety pounds stature, she was just as surprised by my meek appearance. We'd spoken via DM, but it didn't take long to realize we were exact opposites. She'd be pledging a sorority, and I'd hopefully be volunteering for the science department in a lab until all hours of the night. "Hi, Kendall."

Her eyes softened. "Shay?"

I nodded, trying my best to give off the impression that I was like all the other college freshmen super stoked to be living the college life. Don't get me wrong. I was happy to be on my own and starting over. But not the way others were. They saw no supervision, late nights without questions, and parties. I saw freedom from daily stress and the unknown.

"What happened out there?" Kendall's mom asked. "Did your box give way?"

"That's what I get for using cardboard," I lied.

She eyed my box and container. "Would you like help bringing up the rest of your things?"

I blushed. "This is all I have."

"Oh," she said, suddenly looking as uncomfortable as I felt.

"I'm low maintenance. I need very little to survive," I continued, hoping I hadn't insulted my new roommate who seemed to have triple the things I had.

Kendall's dad smiled. "I tell Kendall all the time that less is more."

Kendall rolled her eyes at her dad and then looked to me. "I'm relieved you're a minimalist. Where would all my stuff go otherwise?" She smiled, and I realized that maybe having a roommate who was my opposite would work out better than having a roommate who was as neurotic about school and succeeding as I was.

"Kendall said you're from Colorado," her mother said as she unpacked Kendall's bed linens.

"About thirty minutes from here."

"Wanted to stay close to home?" her dad asked.

*Nope.* "I actually received a full scholarship, so it was a no-brainer."

"Full scholarship?" Kendall asked. "I didn't know that. What's your major?"

"Biochemistry."

Her eyes widened. "So, you can help me with my science classes?"

"Absolutely."

"I sense the beginning of a great friendship," her father said.

I expected sarcasm when I looked to Kendall. But, instead, she just smiled. "Me too."

Relief swept over me telling me—despite the rude girl interaction—that this was going to be a great first year of college after all.

———

Bass of a rap song next door rattled our wall. I'd covered my ears with headphones hours ago. I'd tried to sleep with a pillow over my head. But nothing drowned out the sound—or the vibration of the wall against my bed. I grabbed my phone from the desk beside me. Two in the freaking morning. Now, I wasn't opposed to other people having fun. I got it. This was college. This was the first time most of these kids had been on their own. But classes started in a few hours. And since I had all seven o'clock classes, I wasn't going to be able to function if this kept up. Maybe they didn't even realize how loud it was. I glanced to Kendall's bed. She was sound asleep. The girl clearly slept like a rock.

The song ended and laughter drifted through the wall. I breathed a sigh of relief knowing I could handle laughter. But all too soon the familiar sound of bass returned.

*That's it!*

I kicked my feet out from beneath my worn comforter and trudged into the hallway until I stood outside the room next door. I wasn't trying to be a buzzkill, but it was late and I needed to sleep. I banged on the door with the side of my fist so they could hear me over the music. I waited. The music sounded even louder in the hallway. Hadn't anyone else complained?

The door flew open and the blonde who I'd collided with earlier stood there in only a T-shirt glaring at me. "What?" she snapped.

"I was hoping you could turn down your music. I've got a seven o'clock class, and I really need to sleep."

"No."

My head whipped back. "No?"

"No," she repeated before her eyes drifted over my pajamas. "Are those footie pajamas?"

I glanced down at my pajama choice. "Yes."

She burst out laughing. "Oh. My. *God.*"

"What?" the guy in her room asked as he pulled her door open the rest of the way. "Oh."

*Whoa.* His ruffled dark hair, very bare chest, sleeve of tattoos, and boxers set me off balance for a second. I'd never been that close to a nearly naked guy—not to mention one that good looking—before.

His blue eyes took in my red footie pajamas. "That's something you don't see every day."

"I just need you to turn down the music," I said to him, hoping to appeal to his sense of reason.

"This is college, Little One," he said.

I gasped. "Little One?"

He chuckled as his eyes once again drifted over my pajamas. "If the shoe fits."

"If the shoe fits," I gritted out, "I'd be calling the two of you inconsiderate assholes. But, I didn't do that, did I? I asked nicely."

"Did she just call us assholes?" the mean girl asked.

"That she did," he said to her before his eyes met mine. "Beat it, geek. You interrupted us, and if there's one thing *I* find inconsiderate, it's being interrupted." And without the slightest show of remorse, he slammed the door in my face.

I stood in the empty hallway stewing. My cheeks pulsed with heat. How had I for even one second paid him the slightest bit of attention? There was nothing worse than people who thought they could do whatever they wanted.

But, they had.

And, the music continued to pound off my wall until I left for class the next morning at six-thirty showing me they had no plans to back down.

*Great.*

2

———

SHAY

If my seven o'clock calculus class had been any indication of the rigor of the school work I'd be receiving at Cranmore, bring it on. I sat in the front row of my physics class with my laptop fully charged, and my brain ready to absorb every bit of information Professor Raymond was willing to share. I lived and breathed science and math. It never got old and always required my mind to work overtime. I thrived on the challenge. I yearned for it.

"How'd you sleep?"

My head shot to my right.

The mean guy from next door slid onto the stool beside me at my table with a cocky grin.

Despite his crisp arctic scent wafting its way through my senses, I scooped up my things in one arm and hopped down from my stool. "Not a chance." I walked to the opposite side of the room, taking a seat beside a girl who was typing on her laptop. No way I'd be sitting next to him for an entire semester. Not when I knew what lay beneath the good-looking exterior.

"Okay, ladies and gentlemen," Professor Raymond said

as he walked into class and dropped his briefcase down on the front table. "This is Physics 101. If you're in the wrong place, you best run now because if not, you're in for a hell of a trip."

I smiled as a few students ducked out quickly.

For the next hour, I was in my zone, feeling very much at home amongst terms I knew and knowledge I couldn't get enough of.

"I'll see all of you on Wednesday," Professor Raymond announced as he shut off his presentation. "In the meantime, read pages twenty through fifty in the textbook. There'll be a quick quiz at the start of class, so be on time."

Everyone collected their things and moved to the door. I took my time, hanging back so I could speak to the professor. I approached him once the room cleared out. "Professor Raymond?"

He looked up from his phone. He was younger than he seemed from my seat, the slight gray in his goatee telling me he was probably in his late thirties or early forties. "Yes?"

"I'm Shay Miller."

A smile spread across his face. "*You're* Ms. Miller?"

I nodded.

"Mike Wilson called me about you."

I smiled, knowing my high school physics teacher had made the call.

"He said you'd like to volunteer, maybe in the lab or something," he continued.

"Yes! It's my dream to work in research. I'll even sweep floors if it gets my foot in the door."

He laughed. "We have custodians for that."

"Right."

"Let me think about it," he explained. "I'm sure I could find a role for you."

"Awesome," I said, feeling for the first time that I was right where I was supposed to be.

———

I shot up from a sound sleep that night. The incessant banging on my door had my heart racing and my eyes jumping around my dark room. Kendall's bed was empty. She must've forgotten our door code. I grabbed my glasses and pushed them on, noting it was after midnight on her alarm clock. I climbed out of bed and pulled open the door.

Mean guy stood there with his hands grasping the door frame. "Seriously?" he said.

"What?" I asked, totally confused by his question.

"*You* didn't want to sit next to *me*?"

My lips parted. "You woke me up for this?"

"Yes."

"This is about your ego?"

He dropped his arms from my door frame and crossed them across his chest. "No."

"It is. You can't believe someone doesn't want to be near you."

"Not true."

"Then why the hell are you here?"

"Because I wanted it noted that I was doing you a favor by sitting next to your geeky ass."

"My geeky ass? Is that term used widely or just in your small-minded circle of friends?"

His eyes dropped to my blue footy pajamas. "If the term fits."

"Listen. I can see you struggle. But, let's see if you can understand this." I grabbed hold of my door and slammed it in his face.

I expected him to bang on it. To yell through it. To get mean girl to have his back. But he didn't do any of those things. So, I crawled back into bed and closed my eyes, letting thoughts of mean guy drift from my brain.

And, though I didn't think it was possible, the music that switched on next door was even louder than the night before.

*Asshole.*

3

---

# KASON

I checked the newsfeed on my phone, watching the sick videos of Ousterman catching air on the halfpipe. The guy was a douche, but his tricks were fucking dope. Not that I'd ever admit that to anyone. Especially since I'd be up against him in January in the XGames for slopestyle. I'd qualified in Switzerland back in February. But, with no snow in Colorado until October, getting quality time snowboarding before the Games would be difficult.

"Good morning," Professor Raymond said as he hurried in, running a little late for physics on Wednesday.

It didn't bother me. I sucked at science. But, if I wanted to graduate next year, I'd have to tackle the beast again—because I already failed it last year.

"I hope you all managed to get those pages read because as promised, you have a quiz."

Groans erupted around the room. My eyes darted over my shoulder only to see Little One grinning like a fool. Was she seriously excited about a quiz? She was so damn weird. But I'd give her one thing. She hadn't knocked on Cora's door since Sunday night. And, despite the dark circles under her eyes behind her glasses, she dealt with the noise.

"Once you open your laptops, you'll find the link for the quiz in your emails. Close your laptops when you're finished. You've got fifteen minutes."

*Fuuuuck.*

I opened the quiz link and inwardly cringed. I hadn't read the pages nor would the information have made much sense to me if I had. I knew I struggled with reading. It had been a lifelong thing for me. But I knew how to compensate —usually. Sometimes, I'd used the text reader feature, but with science and math, it didn't help. I stared at my laptop screen, willing the answers to come to me. But after fifteen minutes, I had a feeling I'd need to drop the class. I wanted to be a pro snowboarder. Not a physicist. But if I didn't want my parents to disown me, I needed to get a degree to fall back on. It was the deal I'd made with them long before I had my sponsorship deal with Slopes snowboarding gear. It's why they paid for me to snowboard every weekend since I was ten. Why they hired me a coach to work with me on weekends. Why they paid for my travel to competitions before I had Slopes footing those bills.

"Close your laptops," Professor Raymond said.

I slammed my laptop with a little too much vigor, causing a few students to glance over their shoulders to look at me.

"Now, let's talk Charles's law," Professor Raymond continued. "Who can tell me what it is?"

I glanced around the room, wondering if anyone knew the answer because I sure as hell didn't. Little One's hand shot into the air.

Professor Raymond smiled. "Ah, Ms. Miller."

Ms. Miller? He already knew her name?

"Enlighten us."

"Charles's law is the principle that all gases expand equally for the same rise of temperature if they are held at constant pressure." Professor Raymond opened his mouth to speak, but Little One—Ms. Miller cut him off. "It states that the pressures of all gases increase equally for the same rise of temperature if they are held at constant volume." Professor Raymond again tried to speak, but Ms. Miller continued. "The law is actually now known to only be true for ideal gases."

"I couldn't have said it better myself," Professor Raymond finally said. "Does anyone know where the name stems from?"

Ms. Miller's hand shot into the air. I glanced around but hers was the only one up.

He smirked. "Ms. Miller?"

"The name honors Jacques Charles who experimented with how the volume of gases depended on temperature. It was unfortunate, really, that he never published the work he did back in the late 1700s because others did."

My theory that Little One was a geek had been spot on. *And*, she was a science geek. The best type of geek. At least when I needed help.

*Shay*

I scooped up my things and stuffed them into my backpack, knowing I aced the quiz. I heaved my backpack onto my back and headed for the door. Before I could even step into the hallway, my nemesis stood in front of me, blocking my exit with a skateboard in his hand. "Move," I said.

"No."

"All I have to do is call for help," I said.

He glanced to the bustling hallway filled with students coming and going behind him. "And what exactly do you need help with?" he asked, his blue eyes shifting back to me. They were such a stark contrast to the black shirt he wore.

I clenched my teeth. "Getting you out of my way."

"Do you know how many girls would very much appreciate me *in* their way?"

I couldn't stop my eyes from rolling. "What do you want?"

"There're a lot of things I want. World peace. A star on the Hollywood Walk of Fame. A gold medal—"

"Seriously?" I huffed, hating him bothering me *and* making me late for my next class. "Some of us need to get to our next class."

"Then stop cutting me off. I need something from you."

I scoffed. "Like a reality check?"

"I'm serious. You seem to get all this physics stuff, and I need to get it."

My brows squished together. "They have these things called books. Why don't you open one and read it?"

His features changed and harsh lines tightened around his eyes. "I'm serious, Little One."

"Don't call me that," I snapped.

"I need your help."

A humorless laugh shot out of me. "*You* need *my* help?"

"Yes," he deadpanned.

"So, let me get this straight. When I asked *you* for help lowering the music so I could sleep, you said no and then proceeded to be an even bigger asshole and turn it up."

His gaze held mine. I could see his bravado wavering as he fought to hold eye contact.

"But now you want *me* to help *you*?"

"Yes."

This guy wasn't only an asshole, he was an idiot. "No." I pushed by him and made my way down the hallway and out of the building, not looking back. Why would I? I already knew I bought myself another night of loud music.

4

———

SHAY

"Hey, any chance you'd wanna go to a party tonight?"

I glanced up from my homework at Kendall sitting on her bed. "Is there anything about me that screams party?"

She laughed. "Come on. All you do is study. You've gotta get out a little."

"Says who?"

"Me. And since I'm your roommate who has the privilege of listening to you snore at night, I think I'm entitled to a night out."

I laughed to myself, appreciating her offering to hang with me, but I knew her sorority pledge class friends were a lot more fun than I'd ever be.

She pointed at me. "I can see you thinking about it."

"Oh, I'm thinking about it all right. I'm thinking about what a terrible idea it is."

She laughed. "Come on, if it sucks you can leave."

"*When* it sucks," I corrected.

"Have an open mind. You're going to be a scientist,

right? Don't you need proof before making determinations?"

"It was a hypothesis."

She rolled her eyes. "*Riiiight.*"

"Where's this party?"

"Off campus."

"I don't have anything to wear," I explained, hoping it got me out of the dreadful night it would inevitably be.

"Sure, you do. Your green T-shirt brings out your pretty green eyes."

My cheeks warmed, uncomfortable with the unexpected compliment. No one had ever called my eyes pretty before. "Maybe."

She squealed. "I'll take it."

I glanced to the photo of my mom and me beside my bed. I'd been five when the photo was taken on my first day of kindergarten. She stood behind me with her hands on my tiny shoulders looking so proud of me in my flowered dress with my lunch box in my hand.

"Is that your mom?" Kendall asked, sensing that my mind had drifted from our party talk to the photo.

I nodded.

"Will she be visiting?"

I shook my head. "She died from cancer when I was six."

"Oh, Shay. I'm so sorry. I had no idea."

I shrugged. "It was a long time ago."

She looked at the photo as if it was the first time she'd ever really looked at it. "You look like her."

I grinned, happy to know Kendall could see it. People always said that over the years. And, it made me feel close to her even though I'd lost her so young.

"And, you wore braids back then too," she observed with a smile.

"She used to braid my hair every morning," I said, the vision of those days materializing in my mind's eye. "I'd sit on the floor between her legs, and she'd just go to work on my hair."

"That's why you still wear them," she said.

I considered her words, knowing without a doubt that it was the truth.

———

We stepped out of the Uber in front of an off-campus house. Music blared inside the two-story house and lights cast through the front windows that were devoid of curtains or blinds. People stood outside on the front lawn while others inside could be seen through the windows.

Kendall wore cutoffs and a pretty sleeveless top. I glanced down at my green T-shirt, jeans, and black combat boots that I never left home without.

"You look great," Kendall assured me.

I appreciated her trying to make me feel comfortable with my wardrobe, but it was unnecessary. I was never one to try to fit in. Why bother when I stuck out like a sore thumb?

We made our way up the walkway to a group of girls who beckoned her over. Kendall glanced to me before we approached her friends. "If we get split up, text me to let me know where you are."

"And don't forget, if I'm not having fun, I'm outta here. Which should be in about ten minutes."

She laughed. "It's my mission in life to get you to have fun."

I scoffed. "Good luck with that."

She greeted her friends who swiftly wrapped her in hugs as if they hadn't seen her in years. They shot me polite glances before we made our way inside the house. The music was even louder inside and people holding red cups filled the hallway and rooms. I glanced around, not recognizing a single person in the house.

"Let's get drinks," one of Kendall's friends announced.

My stomach dropped a little. I knew this was college, but I didn't drink—meaning I did it like once in my life. And, I only took a couple of sips of beer. There was a genetic predisposition to addiction, so I knew I didn't want to go down that destructive road.

We followed Kendall's friends into the kitchen and found the keg in the corner. One of them filled the cups, handing one to each of us. I took mine for show, at least trying to fit in. We moved into the living room. People were crammed on a sofa watching a huge television. On screen, snowboarders flew over hills, flipping and doing tricks mid-air. "That's Colorado for you," I said to Kendall beside me.

"What?"

"Guys more into snowboarding than all the pretty girls who showed up to the party."

"Don't you know who lives here?" she asked.

I shook my head.

She leaned into my ear. "Kason McCloud."

"Who's Kason McCloud?"

"An *amazing* snowboarder. He's heading to the X Games in January. Not to mention he's drop-dead gorgeous."

"Little One?" a deep voice called from behind me.

A cold chill rushed up my spine.

"That's him," Kendall whispered to me.

I pulled in a breath then slowly turned to face my neme-sis...Kason McCloud.

He glared at me from across the room.

It made sense now. The shaggy hair. The torn low-hung jeans. The black Slopes snowboarding shirt. The relaxed attitude. The skateboard.

"What are you doing in my house?" he asked.

I fixed a smile in place that actually hurt to hold there. "Partying. What's it look like?" I lifted my cup to my lips and downed the contents for show. Probably not the best idea since I didn't drink and weighed one hundred pounds soaking wet, but desperate times called for desperate measures.

He raised a brow, and I couldn't tell if he was pissed or amused. "Is that so?"

I lifted my chin, giving the impression that I could handle his intimidation if that's what he planned. "Yup."

"Well, then, let's get you and your friends a real drink," he said, sending a killer smile at Kendall and her friends who all fell for it hook, line, and sinker.

*Damn him.*

"Let's go, ladies," he said, turning and heading toward another room in the back of the house.

Having no other choice, I followed them. The effects of the beer I'd downed began to radiate in my cheeks. I stepped into what must've once been a dining room. It now had a bar in the corner with lots of liquor bottles on top of it. Kason walked behind the bar and lined up five cups for the five of us girls. He began pouring numerous liquors into each and topped them all off with a splash of something red. He passed them out to the other girls one by one with a smile until he got to my drink. I expected him to spit in it or something, but he simply held it out, beckoning me closer.

I stayed put, too far to reach it but not budging.

His cocky grin told me he wasn't about to deliver it to me.

*God, I hated him.*

Kendall snatched the drink from his hand and handed it to me.

Kason laughed, and I'm sure he knew we would've stayed in a standoff all night. He stepped out from behind the bar and stopped beside me, leaning into my ear. His cool arctic scent drifted through my senses. "I made yours extra strong."

"Why? Because you don't think I can handle it?"

"No. Because it's the only one you're gonna get. Finish your drink and get the hell out."

I sucked in a sharp breath as high school memories flooded my brain. I hadn't been welcome at any of the cool kids' parties back then. I guess a new location didn't change the fact that I didn't fit in anywhere I went. Well, I had news for Mr. Hotshot Snowboarder. A new place *did* mean a new attitude. And this Shay didn't give a damn. "I guess you'll have to throw me out in front of all your guests then because I'm not leaving. I came here to have fun, and fun I'm gonna have."

He said nothing, though his eyes seemed to darken and his jaw ticked. "We'll see about that." He walked off and I released the breath I'd unknowingly been holding.

"You know Kason McCloud?" Kendall asked, rushing over to me to get the information.

"He's the reason our next-door neighbor plays her music so damn loud at night," I explained.

"She does?" Kendall asked, completely oblivious to the torture I'd been through.

"It seems she and Mr. Snowboarder have a thing going on," I explained.

"Well, that sucks," she said, looking completely let down. "What was he just saying to you? Looked like you guys were talking about more than music."

I sipped my drink, wincing at the strength of it. He hadn't been lying. *Asshole.* "Nothing important."

A few of Kendall's friends played ping pong in the basement, so we spent the next hour or so watching them. The guys they played against were also snowboarders, according to what Kendall told me. Seemed that these guys, along with Kason, were training for the XGames which were held in Aspen in January. I wondered why, if Kason was this pro snowboarder, he even bothered being in school—and why he cared if he passed physics?

"What's she doing here?" a high-pitched voice called from somewhere nearby.

I glanced over my shoulder to find my next-door neighbor wobbling over. Her eyes were shooting daggers my way. *Great.* I turned away from her, not giving her the satisfaction.

"Combat boots?" our neighbor slurred as she stepped in front of me, her nose scrunched in distaste at the sight of my boots. "Do you sleep in those things—oh wait. No, you don't. You sleep in footie pajamas."

It was as if I'd been doused with a bucket of ice-cold water. I wasn't someone who liked attention. Hell, I avoided it at all costs trying to blend into the scenery. But, this bitch just wouldn't quit. "Yup. I do. They're so comfy."

"Just leave," she snarled. "No one wants you here."

Kendall pivoted and crossed her arms. "I want Shay here. So do my friends."

"Oh, look how sweet," she scoffed. "It's the protect-the-nerd-brigade."

I wanted to die. I wanted to crawl into a hole and die knowing every eye in that basement was on us.

"Cora!" Kason called.

All eyes in the basement looked to him standing halfway down the stairs, including my next-door neighbor who I realized now was Cora.

"I've been looking for you, babe," Kason continued. "Come upstairs."

Without another glance, Cora took off for the stairs, her steps just as wobbly but enough to carry her to Kason.

With Cora gone and the air that she sucked out of the room returning, I chugged the rest of my drink and looked to Kendall. "Thank you."

"There's nothing worse than a mean girl." She shrugged. "But I guess someone has to play the role."

We stayed in the basement for another hour, downing more drinks and watching more games of ping pong. The effects of the alcohol started to make things a little fuzzy, and I knew I was done. Needing the bathroom, I made my way upstairs a little unsteady. I ducked my head into every open door.

"It's upstairs," a guy I recognized from a game of ping pong called.

"What?"

"The bathroom. That's what you're looking for, isn't it?"

I nodded.

"It's the room at the end of the hallway. Don't mind the mess."

"Thanks." I climbed the stairs and hurried down the hallway to the open door at the end, relieved to find it unoc-cupied. After taking care of business, I stared at myself in the mirror while washing my hands. I was definitely drunk. I almost didn't recognize myself.

What was I doing there?

I clearly didn't fit in. I'd been told twice I wasn't wanted there. But what the old Shay wouldn't have done was stick up for herself. I was proud of myself for doing it, but I'd be lying if I said I wasn't braced for the repercussions.

I dried my hands with toilet paper, since there was no towel, and tossed it into the basket. I pulled open the door and gasped, "Jesus Christ."

Kason blocked the doorway with his arms crossed. "Are you done making your point?"

"And what point would that be?" I asked, catching the slight slur in my voice.

"That you do what you want. To hell with everyone."

"I just don't care what bullies like you and Cora think."

His head shot back. "Bullies?"

"Bullies. You think you can push everyone around and treat us badly because we're nobodies."

"Need I remind you how badly you treated *me* when I asked you for help?" he challenged.

I balked. "Like you were actually hurt."

"Not hurt. Pissed."

I crossed my arms. "Well, you should be happy to know, I'm getting ready to leave your party. No more loser spoiling your fun."

"You're not a loser."

I cocked my head. "Right."

"You're a bitch, but not a loser."

I laughed to myself. I could handle that.

5

———

## SHAY

I kicked the blankets off my legs as a clammy sweat covered my body. It was my own fault for drinking the amount of alcohol I'd drank. It was clearly trying to escape my body from every lowly pore. I rolled into the center of the bed, hitting something hard—and human.

I sprang up, falling off the side of the bed and landing with a thud on the carpet. Carpet? My dorm room didn't have carpet.

My eyes shot around the unfamiliar room. Snowboards stood in all corners of the space.

*Oh. My. God.*

I looked down at the bra and panties I wore and grabbed for the blanket on the bed to cover myself.

*Ohmigod. Ohmigod. Ohmigod.*

"It's too early," a gravelly voice grumbled.

I froze.

Please no.

Please. *God.* No.

I crawled onto my knees with the blanket wrapped around me, peeking at the person in the bed. Kason lay on his stomach in nothing but boxers, his face turned toward me on the pillow but his eyes closed.

Maybe he was asleep. Maybe he was sleep-talking.

Yup. Going with that.

I searched the room, desperate to find my clothes and boots. I climbed to my feet and tiptoed around the room, snatching my shirt off the dresser, my jeans off the floor, and my boots from the floor by the door.

"Do you really think I don't hear you?" he mumbled.

"Go back to sleep," I whispered. "You're having a dream. A very bad dream."

"My dreams don't usually contain you, Little One. But after last night..."

I chucked my boot at his back with all the strength I had.

He sprang up, shooting daggers at me. "What the hell?"

"That's what *I'm* thinking," I growled, trying to keep my voice low for fear of anyone hearing me. "I would never, even if my life depended on it, come in here willingly. Did you drug me?"

His hair was all disheveled and his eyes sleepy. "Drug you? Are you crazy?" He scrubbed his hands up and down his face.

"How else would I end up in here?" My eyes cast down at the blanket wrapped around me and I felt sick to my stomach. "Wearing only this?"

"It's actually a really funny story."

I held up my palm. "Stop."

He threw his legs off the side of his bed and rested his elbows on his knees, not saying anything for a change.

"Did we?" I cringed, every fiber of my being braced for the worse possible response.

His lips tipped into a cocky grin. "*We* didn't. But, you did make *me* a very happy man."

It was as if the floor dropped out from beneath my feet. "Why?" The word barely left my mouth as the thought of me doing anything to make him happy made my stomach churn.

"*Why?* No girl has ever asked why," he explained. "It's more like, 'when are you gonna let me do that again?'"

My eyes widened and I swallowed hard. "I don't do things like that."

"Well, you did last night—and just know, it was consensual. You were the one initiating it."

"I would *never*."

He shrugged as if he was the innocent victim.

"I don't *forget* things."

"I'm pretty surprised you'd be able to forget something so—"

"I don't like you!" I shouted.

"That's not what you were saying last night."

I closed my eyes, pinching the bridge of my nose. *Wait.* My eyes sprang open. "Where are my glasses?"

He reached for his nightstand, grabbed my glasses, and held them out to me.

Careful not to touch any part of him, I grabbed them and shoved them onto my face. "How did I get in here?" I looked around the room, trying to remember even the slightest memory.

"After we ran into each other outside the bathroom, you asked to see my room."

"I would never ask that."

He shrugged. "You're in here, aren't you?"

I remembered running into him, but then everything grew fuzzy. "You don't even like me."

"I liked you very much last night."

My heart began to throb in my chest. "You have a girlfriend. Where was she?"

"She's not my girlfriend, and she passed out right after I saved your ass from her wrath."

I sucked in a breath remembering that he *had* saved me from her attempt to embarrass me. But that didn't explain why I ended up in his room in only my bra and panties. Nor did it explain why out of everyone at this party, he would want me in his bed. Or why it would ever lead to...something else. It didn't make any sense. I wasn't that kind of girl. "What kind of person takes advantage of a drunk girl?"

His bottom lip jutted out at the notion. "I didn't know you were drunk."

"Bullshit. Sober me would never be into you."

"Don't worry. My ego can handle it."

"I need to get dressed."

"So, get dressed," he said. "It's not like I didn't see you last night. I even have it on video for when I want to relive it."

Blood rushed to my cheeks, the sound gushing in my ears. "You what?"

His lips tipped up in the corners. "You heard me."

I held out my open palm. "Give it to me."

"It's the twenty-first century, Little One. It's not like it's on a tape. It's out there floating in the cloud."

I ground my teeth together, trying to remain calm but knowing it was nearly impossible. I hated him. I hated him with everything I had. "Erase it."

"Nope."

I realized, without a shadow of a doubt, that it was a helpless situation. He was over six feet and double my weight. It wasn't like I could wrestle him for his phone.

And, even if I did manage to somehow get it and destroy the video, he was right. It was out there in the cloud, easily recovered on another device. There was nothing I could do, and that helpless feeling would be the death of me. "I'll sue you."

"For what? I didn't force you on your knees."

My stomach roiled knowing I didn't do things like that. I'd *never* in my right mind do something like that. "I hate you."

"I know."

I chucked my other boot at him, but this time he dodged away from it and it bounced with a couple thuds on the floor behind him.

"Stop that shit. I didn't make you come in here. It wasn't even my idea to record us."

I moved to the opposite side of his bed and sat down so I didn't have to look at his face. I tugged my T-shirt over my head, then shimmied into my jeans before losing the blanket altogether. I shoved my feet into my boots and then walked to the door without looking at him.

"Wait," he called.

I didn't, opening the door and stepping into the hallway.

"Tutor me and I'll erase it."

I stopped short, and the smallest sense of relief washed over me.

6
___

SHAY

"You've gotta get up," Kendall said.

I kept the comforter over my head, not wanting to see or talk to anyone. I was mortified that I had to do the walk of shame that morning. I didn't want Kendall and her friends to think I was that type of girl. Because I wasn't! "Tell me again what happened."

She sighed and dropped down onto the side of my bed making it droop slightly with her weight. "I went looking for you when it was time to go, and I ran into Kason in the upstairs hallway."

"Was he wearing clothes?"

She giggled. "Unfortunately."

"What did he say?"

"He said you'd thrown up in the bathroom, and he was gonna take care of you."

I scoffed. Taking care of me was not exactly what had gone down. Ugh. No pun intended!

"Was I wrong to leave you with him?"

You could say that. "How could you know he was lying."

"Who says he was lying?" she asked. "Just because you don't remember getting sick, it doesn't mean you didn't."

If I'd gotten sick, why hadn't he told me? "I'm sorry this happened."

"Don't be crazy. If you knew how many nights I've spent praying to the porcelain gods, you wouldn't be apologizing."

"I just don't...do that sort of thing." *Like ever.*

"Oh, now I feel guilty for making you come with me."

I pulled the comforter off my head and looked at her guilt-ridden face. "No one's to blame but me. I should know I can't handle my liquor."

My phone pinged somewhere near my bed.

Kendall grabbed it off my desk for me. "It's a text from Snowboard Hottie," she informed me seeing the screen.

"What?" I gasped, the comforter falling off me as I jolted up and checked the screen.

SNOWBOARD HOTTIE

Library. 8. Tomorrow nite.


*Kason*


I chose a table in the far corner of the top floor of the library, hoping no one saw me with Little One. Even though I'd let her believe things had escalated between the two of us, I wasn't about to touch a virgin—because she was *definitely* a virgin. And not *at all* my type. But, I'd be lying if I said I didn't love watching her squirm at the thought of going down on me. Truth be told, it was the only thing I could think of to get her to tutor me. Walking into her leaving my bathroom had set the idea in motion and knowing she was on the verge of passing out, made it happen.

I pushed in my earbuds as I waited for her to show up, blasting the songs I usually practiced to. I closed my eyes and visualized the stunts I wanted to nail at the Games. Visualized the crowd cheering as I landed tricks most only wished they could pull off. Visualized accepting the gold medal after my final run. I was all about positivity when it came to snowboarding. No use worrying that I wouldn't pull off a trick. It was more important to assume I would.

A loud thud on the table followed by a gust of air caused my eyes to spring open. Little One stood there with her arms crossed and a stack of books piled high in front of me.

I tugged the earbuds out of my ears, the music still pouring through them.

"I don't appreciate being ordered around," she growled.

"Noted. Next time I'll give you two choices."

She rolled her eyes and slipped into the seat across from me. She looked different than she had yesterday morning. Less ready to kill me. But, she still wore her glasses and those braids that only looked hot on snow bunnies in beanies. "Open to page twenty. I assume you didn't bother to read it."

"Was I your first?" I asked, totally wanting to watch her get fired up.

She glanced up, pegging me with her eyes. "If this is how you plan to spend our tutoring session, you aren't going to learn anything."

"So, you're not gonna tell me?"

She closed her eyes, and I could see the irritation grasping hold of her features. She was trying to stay calm even though I knew all she wanted to do was put in her time and get the video—the one that didn't actually exist.

And, as much fun as I was having teasing her, *she* wasn't having fun. Since I wasn't a complete douchebag—and I needed her help, I stopped. "Okay. Page twenty." I opened my book to the page.

"Take a look at the equation at the bottom. Do you see where it talks about orbital speed?"

I nodded.

"It's explaining that the speed required of a satellite to remain in an orbit around a central body—like a planet or the sun—is dependent upon the radius of orbit and the mass of the central body. The equation expressing the relationship between these variables is derived by combining circular motion definitions of acceleration with Newton's law of universal gravitation."

"It's like you're speaking a different language."

Her shoulders deflated.

"I never said this would be easy."

"Okay. So, look at the equation. $v = SQRT (G \cdot M_{central} / R)$ where $M_{central}$ is the mass of the central body about which the satellite orbits, R is the radius of orbit and G is $6.673 \times 10^{-11} \ N \cdot m^2/kg^2$."

"Can we maybe start with what radius is?"

"Are you joking?"

"Am I smiling?" I deadpanned.

"Radius is a line segment extending from the center of a circle or sphere to the circumference."

"Oh, right," I said, kind of remembering that from a high school math class.

She spent the next hour reviewing terms I'm sure everyone knew but me. And, while I knew it annoyed her to no end to have to start from jump, she did it without complaining.

"You're really smart," I said at the end of our session as she stuffed the books back into her backpack.

"You're really dumb," she countered, though I knew she didn't mean it. She just hated me.

"I'm dyslexic," I explained, watching the realization cross her features for a split second before she squashed it. "I hide it well. All the tutors my parents hired couldn't help, so chances are you won't be able to either."

"Sounds like a challenge," she said without looking at me. "How have you been able to get by?"

"By talking pretty girls into doing my work for me."

She glanced at me, her eyes narrowed.

"Joking. Sort of."

She shook her head, put off by my words I assumed.

"I've got techniques I use," I explained.

"Like what?"

"Dictation apps and flashcards. But since I'm super busy traveling most of the time, studying kinda falls by the wayside."

"Why are you even in school if your focus is snowboarding?"

I leaned back in my seat and crossed my arms. "So, you do know who I am?"

"Someone told me," she said as she stood up. "Not that it meant anything to me. I don't follow sports."

"You should check out some of my videos. You can get them online."

She heaved her heavy backpack onto her back. "No, thanks."

"Again, with the ego-crushing. Is that your thing?"

She shrugged before taking off and leaving me alone in the corner of the library.

I had to hand it to her. I didn't think she'd last the whole hour. But she had. Maybe Little One had more determination than I gave her credit for.

7

———

SHAY

I lay on my bed, researching everything there was to know about dyslexia on my laptop. Nice wrench Kason tossed into the torture that was tutoring him. I figured I'd walk him through the first few chapters, give him some formulas, and he'd erase the video. But now that I knew he wouldn't grasp the information unless I spoon-fed it to him, I needed some quick fixes.

There was no way I'd ever be able to relax with that video hanging over my head—or the idea that I'd done something with him so out of character for me. It ate away at me. Not knowing if I'd do something to make him leak it. Not knowing if he watched it nightly. Not knowing if he showed his friends. Had I become a laughing stock at his house?

I'd wracked my brain for some sliver of a memory. Some emotion. Some something. But I couldn't for the life of me remember anything happening between us. How could something I'd never done before—something I would've only done with someone I loved—be so easy to forget?

I needed to be done with Kason McCloud. Then maybe, I could regain my sanity. So, I did the only thing I could. I wore a brave face and endured whatever came my way—like I'd been doing my whole life—I could get through it. I *would* get through it.

My phone rang beside me and I glanced to it. A cold shiver rushed up my spine when I saw the number. I'd somehow been able to shut that part of my life out while I was at school. If I pretended it didn't exist, it didn't. So, I let the phone continue to ring until the screen lit up with a missed call.

I released a long breath before deleting the call.

*Kason*

"What's up with Cora?" my best friend Thayer asked as we skateboarded across campus, giving people a show whenever we came upon a metal railing or a bunch of steps.

"Dude, she won't leave me the hell alone," I explained.

"It's like you made a deal with the devil when you agreed to let Slopes sponsor you," he said. "He'll drop your ass if you hurt his daughter."

"Look, I'm not against screwing her when the need arises, but she wants more and I'm obviously not lookin' for that."

"Just be honest with her," he said as he kick-flipped over a curb.

"She brings up my sponsorship every time she feels like I'm pushing her away."

"Dude, she's hot and all. But you can't have some girl holding your sponsorship over you. Especially, when there are plenty of other sponsors who'll line up if this one goes south."

"They all make you jump through hoops, no matter

who you're with," I said as I ollied. "They're never satisfied. Either they want more social media posts with sick tricks or they want you sporting their shit, no matter how ugly it is."

"Don't you wish it was just about snowboarding? Like it was when we were two ten-year-old-punks tearing up the mountain for kicks?" Thayer asked.

"Sometimes. But, you know, once you get a medal and pull off tricks no one else has, that high just keeps you coming back."

"You think you'll get gold in Aspen?" he asked.

"Yes."

He laughed, knowing I was a cocky son-of-a-bitch. He'd known me longer than anyone I chilled with these days. He also knew how bad I wanted gold. Bronze and silver had been amazing, but I needed gold this year. Thayer was just as good as I was on a snowboard, but he hated jumping through hoops for sponsors so he didn't. At least that's what he said. I wondered if it had more to do with losing his mom last year that made him lose his desire. But, since he didn't talk about her, I didn't press him. "Hey, what's the deal with braids?"

I nearly choked. "What?"

"I saw her go upstairs Saturday night and she never came back down."

*Fuck. How was I explaining that shit?* "She's helping me with something," I explained, leaving out the specifics. He may have been my best friend, but he didn't need to know how bad my school struggles really were. I'd always just played it off as if I didn't give a shit. There was something about letting people know how bad my struggles really were that made me feel vulnerable. That's why I couldn't believe I'd told Little One. When she called me dumb, it set something off inside me. Even though I knew she was joking, it was like I still needed to prove to her that I wasn't.

"I *bet* she's helping you with something," Thayer said, busting my balls.

Laughter burst out of both of us as we made our way across campus.

8

———

SHAY

I peeked across the classroom at Kason, wondering if the work we put in Sunday night helped him pass the unexpected quiz Professor Raymond assigned. His pen moved across the paper, giving nothing away. When class was dismissed, he ducked out before I was even finished packing my backpack. In the hallway, I spotted him holding a skateboard and talking to some other skateboarders. He caught my eyes but quickly looked away. I didn't know if that meant he failed the quiz and he was cursing my tutoring skills, or if he didn't want anyone to know we knew each other. Likely, both.

I stepped outside and began my hike across campus, admiring the old brick buildings and ivy covering the front of many of them. It was one of the things I first noticed about the school when I toured it last year. I wondered what the buildings had looked like before they'd been victimized by the troublesome ivy. Then, I realized that the ivy is what gave them character. It's what made them appear stronger, withstanding such an intrusion.

"Shay!"

I spun around, spotting Kendall hurrying around groups of people trying to catch up with me. She appeared to be alone for a change. Her pledge sisters had invaded our room and joined us at meals recently. They were nice, but I really had nothing in common with them—especially when all they wanted to do was talk sorority stuff. "Hi," I said.

"Where're you heading?" she asked, keeping pace with me.

"Intro to Art. You?"

"Intro to Drama. We're reciting monologues today."

"Is that what you were practicing in your sleep?"

She laughed. "I was not."

I nodded. "Julia Stiles poem from *Ten Things I Hate About You*, right?"

She laughed even louder. "Oh my God."

"If your sleep-talking's any indication, you'll do great."

"I was up so late practicing, it must've been on my mind while I slept."

"How could you concentrate with the music playing so loud next door?" I asked.

"There was no music playing."

Oh, my *God*. There hadn't been. How had I not realized that? I'd heard her sleep-talking. I'd slept soundly. Had they given up torturing me?


*Kason*


I rushed to the table in the corner of the library hoping I beat Little One there. I hadn't.

She sat with her arms across her chest glaring at me. "Your time might not be precious, but mine is."

"Sorry," I said as I slipped into the chair across from her

and dropped my bag to the ground. "Thayer and I went to Winter."

Her eyes narrowed. "What's Winter?"

"An indoor slope."

"There's such a thing?"

"You must not be from Colorado," I said.

"Actually I am. I'm just not interested."

I scoffed. "That's kind of rude. I find what you do interesting."

"Such as?" she challenged.

"Um...well...physics."

She rolled her eyes.

I reached down and grabbed my physics book, knowing I needed to be serious and focused or she'd walk out on me. "Which page?"

Her lips twisted as she appeared to consider something. "I want to try something."

"Okay."

"Pull up one of your snowboard videos," she said.

I smirked. "Couldn't resist, could you?"

"Stop being an idiot."

I pulled out my phone and pulled up the highlight reel I'd filmed for Slopes when they needed social media content. I handed the phone to her. "Try not to be too impressed."

She took the phone and watched intently. How could she not be impressed? I nailed every trick—at least every one that made the highlight reel.

I watched her eyes as they took in my inverted aerials, double grabs, and back twelve doubles. Her features didn't change. She appeared unfazed by my skills. What the fuck?

She handed me back my phone. "Okay."

"Okay?"

She nodded, opening her notebook and scribbling something down. She spun it to face me and I could see she'd jotted down some numbers, letters, and symbols. "A snowboarder gains speed by converting gravitational potential energy into kinetic energy of motion. So, the more a snowboarder descends a hill, the faster he goes. There were a bunch of instances where you were going down a hill in that video. Since the side of the mountain was steep, you needed to prevent yourself from going too fast and losing control."

"I'm a pro. That's child's play."

She rolled her eyes, clearly put off by my unwarranted commentary.

"To stop yourself from skidding on the snow, you used a zig-zag pattern. You probably don't even realize it, but that creates frictional resistance with the snow and prevents your speed from reaching dangerously high levels. Less experienced snowboarders probably skid around their turns, right?"

I nodded.

"Well, that happens because the snowboard is tilted on its edge and the exposed base of the board plows into the snow head-on." She showed me with the slant of her hand. "I assume it results in a significant loss in speed."

"Yeah."

"This happens because the plowing action generates frictional resistance with the snow by physically pushing it. This resistance is significantly more than the resistance seen if the snowboard were to glide on the snow with the base of the board flat on the snow. The board is pointed in the same direction as its velocity—which is the same as the velocity of the snowboarder. The necessary requirement for minimizing snow resistance and maximizing speed."

Though I normally struggled to keep up with science

"language," Little One's snowboarding example helped me relate to the information so I could visualize it.

She tapped the tip of her pen on the notebook, showing me the letters she'd written earlier. "This allows the snowboard to go around the turn without any skidding, since the snowboard is always pointed in the same direction as its velocity."

"I think I get it," I said.

Her brows inverted. "You do?"

"More than I did when I got here."

She nodded, though I couldn't read her expression. Was she happy she'd helped me or indifferent since she hated me?

"For someone who knows nothing about snowboarding, you sure do know a lot about it."

She shrugged. "It's basic science."

"I think you need to hit the slopes and test your examples for yourself."

She shook her head. "That would be a disaster. My coordination is what you call lacking."

"You? I never would've thought that."

She leveled me with her eyes.

I chuckled. "Everyone has to start somewhere, Little One."

"I'll be staying on solid ground."

"Suit yourself. But, you'll never know what you're missing out on."

She shrugged, my challenge not the least bit appealing to her.

"Why don't you wear contacts?"

She glanced up, her old glasses magnifying her green eyes. "What?"

"You've got pretty eyes," I said, just noticing the dark green ring around her emerald eyes.

"Stop."

"I'm serious," I insisted. "Why do you hide them?"

She stared down at the pages in front of her, probably plotting my imminent death. "Contacts cost money which I don't have."

"Tuition bleed you dry?"

"I wouldn't have even been able to afford tuition if it wasn't for my scholarship."

"Geez, sorry to hear that."

She shrugged. "It's only temporary. I won't end up like my parents."

"That bad?"

"Worse."

I wasn't sure what to say. I hadn't expected such honesty from her. But then again, I didn't really know her.

9

___________

KASON

Worse.

That word played through my mind as I sat on a crate behind the counter at Blades, my buddy Jesse's ski shop. It wasn't busy during the off-season, so Thayer and I usually just chilled there while we weren't in class or skateboarding.

"McCloud."

I glanced to Jesse standing in front of me. "What?"

He and Thayer laughed.

I looked between them. "What?"

"You didn't hear a word I said, did you?" Jesse asked.

"Sorry, bro. What'd you say?"

"We were just saying that if VonBuren doesn't make it back from rehab by January, it's only Ousterman you need to worry about."

"Kason doesn't worry about anyone," Thayer said, always having my back, even though he should've been competing too. "Right, Kason?"

I shrugged, spinning the wheels on my skateboard.

"I hear Slopes is throwing one hell of a bender next weekend up at the mountain," Jesse said.

I rolled my eyes. "Just an excuse to get us all in one room wearing their shit disguised as a charity event."

"Such a hardship," Jesse laughed. "Hey, if you're hating on Slopes, I hear Kincaid's chomping at the bit to sponsor you."

I frowned and nodded, having heard the same rumor.

"Dude. You know that means you've made it if they want to sponsor you," he said.

I shook my head. "You know I signed an exclusive contract with Slopes. I can't accept Kincaid's offer."

"Their very *generous* offer," Thayer added.

"Rookie mistake," I said, knowing when I first got my Slopes' offer, I was stoked. The money they offered upfront covered my travel and competition expenses all over the world. But, now I realized that came with a price. I was trapped in a contract that dictated more than I bargained for. I'd felt like a prisoner since Cora started holding my sponsorship over me, and her father started telling me which competitions they'd pay for—which I now had a sneaky suspicion was dictated by said daughter who didn't want me traipsing across the globe. My boys who signed on with Kincaid from jump had all the freedom in the fucking world.

"You could always piss off Cora so Daddy will kick your ass to the curb," Jesse said.

My eyes widened. Since a contract was binding, I hadn't considered trying to get out of my contract. But, if they *let* me go...

"She is the one holding the sponsorship over your head," he continued. "Right?"

How had I not thought of that before? I mean, I knew it was a totally shady thing to do.

"There's got to be another way to get out of it," Thayer said, always the straight shooter.

"Yeah. Maybe you're right," I said.

"Dude, rule number one," Jesse said. "Don't mix business with pleasure. Because, if there's no longer pleasure, get yourself outta there as fast as you can."

Maybe he was right. Maybe desperate times called for desperate measures.


*Shay*


Professor Raymond passed test booklets out to each table. The snowboarding examples really seemed to help Kason understand the ins and outs of circular motion and gravitation. We still needed to cover free body diagrams and Newton's second law. But, he had enough background knowledge to at least put in a fair effort. I never promised an A. It'd be a miracle if he pulled off a D.

I opened the test booklet and checked the questions. Kason would know the first few, though he'd struggle on the last few. I glanced over my shoulder at him. As if he knew I was looking, his eyes shifted to mine. By the look on his face, he had read the questions and knew what I knew. I nodded subtly before turning to my test.

I flew through the questions, finishing my test before most probably even started the second question. I grabbed my backpack and looped my arms through the straps, dropping my test booklet on Professor Raymond's desk on my way to the door. He smiled, probably because he was sure I aced it. I peeked at Kason before I stepped into the hallway. His pen moved furiously across his page like a man on a mission. Hopefully, he'd pass. That way, we could go our separate ways, and I'd never have to speak to Kason McCloud ever again.

———

I sensed someone hovering over me at my corner table in the library. I yanked off my headphones, letting them hang around my neck as I glanced up. Kason stood there with his hands in his jeans' pockets, his backpack on his back, and a beanie covering all but the ends of his hair that curled under the back of it.

"What are you listening to?" he asked as he slipped off his backpack.

"Tesla."

"I thought that was a car."

"And a rock band."

He dropped into the seat across from me. "Didn't take you for a rock fan."

I shrugged. "I like eighties and nineties rock."

"Can I listen?"

"Why?"

"Because I'm interested."

I sighed, wishing I could just tutor him and not have to play nice. I pulled off my headphones and handed them to him. The sooner we got this charade over with the better.

He put them on, his eyes lifting to the ceiling as he listened to the song I'd been listening to. "What's the song?" he shouted, clearly not realizing how loud he was in the quiet library.

I motioned for him to take them off.

He pulled them off.

"'What You Give,'" I explained. "It's my favorite."

"I like it."

"Liar."

"I'm serious. It's good. It's slow then it surprises you and gets hard."

I held out my hand, requesting my headphones back. He passed them to me, and I tucked them into my backpack.

"What are we doing tonight?"

I opened my notebook to a drawing of a snowboarder with different lines and angles labeled with letters. I turned it so he could see it, while I looked at it upside down. "The line passing through points P and G..." I pointed to the diagram with the end of my pen and traced the line from P to G for him. "This is defined here as the angle of lean of the snowboarder."

"Did you draw this?" Kason asked, leaning over the picture.

"Yes." I tapped my pen on the drawing, trying to get him to focus. "G is the center of mass of the system which consists of the snowboarder plus the snowboard, which together can be treated as a rigid body."

"This is really good," he said, seemingly ignoring everything I just explained. "You're really talented."

I pulled in a silent breath begging God for the strength to endure his ADHD which I assumed he had, in addition to his dyslexia. "P is the approximate contact point between the snowboard and the snow. L is the distance between point P and point G which you see is just about the center of the snowboarder's stomach."

"Right here?" he pointed to the line running from the board to the snowboarder.

I nodded.

"That looks more like his belly button."

"What?"

"G."

"Fine. G can be his belly button."

Kason smirked, liking that he got his way. Little did he know, I was trying to get this over with and would agree to most things at this point so he'd erase the video.

"Now this is the centripetal acceleration of point G—"

"The belly button?"

I huffed. Did he really think I wanted to be there? Did he really think it was fun for me to be explaining basic physics to someone who was blackmailing me? "This acceleration is in the x-direction and points toward the center of the turn, at a given instant $F_1$ is the contact force in the x-direction, with the snow, acting on the snowboard at point P."

He stared at the drawing as I traced the area I wanted him focused on.

"$N_1$ is the contact force in the y-direction, with the snow acting on the snowboard at point P."

"I think my head might explode."

"It's not going to explode," I assured him.

"How do you know?"

"Because, only six people have ever died from their head exploding, so statistically, with over seven billion people in the world, there is a slim chance of it happening to you."

"You're lying," he said.

"I'm not. It happened to a chess player in Russia in the nineties. It's called Hyper Cerebral Electrosis. Those who've suffered from HCE were said to be highly intelli-gent with great powers of concentration—so no need to worry."

He laughed. "I still don't believe you."

"Look it up. It happens when the circuits of the brain become overloaded by the body's own electricity. During time of intense mental activity—like a game of chess—when excess currents are surging through the brain, the explosions are said to happen."

"Wow. You're not kidding."

I shook my head. "No, it's pretty scary."

"I think you may be a candidate for HCE," he said.

"You worried about getting my brain bits all over you?"

He grimaced. "That's disgusting."

I snickered. "You brought it up."

"Was that a laugh? Did Little One actually just laugh?"

"It won't happen again."

"I hope it does."

The way his eyes stared into mine made me feel all sorts of weird things. Good-looking guys did not stare at me. And just because this one was a grade A asshole, it didn't mean it wouldn't affect me. "Did you pass Raymond's test?" I asked, swiftly changing the subject.

"I didn't tell you? I got a D. I think he only gave it to me since I was the last one in class taking the test, and he wanted to go home."

"Well, you passed. And, you're going to pass the next one if you focus." I tapped my pen on the drawing, pulling his attention back to the line my pen was now tracing. "Note that v is the instantaneous velocity of the center of mass G. This velocity is pointing off the page. The center of mass G has zero acceleration in the y-direction. Therefore, the forces in the y-direction acting on the system must sum to zero."

"Okay."

My brows shot up. "You get it?"

"No. I need a break because my head hurts—but we both know my head won't really explode, so I just need a breather."

I laughed to myself—which told me I needed a breather too. I did not find guys like Kason McCloud funny. I hated guys like him. *Him* specifically. I pushed my chair back and stood.

"You're not leaving, are you?" he asked.

"I'll be back." I grabbed my phone and took off for the restroom. If he thought *he* needed a break, he had no idea how difficult it was to sit with him and not want to beg him to erase that video every five minutes.

I used the restroom then got a drink from the vending machine, taking my time so I could relax. Because any time I thought of the video, my stress level shot through the roof.

When I returned to our table, a pretty brunette was sitting on top of it and laughing at something Kason was saying. I cleared my throat.

She turned to look at me. "Yes?"

"You're sitting on my assignment."

She looked down at the papers she was sitting on. "Oops." She scooted herself off the table with a giggle. "You have my number, Kason."

"I'll hit you up this weekend," he said.

"You better." She turned and disappeared from our corner of the library.

I straightened the papers on the table, annoyed by the intrusion. "It's a wonder she found you all the way back here," I mumbled before sitting back down.

"Why's that?"

"Well, since we're hiding back here so no one sees us together—"

"Not true," he said.

"Totally true. I don't want people seeing us together."

"Well, I don't care if people see us together," he said.

*Yeah, right.* "Can we just get back to the physics?"

He laughed. "It's why we're here, isn't it?"

10

————

## KASON

Thayer spotted for me as I lay on the weight bench lifting in the campus gym. Until it snowed, I needed to increase my workouts. I pressed one more before dropping it into the rack.

"I think you need to add a switch backside triple cork 1440," Thayer said as I sat up and wiped my face with a towel.

"Amos did one in his final run last year." I stood up so Thayer could take my spot on the bench. "I don't want anyone thinking I'm not original."

He lay back and grasped the barbell. "Oh, you're definitely original."

I laughed as I spotted for him. "Did you know a person's brain can actually explode?" I asked as he began bench-pressing.

"Bullshit."

"I swear. Apparently, it happened to some chess player in Russia."

"Wow."

"Right?"

"You better land your tricks in Aspen so you don't need to worry about that happening to you."

"It only happens to super smart people."

He burst out laughing after he returned the barbell to the rack. "Well, then you have nothing to worry about." He sat up and wiped his face with his towel.

"Asshole."

"Kason?"

*Fuck.*

Cora stood there in booty shorts and a crop top, her arms crossed and her eyes narrowed. "I called you last night when you didn't come over? I was worried. But, I can see you're okay."

Thayer stood. "Thanks for the workout, bro. See you at home," he said as he hightailed it out of there.

*Traitor.*

Cora took his spot on the weight bench. "What's going on?"

*Here goes nothing.* "Listen."

"I am," she said, clearly annoyed with me for blowing her off last night.

"Things are starting to get busy. I really need to focus on training."

"So, train. I'm not standing in your way."

I sighed. "You know I haven't made you any promises."

She looked angry. "You sure about that? Because I'd say every time you were fucking me, you were making me promises."

A few guys nearby lifting weight turned to look our way.

I lowered my voice so Cora would take the hint and follow suit. "We're in college, Cora. We're horny. We hook up. We have fun. We move on."

Her eyes widened and she got louder. "You've got to be kidding me."

"I don't know what you're looking for here."

"I'm looking for you to admit that I'm not the kind of girl you fuck and ditch."

Everyone in the weight room was now looking our way.

*Fan-fucking-tastic.* "Will you lower your voice before people start recording this?"

"Oh, and ruin the good name of Kason McCloud?" she said. "Why would I ever want to do that?"

She was trying to cause a scene, and I wasn't about to play into it. "If you can't control whatever the hell you've got going on, I'm outta here." I took off for the door.

"This isn't over, Kason!" she called as I walked away.

Hopefully not. Because when Daddy caught wind that I was kicking his little girl to the curb, maybe he'd drop his sponsorship and I could go with Kincaid.


*Shay*


I made my way through the stacks to the back corner of the library. To my surprise, Kason sat at our usual table wearing headphones.

I dropped my bag onto the table.

Kason glanced up and smiled.

I found it strange that the small gesture could appear so familiar. Yet, so torturous.

"Hey." He pulled off his headphones. "Guess what I'm listening to?"

I shrugged. "No idea."

"Tesla."

"Why?"

"Because I told you I liked their sound."

I sat down across from him and pulled out my laptop.

"I've also been listening to Slaughter and Bad Company."

I flipped open my laptop and searched for the website I needed, wondering why he was trying so hard to take an interest in me.

"Did you have a nice day?" he asked.

My eyes lifted from my laptop screen. "What?"

"Your day. Did you have a good one?"

Now, he was asking me about my day. What alternate universe were we living in? I shrugged and spun my laptop to face him. "I made you a quiz using all the terms we covered so far in class."

"You made this for me?" he asked as he looked at my screen. "When?"

"I did a little last night and then some this morning."

If I didn't know any better, I could've sworn a look of regret passed over his features. "This is really cool. Thanks for doing this for me."

Thanks? Did he really thank me? Didn't he realize I didn't have a choice?

"Why are you so good at physics?"

"I'm interested in it," I said.

"Yeah, but why?"

"I'm gonna be a biochemist."

"Seriously?"

"I want to develop cures for diseases."

"Oh," he said. "Any particular disease or just diseases in general?"

I considered my words carefully, not wanting to open myself up to questions I wasn't going to answer. "Addiction."

"What happened to 'just say no'?"

I shook my head, knowing it's what we'd been taught in school for years. But it was wrong. "Addiction is a chronic disease. It changes brain function. Scientists thought pleasure alone was enough for people to seek an addictive substance or activity. But, research tells us it's more complicated."

"What's that mean?"

"Dopamine contributes to the experience of pleasure, but also plays a role in learning and memory—two elements in the transition from liking something to becoming addicted to it."

He stared at me with narrowed eyes, and I couldn't tell if he was trying to understand or was completely lost the second I opened my mouth.

But I couldn't stop. I loved talking about science, especially when it came to how I was going to change the face of the science surrounding addiction one day. "The brain registers all pleasures the same way. Repeated exposure to an addictive substance or behavior causes nerve cells in the nucleus accumbens and the prefrontal cortex to communicate in a way that combines *liking* something with *wanting* it. That's what causes us to go after it to seek out the source of pleasure. Hence, addiction. If I can just discover the link to addiction and the solution to stopping it, we'd have a lot less heartache in our world."

"Wow," Kason said.

"What?"

"That's pretty impressive."

I shrugged.

"I didn't understand half of what you said, but I know you're going to do something really amazing one day."

Heat rushed to my cheeks. Compliments made me

uncomfortable. "I may not be able to flip on a snowboard, but this is my rush."

He nodded, seemingly understanding. "I can teach you to flip."

I laughed. "I can't even stand on a snowboard. No way I'd ever be able to flip."

"You never know unless you try."

I rolled my eyes.

"What are you doing this weekend?" he asked.

"I'm not going snowboarding with you."

"Whoa. Retract the claws, Little Genius. I wasn't asking you to go snowboarding since there's no snow yet. I was just wondering if you were busy."

"Why?"

"Because I need a date for a charity event."

I balked. "*You* need a date?"

"Don't sound so surprised."

"What about mean girl?" I asked, curious what happened to the power couple. They seemed so right for each other.

"We're taking a break."

"So, she kicked you to the curb?"

He chuckled. "Not exactly."

"How about little-miss-sit-on-the-table-and-spread-her-legs?"

He laughed. "Did you really just say that?"

"Was she not sitting on the table with her legs spread the other night?"

"No. She closed them once you walked over." His lips slipped into a cocky grin.

"I rest my case." I opened my notebook to a blank page so I could take notes while he took the quiz that he had yet to start. "What's the charity?"

"No idea. It's not really about the charity."

"Why not?"

"My sponsor throws it to raise money, though what they really want is to sell their product. Having me and all their other athletes there is the enticer for people with deep pockets to be there too."

"That's shitty."

"Yup. The real word blows."

I held my tongue. He didn't know the half.

"So?"

"So, what?" I asked.

"You wanna go with me?"

"No."

"Why not?"

"Because I don't like you."

He chuckled. "Tell me how you really feel."

"Well, you're a complete douchebag who—"

He waved his palms in front of me. "Whoa. I wasn't serious."

"Then why'd you ask?"

He shook his head, obviously confused by my candor. "I thought you'd want to help a guy in need."

I scoffed. "You're a guy in need?"

"Yes, in need of a date."

"Well, besides the fact that I don't like you, you have a video of me and you're blackmailing me with it. Need I say more?"

"You make it sound so—"

"Disgusting?"

"I was going to say—"

"Wrong?"

He continued, "More like—"

"An asshole thing to do?"

He huffed, clearly not liking me calling him out on his scheme. "You win."

"Thank you. I'm sure you won't have any trouble finding some willing female to go to a charity event with you. Aren't you like Mr. Big Shot Snowboarder?"

His lips twitched. "I like to think so."

I rolled my eyes, hating that even when I hated him, he could be amusing. "Well, it's still a no from me."

## 11

## SHAY

I lay on my bed as Kendall was getting ready for a fraternity social. I was mesmerized that she knew how to apply makeup like those Instagram models who looked perfect without filters. She knew what colors needed to blend on her eyes to give them that lift and shine. And, her blush brush swept across the apples of her cheeks giving her that flushed look.

Because my mom died when I was six, I didn't have a woman around to buy me makeup or teach me about things like skincare. Instead of learning on my own, I said to hell with it all. I didn't need it. And, while I was a firm believer that beauty on the inside was what should matter, just once I would've liked someone to think I was pretty on the outside.

There was a knock at our door. Kendall dropped the lip gloss she just swiped on and rushed to the door, pulling it open and stepping back when it wasn't who she expected.

"Is Little One here?"

I gasped.

"You mean Shay?"

I stood from my bed and moved to the door. "What are you doing here?"

His light blue button-down shirt rolled at the sleeves displayed his sleeve of tattoos and made his eyes bluer than normal. And, instead of jeans, he wore khaki cargo pants and sneakers. "I asked you to go to that charity event with me," he explained.

"And I said no."

"Go get dressed," he insisted. "I need you."

"No."

Kendall's eyes jumped between the two of us, clearly unaccustomed to our usual banter since it happened while we were alone in the corner of the library.

"I came all the way here to get you."

I rolled my eyes. "Those three miles must've been taxing."

"See? I was willing to endure the journey for you."

"I have no idea why you'd think I'd change my mind."

He crossed his arms. "Oh, I'd say there's one *big* reason that you would change your mind."

"What's that?" I dared him with my eyes to say it in front of Kendall.

"Go with him, Shay," Kendall interrupted.

I turned toward her and scowled.

"It could be fun," she explained.

"Whose side are you on?"

She stifled a smile. "It's for charity."

I pointed at Kason. "He doesn't even know what type of charity it's for."

"Actually," he began. "I do. It's for UPRISE. It supports underprivileged kids in the Denver area."

*Dammit.* Charities like that had always been a savior for

me when it came to the food and necessities I needed when my dad was on a bender, disappearing for days at a time.

"That thing I need to get rid of..." he began.

My eyes widened. Was he saying what I thought he was saying?

"It's gone after tonight."

I inhaled sharply. If I went with him, would this all really be over? Would he erase the video? "I have nothing to wear."

His lips slipped into a small grin. "I've got it covered."

I stared across the space between us. Him in all his snowboarder dude glory. Why was he so desperate to go with me to this event? He could've asked any girl and, unlike me, they would've loved to go with him. There had to be more to it. But if I didn't go, there was no chance of him erasing the video any time soon.

"What do you say, Shay?" he said. "You in?"

"You called me Shay," I said.

"It's your name, isn't it?"

"You didn't know that until Kendall said it."

"Not true."

"Very true," I ascertained.

"You two are hysterical," Kendall said, still standing nearby witnessing the whole ridiculous scene between us.

I shot daggers her way. "We are not. He's a jerk."

"A jerk who you're going to a charity event with," he added.

I growled deep in my throat, hating that he had the video hanging over me. But not for long. "Fine. Let's get this over with."

## *Kason*

I glanced over at Shay in the passenger seat of my Jeep, still amazed it didn't take more arm twisting to get her to go with me. She was so small and fragile-looking on the outside. But on the inside, she was fierce and fiery and could eat a guy like me for breakfast if I wasn't careful.

"Stop staring at me," she said, though her eyes were focused out the passenger window.

"I'm not staring."

Being in such close quarters was new for us. In the library, the space was so big, it never felt as if we were truly alone. But now, with nothing between us but a center console, I was very aware of our proximity—not to mention, the fact that I didn't really know Shay. She was right. I only learned her name from her roommate. "Are you excited?" I asked, dumbly.

"No."

My eyes jumped between Shay and the road. "Do you always say what you're thinking?"

"Yes."

"It's actually refreshing."

She looked at me. "Why's that?"

"I'm just used to people telling me how awesome I am."

She groaned.

"I'm serious. It's like I can do no wrong because I can land tricks on a snowboard. And, while I *can* pull off some sick tricks, it's not who I am. It's what I do. So, when they blow up my ego, it's for something superficial. Does that make sense?"

"Oddly. Yes."

A humorless laugh escaped me. "I've never said that out loud before."

"Why not?"

"I guess I didn't want anyone to think I was whining about my success."

"It's not whining if it's the truth. And, if you can't be open with your friends, they're probably not your real friends."

She was right. I knew my boys were my boys because they were there when I wasn't winning medals. It was my competitors who acted like they were my friends, but I knew they didn't really have my back. Instead, they hoped I didn't nail my corks, flips, and jumps because then they could take my place.

Before long, I hit my blinker and turned into the small parking lot off the main strip in town. As I parked my Jeep and cut the engine, Shay looked around, likely worried I planned to do something sinister in the empty parking lot. We were clearly not at the ski resort where the event was being held, so I understood her confusion. "Come on," I said, pushing open my door and stepping out. I waited until Shay stepped beside me before taking off for the small boutique. The bell on the front door jingled as we stepped inside.

"Kason? Is that you?" My sister Giselle rushed out from the back room with a huge smile on her face. But it wasn't directed at me. It was directed at Shay who looked completely out of her element in the prissy shop because she was wearing a black T-shirt, jeans, and combat boots. "You must be Shay?"

Shay nodded, obviously unsure what to make of this stranger walking around her in a circle, sizing her up.

"I'm Kason's sister Giselle. I own the shop."

Realization swept across Shay's face at our similarities. Giselle and I had the same dark hair and blue eyes. "It's nice to meet you." Shay took in all the dainty clothes in the boutique. "You have a beautiful shop."

"Thanks." Giselle gave her one more once over. "I have the perfect dress for you."

You'd have thought Shay was a deer caught in head-lights by the way her eyes widened. "I can't wear a dress."

"Of course, you can," Giselle assured her. "You've got a great body, and I've picked out the perfect one for your skin tone."

"No, I mean..." Shay's voice drifted off.

My sister and I exchanged a glance, both realizing that Shay didn't want to say whatever it was she was thinking in front of me.

"I'm just gonna go wait outside," I said, walking toward the door and leaving them alone inside. Though I was curious what they would talk about, I stepped onto the side-walk. The night air carried a slight chill and I knew snow-boarding season would be here soon. My phone pinged and I checked the screen.

JESSE

She already asked where you were.

I sent off a quick response.

ME

Be there in 30.

I leaned against the building and scanned my news feed, checking if Ousterman or any of my competitors had been posting any footage. I knew some of them were training overseas while I was stuck being a college student.

My thoughts drifted back to the car ride to the boutique. I'd been honest when I told Shay that I'd never talked about the attention I received before. It sucked not knowing who I was without snowboarding. I'd made a lot of mistakes in my life, and I was by no means a saint. On the contrary, I'd certainly become the devil when it came to Shay. She may have started things when she acted like a little brat about the loud music that first night, but I hadn't helped by holding the fake video over her head. And, now, I was using her to push Cora over the edge. Shay didn't deserve it. I just didn't know how to stop at this point.

My phone pinged. I expected it to be Thayer or even Jesse again, but it was Giselle.

GISELLE

Get in here.

*Oh, man.*

I pushed myself off the wall and moved inside, stopping short when I came face to face with Shay—at least I thought it was Shay. Yup, she was wearing combat boots. But that was the only sign it was her. She wore a sleeveless green dress that showed off the curves she hid beneath her normal T-shirt and jeans. My eyes jumped to Giselle. "Where's Shay?"

"Stop it," Giselle chided me. "Doesn't she look beautiful?"

I took in Shay's hair, no longer in braids, but pulled off her face and knotted into a stylish bun. I think my sister even put some blush on her face because her normally pale cheeks held a splash of pink. I wasn't sure about her eyes because, as usual, they were hidden beneath her glasses. "You look nice, Shay."

She said nothing, just stared down at her damn boots.

I looked at my sister. "Don't you have some shoes she can wear?"

"Nope. I think her boots look awesome." She and Shay

exchanged a strange look. I was missing something. I just didn't know what it was, and neither of them was going to tell me. "Besides, you're going to a charity event with a bunch of gnarly snowboarders. The boots are apropos."

"Gnarly?" I asked.

"You don't think I've been around you and your boys long enough to follow the language?" Giselle asked.

I laughed, but she had a point about Shay's boots. I wasn't exactly dressed to the nines in my cargo pants and collared shirt for the event. I'd also yet to pull on my ugly pink Slopes beanie I'd need to wear into the event to represent.

"You ready?" I asked Shay.

She nodded.

I motioned with my arm for her to lead the way out. Giselle nabbed the back of my shirt. "Be good to her," she whispered. "She's more fragile than she looks."

My brows hitched together. "Yeah, okay."

"Promise me, Kason."

There was something about the desperation in Giselle's voice that haunted me as I drove the winding road up to Bear Mountain. Not to mention Shay sitting beside me not saying a damn thing.

"Giselle and I are complete opposites," I said, needing to fill the uncomfortable silence.

"She's the nice one," Shay said.

I laughed. She wasn't lying. "I walked right into that, didn't I?"

She nodded.

"Do you think we're ever gonna be friends, Shay?"

She took me by surprise and looked at me. "Not if you don't erase that video."

I opened my mouth to respond—to tell her I didn't have

a video—but I knew that if I told her the truth, she would've called an Uber as soon as we reached the event. I needed to be seen with her. I needed tonight to happen, and then I'd tell her the truth. It was only fair. She'd done her part—actually, she'd gone above and beyond her part. And, I owed it to her to do mine.

12

———

SHAY

I was so out of my element it hurt. I didn't wear dresses. I didn't wear my hair up in a pretty bun. I didn't wear makeup. And, I certainly didn't hang out with asshole snowboarders who blackmailed me.

"It's this way," Kason said, leading me toward a banquet room inside the lodge. He tugged a bright pink beanie with *Slopes* in white lettering over his head. As usual when he was wearing a beanie, his hair curled over the back edges of the hat.

"That's certainly some pink you've got going on," I said as I followed him, trying to keep up so I wasn't left alone once we got inside.

"It's Slopes' color. It's awful."

We stepped into the event room. The walls were dark wood, the ceiling was high, and music reverberated throughout. Kason stopped short, and I nearly bumped into him. Some photographers approached and one of them asked, "Mind if we get some pictures?"

I stepped to the side to let him get his picture taken. He wore a smile for the photographers that didn't reach his eyes. I wondered if this was as dreadful for him as it was for me.

"Thanks, guys," he said to the photographers before moving to me.

"So, you're a model, too?" I said.

"Right." He placed his hand on the small of my back and guided me toward a rowdy group of guys milling by the bar.

The brief contact had me *very* aware of the feeling of his hand on me.

"*Heeeeey*," Kason's friends cheered when they spotted him.

He laughed as he was pulled into bro hugs. Once he was released by the last guy, he stepped next to me. "Guys, this is Shay."

They all said hey or lifted their chins to acknowledge me.

I smiled but said nothing.

"You want a drink?" Kason asked me.

"Yes," I answered a little too quickly.

He laughed and moved to the bar.

I stood on the outskirts of the group of guys, not really knowing what to do with myself now that Kason had left my side.

"You and Kason a thing?" one of the guys asked me.

I nearly choked on my laughter. "God, no."

"Oh my God." He laughed. "You're funny. He definitely needs someone like you in his life. You know, to keep him grounded."

"Yeah, well, our friendship is temporary."

"Hey, Shay." It was a guy I recognized from Kason's party. His blond shaggy hair fell over his forehead and almost touched his green eyes. "I'm Kason's roommate, Thayer."

"I remember you from the party. Thanks for the directions to the bathroom."

He smiled. "I'm all about helping damsels in distress."

"Oh, Shay is definitely not a damsel in distress," Kason said as he stepped up beside me and handed me a red drink.

I took it, lifting the straw to my lips and sipping down half the drink. It was sweet and strong. But, knowing how much trouble I'd gotten into the last time I drank, I slowed down.

"What is *she* doing here?"

*Shit.*

I didn't turn around, but all the guys around me did and amusement played across their faces.

"Relax, Cora. Shay's here with me," Kason explained. "We're friends."

"*Friends?*" her question mirrored my thoughts. "Is she the reason you...we...?" She huffed her frustration.

I turned to find her fuming in a red strapless dress and high heels that showed off her killer calves.

Kason sighed. "Let's go outside and talk." He slipped his hand behind Cora's lower back and guided her toward the door.

Unlike me when his hand guided our way, she moved away from it and walked ahead of him.

"Someone's in trouble," Thayer said.

The other guys laughed.

"Isn't that what he was going for?" One of them asked.

Thayer's nervous eyes jumped to me.

I suddenly realized I was involved in something I wasn't aware of. *Dammit, Kason. What are you doing now?* "Tell me what's going on," I said to Thayer.

"If Kason didn't mention it, maybe we shouldn't," the guy I didn't know said.

Thayer shoved him away from us. "You're the one who opened your damn mouth, Jesse." He looked back to me and lowered his voice. "Kason wants out of his deal with Slopes."

"Why?" I asked.

"It's a sucky deal."

"So, can't he just get out of it then?"

He cocked his head. "Cora's father owns the company. This is his event."

"I'm not following."

"Kason knew showing up with someone else would make Cora force her father to drop his sponsorship."

Heat rushed to my cheeks and that feeling I had when he initially asked me to go to this event returned. What would make Cora angry enough to demand her father drop Kason's sponsorship? Him showing up at her father's event with someone she hated. Someone opposite of her in every way. I had to hand it to Kason, he went big with this one. And, while I felt foolish being a pawn in this game he was playing, I knew after tonight, I'd no longer have a video of me doing unthinkable things hanging over my head. And, I'd be rid of him. So, if he needed a date who'd get him out of his sponsorship, that's exactly what he'd get.

The finish line was near.

I could almost taste it.

"Don't be mad at Kason," Thayer said. "He does a lot of stupid stuff."

Tell me about it. "I'm not mad."

"You're not?"

"Nope." A television screen over the bar played clips of Kason snowboarding. I found myself being drawn into the fluidity of his moves. The height of his jumps. The flawless-ness of his flips.

"Impressive, huh?" Kason asked as he stepped up beside me, the heat of his body so close to mine catching me off guard.

"You take care of all that?" I asked.

"I sure hope so."

"I know why you brought me here," I said, my eyes breaking from the television and moving to his.

His face contorted with regret. "I didn't want you to find—"

I held up my hand. "I don't care. As long as you do what you agreed to do at the end of the night, we're good."

"Really?"

"Well, not good like we're ever gonna be friends. But good in terms of why I'm here and what I get out of it."

His eyes clouded over, and I could've sworn I caught anger flitter across them.

We spent the next hour hanging by the bar with his friends. When some men in suits whisked him away, I took the opportunity to use the restroom.

As I washed my hands, I almost didn't recognize myself in the mirror above the sink. Giselle had applied eye shadow and blush—against my will. But, even I had to admit, it transformed my face into someone who almost looked pretty.

"You couldn't even leave the ugly boots home for one night?" Cora glared at me as she stepped inside the restroom.

"I think they add to the outfit," I shot back.

She balked. "As if."

I contemplated trying to get by her, but she leaned against the door.

"Are you enjoying your night?" she asked.

"Immensely."

Her eyes narrowed. "It's comical really. Him bringing a charity case to a charity event."

Her cold words pierced something deep inside of me. And I hated that they did. I was tougher than that.

"What? You didn't realize that's why you're here?"

I let her spew her venom. It was no worse than what I'd heard growing up.

"Say something," she urged.

I said nothing, just stared at her with blank eyes that I knew she couldn't read. I'd perfected that look a long time ago. And no mean girl was going to break through their impenetrable wall.

"He doesn't love you," she taunted.

I scoffed to myself. Of course, he didn't.

"Shay?" Kason called from outside the restroom.

"You gonna run?" she asked. "It's what all girls do when Kason calls."

"In here," I called, not giving her the satisfaction of "running."

"You okay?" he called.

"Yes. Just catching up with Cora," I assured him from the other side of the door.

"Oh," he said, his voice drifting off at my odd response.

"Now, if you'll excuse me," I said to Cora. "My date is waiting." I walked to the door and waited for her to move. Of course, she didn't.

"A nice dress and some makeup won't change what you are," she gritted through clenched teeth.

"Oh yeah? What's that?" I asked, ready for whatever cruelty she intended to give.

"Trash."

"Wow. I expected something a little more creative from you." I reached around her and yanked open the door, causing her to jump as it hit her in the back. "Ah well, maybe next time," I said as I walked right into Kason standing outside the door. Relief spread over me at the sight of him. Sure, I could deal with mean girls, but I wouldn't lie and say their venom didn't sting.

"What's going on?" he asked.

"Just mean girl being a mean girl."

His eyes shot to the closed door. "What did she say?"

"Nothing I haven't heard before."

His eyes shifted back to me and regret plagued them. "Shay?"

I shook my head. "It's fine."

His hand unexpectedly slipped into mine. I tried to pull it free, but he linked our fingers, holding on so tightly I had no other option but to follow him back toward the banquet hall. His hand was warm and provided a sense of security I wasn't used to. And, man, did I hate that.

We stopped in the doorway of the busy room. Inside, people ate food at large round tables while others stood in line at the monstrous buffet tables. Music blared and rowdy snowboarders watched the giant screens around the room displaying jumps and flips and howling at the exciting displays. Kason didn't lead me toward his friends. Instead, he turned and led me toward the exit.

I looked over my shoulder. "Don't we need to go back in there?"

"No."

"You gonna tell me why not?"

"No."

"Did I do something to make you upset?" I asked, unsure why he was suddenly being curt.

"Don't be ridiculous."

I said nothing. I only needed to make it through the rest of the night and then I'd be free.

We stepped outside and the night air held a welcomed chill. The exchange with Cora had left my body heated. Kason didn't release my hand as he moved me toward the foot of the mountain behind the lodge. Obviously, there was no snow, but he walked us over to the ski lift that sat still at the boarding station. The chair at the bottom dangled a couple of feet above the ground. Kason sat down on it and pulled me down beside him.

We sat in silence for a long time with darkness surrounding us and the seat beneath us swaying slightly. The chill in the air and the eeriness of the looming mountains all around us sent a shiver rushing up my spine.

"I know the deal was if you came with me tonight I'd erase the video," he said, breaking the silence.

I glanced to him.

His eyes were fixed on the space in front of us. "But, I still really need you to tutor me."

"You know I'm only doing it because...well because I had to. I don't have time to keep helping you while focusing on my own work."

"I need you, Shay."

My head hitched back. He wasn't joking around. The pleading in his voice told me it was the truth. His eyes drifted over my dress all the way down to my boots then back up again. He stopped at my eyes, staring into them. He lifted his hands to my glasses. My heart foolishly sped as he pulled off my glasses and continued gazing into my eyes.

I felt myself getting lost in the way his blue eyes resembled ice in the darkness. I'd always wanted to be on the receiving end of a look like that, but I needed to remember, not only was he blackmailing me, he'd brought me there to make Cora angry, not because he wanted me there. "Stop looking at me like that."

"Like what?"

"Like we're even going to speak after tonight."

His jaw ticked.

I wondered why that had made him angry.

"You don't even realize how pretty you are, do you?" he asked.

"You're only saying that because of the dress *you* got me."

"I can't even see a dress right now, Shay."

My traitorous stomach flipped over itself. Why was it *him* who was saying nice things to me? Why couldn't it be some guy who was kind and considerate and who loved science as much as me? Why did it have to be someone who'd hurt me for his own gain? Someone who wanted what he wanted and to hell with anyone who stood in his way.

"Why do you try to hide behind your glasses and boots?" he asked, his eyes unwavering.

"I don't need to try to be other people's idea of pretty. I just need to be me. Someone will love me for me."

He closed his eyes as if pained by what I'd said.

But I hadn't been lying. Sure, I liked the way he was looking at me. Who wouldn't? But it was because of makeup, a dress, and a stupid hairstyle that made him say I was pretty.

He opened his eyes and slid my glasses back onto my face. "I need to tell you something."

"Okay."

"I know I'm a complete asshole for not telling you sooner, but it was done out of desperation."

"I already know you used me to piss off Cora."

"Not that."

"Then what?"

"The video."

My stomach lurched and I was terrified to even ask. "What about the video?"

"It doesn't exist."

"What do you mean it doesn't exist?"

He winced. "Nothing actually happened between us."

I jumped to my feet, unsure what to do at that moment. "Nothing happened?" I asked, needing confirmation if I was going to be able to truly process it.

He shook his head.

"But..." my voice disappeared, a range of emotions flooding my body. There was no video. I hadn't done anything with Kason. I hadn't not remembered something. I could breathe. I could finally breathe.

But, if there was no video and we hadn't done anything, Kason had lied. And not just once. All this time he could have told me the truth, but he held the lie over me. He'd caused me unnecessary stress. Caused me to question everything I knew to be true about myself. "How could you do that?" I whispered.

"I needed your help, and you wouldn't give it willingly."

"So, you lied to me?"

He nodded. "I'm so sorry I hurt you, Shay. That was before I knew you."

"You don't know me. You know nothing about me."

"I know you're smart. And you don't take shit from other people."

I scoffed. Wasn't that the opposite of what I'd done with him?

"And maybe I don't know your backstory, but I do know

you're someone who helps other people, even when you don't want to. And you've got a really pretty smile when you just allow yourself to show it."

"I need you to take me home. Actually, I'll get my own ride. Stay with your people. You and Cora deserve each other. You both treat people like they're nothing." I took off toward the lodge.

"Shay!" he called.

"Let it go, Kason. This was never going past tonight." I hurried around the side of the lodge and out to the parking lot, walking as quickly as I could and as far away from the building as I could get. I ordered an Uber and waited on a boulder on the side of the road, far from any prying eyes.

My phone pinged with a text.

SNOWBOARD HOTTIE

I'm sorry.

But was he? Did he know how it felt to think you'd done something out of character, something you couldn't remember no matter how hard you tried? Because that's what I'd been going through for the past few weeks thanks to his selfish desire to get me to tutor him.

Well, at least I knew the truth.

Now, I'd never have to speak to him again.

# 13

## KASON

I lay in bed staring up at my ceiling. Sunlight filtered into my room, but I had no desire to leave my bed. Last night had been a shit show of epic proportions. And, I'd yet to get a call from Cora's father dropping my ass. Great idea that was.

My phone rang. I grabbed it off my nightstand only to find Giselle's name on my screen. I contemplated letting it go to voicemail since I really wasn't in the mood to talk, but I answered it anyway. "What's up?"

"How was last night?"

"Sucked. Had to kiss a lot of ass."

"Not what I meant. How'd it go with Shay?"

"What do you mean?"

"She's different than the girls you usually date."

"Shay and I aren't dating. She was helping me get rid of Cora once and for all. And, hopefully, my ticket to getting out of my contract with Slopes."

"Wait, what?"

"You heard me. It was just a one-night thing."

Silence filled Giselle's end.

I knew I'd disappointed her. I fucking hated when I disappointed her. We may've only been two years apart, but I still wanted to make her proud. And, after what I just admitted, I knew I hadn't. I sighed heavily. "Say it."

"You promised you'd be good to her," she said.

"She knew it was just for the night. I made her no promises." Except, of course, the promise to erase the non-existent video.

"I love you, Kase, but you're a real asshole sometimes."

"Never claimed not to be."

"She'd be good for you."

I didn't respond.

"Don't cut someone like her out of your life. She's not the kind of girl you use and then throw away."

"And you know this because of the twenty minutes you spent with her?"

"You can learn a lot about someone in a short time if you pay attention." With that she hung up, leaving me to wonder what the hell she knew that made her care about Shay so quickly.

I mean, I guess I could see how people could like Shay. It was hard *not* to be drawn in by her intelligence, sass, and no-bullshit attitude. Because I knew, something inside me changed when I couldn't find her at the event. I thought she'd taken off. I thought I hadn't had the chance to come clean to her. That feeling caused a giant void in my chest—one that came out of nowhere.

*Then*, I saw her face as she left the restroom. It nearly broke me. As hard as she tried to conceal her sadness at whatever went down in there with Cora, I could see it. It lasted no more than a second, but it was replaced by a sense of relief when she found me standing there. *Me*. It was as if she was actually happy to see me for the first time. And, in that moment, I wanted to protect her. Protect her from all the mean girls out there. Protect her from people who couldn't see the true beauty she was. But I couldn't do that with the lie hanging over us. Unfortunately, I realized too late that there was no way to tell her the truth without it ending...well, the way it did.

———

"You gonna pout all day?" Thayer asked from the driver's seat of his truck the next day. "Because today's gonna blow if you are."

"Maybe." I didn't leave my room all day yesterday. I felt like shit after speaking to Giselle—not to mention my hand in how everything played out Friday night. "Do you think I'm an asshole?"

"What?"

"Giselle said I can be a real asshole."

"You can be."

I gave him a look.

But Thayer wasn't intimidated by a look, ignoring me and pulling into the parking lot at Bear Mountain. "Can you even believe there's snow in October?" he asked, our deep conversation clearly over.

"It's Colorado. Anything's possible."

We hopped out of his truck and breathed in the crisp morning air. We'd left our house before the sunrise, wanting to get there as soon as they started running the lifts. We grabbed our snowboards and trekked toward the lodge.

We caught the first lift of the day up to the summit so we could take the first run of the season. The view never got old as the cable carried our lift swiftly up the incline. The mountains were where I felt most at home—and alive.

"So," Thayer said. "What went down with you and Shay? I knew not to ask when you came back in without her, but I figured a couple of days passed, so..."

I didn't want to admit to anyone what I'd done. But Thayer was my best friend—as close to a brother as I was ever gonna get. And, just as nosey. If he still liked me after I stole his girl in ninth grade, he'd see my screw-up for what it was. A terrible lapse in judgment. "I did something shitty to her."

"Worse than taking her to the event to rile up Cora?" he asked.

I nodded.

Disappointment flashed in his eyes. "How shitty?"

"I sort of blackmailed her into tutoring me."

"How do you sort of blackmail someone?"

Hearing him say it made the whole situation sound even worse than it was. "Fine. I totally blackmailed her. And it all came to a head the other night."

"What the hell were you holding over her?"

"Don't make me say it."

"Dude," he prompted.

A long breath whooshed through my lips in a white puff of air. "I told her I had a video of her."

His eyes narrowed. "What kind of video?"

I nodded, not really needing to say anymore.

"Jesus Christ."

The disappointment in his voice told me what I already knew. I was a complete asshole. "I know."

"And now she hates you?" Thayer ascertained, probably happy that she saw me for who I really was.

I nodded.

Our lift approached the top and we hopped off, making our way toward the summit in silence. The sun rising over the horizon was a sight to behold. I just wished I didn't feel so damn shitty on the inside.

"You need to start thinking about other people," Thayer said as he stopped at the top of the mountain.

I moved beside him and stared down at the untouched snow before us.

"You need to realize lying to people and not facing the truth isn't the way to live your life. You need to realize your lies can hurt other people whether you intend them to or not. You need to be a better guy for all the girls you hang with and all the snowboarders who idolize you."

"I suck, alright?" I said.

"Was it worth it?"

"Hurting Shay?"

He nodded.

"No."

"Then, learn something from this shit. Trying to get out of your sponsorship contract in a shady-ass way doesn't seem so important now, does it?"

"Obviously no."

"Well, you need to fix it," he said.

"If there's someone who could hold a grudge, it's gonna be that girl."

"Then do something nice for her. Girls love that shit."

"Something nice?"

"Yeah. What does she like?"

I thought for a moment. "Physics...eighties and nineties rock music...combat boots."

"Well, that's a start." He dropped in, taking off down the mountain without me, probably needing space from his asshole best friend who proved yet again to be even more of an asshole than he'd been the day before.

I dropped in. My board drifted over the fresh powder as

if no time had passed since my last run. I took each turn with the precision I always did, but Shay's voice manifested itself in my mind. I found myself paying attention to the curve of my board, allowing myself to slide a little to see what she'd explained when trying to relate snowboarding to physics.

She'd known what would help me. And used that. She'd spent time preparing to help me, all the while I'd been manipulating her. What kind of person did that?

Shay and I never would have gotten to a good place because she never forgot why she was tutoring me. She never forgot I was blackmailing her. I wondered if we would have gotten along if I hadn't forced her to tutor me. Would she have ever let her guard down with me if I didn't have some video of us hanging over her head? Would things have been different if I'd never lied?

Maybe my honesty Friday night—albeit a shock to her—created a clean slate for us.

Maybe Thayer was right.

Maybe I needed to do something nice for her so she could see I wasn't the guy she thought I was.

## 14

———

## KASON

I arrived to physics class early Monday morning, hoping to speak to Shay. I hated the way we left things the other night. And, after what Giselle *and* Thayer had said, I knew I needed to make things right. But Shay wasn't at her table when I entered the room. I scanned the other tables, wondering if she changed her seat, but there was no sign of her. I moved to my seat and the girl who normally sat next to me tried to make small talk, but all I could focus on was the door.

"Good morning, everyone," Professor Raymond announced as he strolled into the classroom, closing the door behind him. "Open your books to page one hundred and ten. We're going to continue our discussion on Kepler's Three Laws."

The classroom door squeaked open and Shay hurried in, mumbling her apologies to the professor as she passed by him. Her braids were back and no makeup touched her pale cheeks as she slipped into her seat. This was the Shay she shared with the world. The one you could take or leave for all she cared. But, for some reason, I didn't want to leave her. I wanted her to tutor me. I wanted her to put me in my place. I wanted her to hate me. At least it meant she felt something. Because, knowing she didn't, sucked.

"Does anyone know what Kepler's three laws of planetary motion are?" Professor Raymond's eyes scanned the room.

My eyes went right to Shay. She opened her laptop but didn't offer to answer his question. That was completely unlike her. I knew she knew Kepler's three laws. Why wasn't she answering?

"Anyone?" Professor Raymond asked, looking to Shay.

Still, she didn't offer an answer, instead staring into her laptop screen.

"I think..." I began. "There are three."

Laughter erupted around the classroom.

I hadn't meant to entertain them. I was just racking my brain for what I'd learned. "The Law of Harmonies," I continued before he thought I was being a dick.

"Very good, Mr. McCloud," Professor Raymond said as if he was just as shocked as I was that I knew the answer—or at least part of it.

Shay didn't look in my direction.

"The Law of Ellipses," I continued, having no idea how I remembered that one.

Professor Raymond smiled, seemingly impressed.

"And the Law of...Equal Areas," I said.

Professor Raymond smiled. "Perfect, Mr. McCloud."

I exhaled.

The girl beside me smiled at me, impressed by my newfound intelligence. But she wasn't the girl I wanted looking at me. The girl whose attention I wanted did not look at me then or for the remainder of the class.

When Professor Raymond dismissed us an hour later, I

stuffed my things into my bag and grabbed my skateboard, ready to walk out with Shay. But, before I could meet up with her, she walked up to Professor Raymond to speak to him. Not wanting to look like a creepy stalker, I walked out of class and stopped in the hallway. Not giving up that easily, I leaned against the wall and waited for her.

The door opened a few minutes later. I pushed off the wall and attempted to approach her, but she and Professor Raymond were caught up in conversation as they walked down the hallway together, ignoring me completely.

*Dammit.*

*Shay*

"So, I've been brainstorming some things and knew you were the one to ask," Professor Raymond said as we made our way out of the building together.

"Okay."

"Well, you obviously don't need to be taking my class."

"What? I love your class."

He chuckled. "No, I just meant, you're quite capable of teaching it with all the prior knowledge you possess."

My eyes flashed down as my cheeks warmed. "I don't know everything."

"Stop being modest. I know you want to volunteer and, up until now, I wasn't sure how I could best utilize you."

"What do you have in mind?"

"Well, I don't have a TA this semester. But, I've never heard of a freshman serving as a TA, so I don't really think that's an option. I was actually hoping you could play a more behind-the-scenes type of role for me."

My brows furrowed.

"Let me cut to the chase. More than half of the students in your class are failing."

My eyes widened, though thinking about it, besides Kason tossing out that answer today, I was the only one in class who ever participated.

"I don't want the dean questioning me about my teaching because these students don't have the work ethic you do. So, I was looking to set up a study group. And, I'd like to have you tutor those who show up."

"Oh, I..."

"I can't pay you, but I assure you, it will look great on a resume."

"I'm sure it will, but when I asked about volunteering, I was hoping you might need someone in the lab."

"You did say you'd sweep floors," he reminded me.

"I did say that, didn't I?"

———

Frustrated with the way my conversation with Professor Raymond had gone earlier, I ate an early dinner and decided to shower before bed. I didn't want to tutor people who didn't want to put in the effort to pass his class. I wanted to be swept up in science research in a lab somewhere. But, I shouldn't have been surprised. Given the way things had been going for me lately, this was par for the course.

I made my way to the bathroom in my shower robe and untied combat boots. I pulled open the door to the bathroom and jumped back when Cora stood there glaring at me. In no mood to deal with her, I tried to move around her.

She shifted her hip so I couldn't.

"Look," I said, wanting nothing more than to be away

from her. "We live next door to each other. Can't we just agree not to bother with one another? I know I'm fine with it."

Her eyes dropped to my boots, as usual ogling them with distaste. "Since day one you've been getting in my way. And now you think you can show up to my father's event with my man and we can just ignore each other? That's not how things work in the real world."

"For your information, I hate your man. I was forced into going to that stupid event. You can have him. Seriously. He's all yours."

Her mouth opened then closed as if she hadn't expected me to relent so easily.

"Now, can you move so I can shower?"

She stared me down for a long time, seemingly unsure what to make of the information I'd given her. Unexpectedly, she stepped out of the way.

I moved away and into a warm shower, letting all thoughts of selfish assholes flee my brain.

# 15

## KASON

I arrived to physics before the rest of the class. But just like last class, Shay had ducked in at the last minute, avoiding eye contact with me at all costs. The fact that she thought she could avoid me for the rest of the semester had me pulling out my phone and texting her.

ME

Hi.

She pulled out her phone to check it when it must have vibrated with my text. She instantly shoved it back into her bag without responding.

"We'll be having a test on this unit next Monday," Professor Raymond announced at the end of class. "And I have some exciting news," he continued. "Since many of you seem to be struggling this semester, I've set up a study group to assist with your study skills."

I scoffed. *Sounds exciting.*

"Ms. Miller will be leading the group."

*Wait. What?*

"The study group will run from seven to eight on

Wednesday nights in the conference room by my office starting tonight."

*Holy crap.*

Shay Miller didn't want to look at me or return my texts, but I knew where I'd be Wednesday nights. And there wasn't a damn thing she could do about it.

———

I walked into the dark building, searching for the conference room a few minutes before seven. There was one other guy outside the door at the end of the hallway. "Are you here for the study group?" I asked.

He nodded.

I peeked in the window, noting Shay alone inside at the conference table looking at her laptop screen. I looked to the guy who stood in the hallway with me. "I'll give you fifty bucks to leave."

"What?"

"I'll give you fifty bucks to leave," I repeated.

"Are you serious?"

"Deathly."

"Okay."

I grabbed my wallet from my back pocket, pulled out a fifty, and handed it to him. "Thanks, man."

The guy nabbed the cash then took off.

A sense of relief washed over me as I checked my phone. It was seven and no one else was there. I twisted the doorknob, causing Shay to glance up as I stepped inside the small room. Disappointment spread across her face.

"Looks like it's just you and me," I said with a smile.

She closed her eyes as if pained by the notion.

I sat down at the table in the seat next to hers. "Just like old times, huh?"

"Why are you here?" she asked.

"Because I need a tutor. I told you that."

Her eyes shot to the closed door. "No one else is out there?"

"Nope."

She closed her laptop. "I'm gonna tell Professor Raymond this was a bust."

"But *I'm* here."

"Right." She packed her laptop into her backpack.

"What's it gonna take for you to help me?"

"Hell freezing over." She rolled back in her chair and stood up.

"Seriously, Shay? I'm sorry about what happened between us."

She balked. "Nothing happened between us. That's the point. You made me think something did."

"I know. And I'm sorry. It was a mistake."

"Is that how things work in your life? You say sorry and all is forgiven?"

I didn't say anything.

"Because in my world, people who use you and lie to you get what's coming to them." She heaved her backpack over her shoulders and walked to the door just as it opened.

Professor Raymond stepped inside. "Looks like we got one."

Shay froze.

"Hey, Professor," I said. "I'm so glad you arranged this because I'm struggling to keep up in your class. But speaking from experience, Shay is an awesome tutor."

He glanced to her backpack on her back. "Did you just get here?"

Shay stood awkwardly with her hands grasping the straps of her backpack. "Yup," she lied. "I was running late." She turned slowly and glared at me as she pulled out a chair and removed her backpack.

"Don't mind me," Professor Raymond said, pulling out a chair at the end of the table. "I'm just going to do some work down here. Pretend I'm not even here."

Shay huffed as she sat down, retrieving her laptop from her bag and opening it on the table.

"That quiz you made me for the last test was a lifesaver," I said, making sure Professor Raymond heard.

He smiled.

"Maybe we can do another one of those," I suggested to Shay, knowing she was hating every second of this.

"Great idea," she said through clenched teeth. "But how about I show *you* how to set one up. You can input the words and definitions. That way *you're* learning as you create the quiz."

"Brilliant idea. Professor Raymond was smart to get you."

She leveled me with scathing eyes.

I smiled, but my smile was short-lived. I realized by having me do all the inputting, we were sitting in silence and she barely had to speak to me.

*Damn her.*

At ten minutes to eight, Professor Raymond slipped out, citing a dinner date.

"Thank God," Shay said as soon as he was gone, closing her laptop and packing it into her bag.

"Whoa. It's not even eight yet," I argued.

"So?"

"So, I get you until eight."

"You don't get *me*, Kason. You get physics."

"You can't hate me forever."

She grabbed her backpack. "Watch me." She yanked open the door and walked out of the conference room.

I stuffed my things into my bag and ran after her, catching up with her outside the building. "I'm not letting you walk home alone. I've got my Jeep."

"I'm not going anywhere with you," she said as she continued walking.

I kept pace with her. "Well, I'm not letting you walk alone."

"Well, then enjoy the walk." She quickened her pace, taking the path toward her dorm as I slowed to a stop.

My Jeep was parked there, but I couldn't just let her walk alone across the dark campus. I took off after her, following on foot.

The five-minute walk to her dorm was steeped in silence. A long ominous silence. I considered apologizing again, but it would likely only irritate her and not have the outcome I was hoping for.

When we reached the dorm, she flashed her key card and opened the door. I expected her to at least glance back at me once she stepped inside, but she didn't. And, I couldn't even blame her.

16

———

## KASON

Another long week of Shay not acknowledging my existence in physics class passed. I didn't want to be the asshole she, and everyone else apparently, thought I was. Yes, I was a guy who screwed up. But I deserved a do-over. The girl just wasn't budging.

And, since I wasn't a patient guy, I did what any desperate guy would do, I headed to study group Wednesday night. I cursed under my breath when I spotted the guy from the first week standing outside the conference room. Was the douche trying to extort me or was he really here to study?

"What's up, dude? She in there?" I asked.

Excitement flashed in his eyes, dollar signs no doubt cha-chinging in his brain.

"You going in?" I asked as I grabbed the doorknob.

Disappointment crossed his features. "I'm not sure," he said as if he was still holding out hope that I'd offer him money again.

I left his ass in the hallway and walked inside the conference room, more nervous than I realized. My heart began to pound as I found Shay on her laptop, her eyes focused on her screen. I quietly closed the door behind me, pulled out the rolling chair, and sat down.

Shay still didn't look away from her laptop screen.

"Hey, Shay."

She said nothing.

"Did you have a nice day?"

She said nothing.

*Okay.*

"Hey, you two," Professor Raymond said as he swept into the room, taking a seat at the head of the conference table with a stack of papers.

"Hey," I said, never so happy to see the professor. Now Shay *had* to talk to me.

"Hi," Shay said to him, finally speaking.

"Don't mind me," he continued as he popped his earbuds into his ears. "I've got a bunch of essays to correct."

I looked to Shay. "I read Monday's homework. I'm a total pro on Kepler's now."

She finally looked at me with cold eyes, probably glad the professor couldn't hear us because of his earbuds. "You knew a few basic terms."

I cocked my head, hating the coldness she was exuding. "Shay?"

She huffed. "You're here for help. So, I'll help. But that's all you'll get, or I swear I will leave."

"Agreed," I said, taking whatever small morsel she'd toss my way.

She exhaled as she grabbed her notebook from her backpack. She opened it and flipped through until she found a blank page inside and pushed the open notebook toward me. "Suppose a small planet is discovered that is fourteen times as far from the sun as the Earth's distance is from the sun. Use Kepler's Law of Harmonies to predict the orbital period of such a planet."

I stared at her as if she'd spoken a language I didn't know. Because let's be honest. *That* was a language I didn't know.

She pulled her notebook back and jotted something down on the page before facing it back toward me. "This is the given."

I glanced at the paper. $T^2/R^3 = 2.97 \times 10^{-19} \, s^2/m^3$

She sat back in her chair and her eyes returned to her laptop screen. "Let me know if you need me."

Again, she'd given me a task to keep me occupied and her from having to speak to me. *Damn her.*

I spent the next thirty minutes trying to work out the problem. Much of the paper was filled with scribbled out math, and I realized whatever I'd been working on made no sense. I had no idea what I was doing. It was one thing to remember a few definitions, but I sucked at the math part. I finally turned the paper toward Shay. "Am I even close?"

She pulled her attention away from whatever she was doing on her laptop and glanced down at my work. "Well..." Her eyes moved over the messy paper. "Your first mistake was you didn't rearrange to solve for $T_p$."

"Oh, of course, I didn't rearrange for $T_p$."

"Do you really understand that?" she asked.

"Hell no."

Her shoulders dropped on a huff. "Here." She jotted a formula down on the paper, explaining each step she took as she wrote it. I listened to everything she said and followed along on the paper, trying to grasp something that made no sense at all. "So, $T_{planet} = 52.4$ yr," she explained as she wrote it.

"Of course, it does," I mumbled.

"Nothing?" she asked, noting my confusion.

I shook my head.

"Let me think about how to approach this. We can try again next week."

*Next week?* "Okay."

"You're not a lost cause, Kason," she said as she closed her laptop. "You just need a little assistance."

"Well, I appreciate your patience. I know it can't be easy to explain something that's so easy to you to someone who only sees gibberish. Let me get you a coffee or something for all your help," I offered.

"I'm fine. I need to get back to the dorm."

"Hot date?" I joked, not wanting her to leave yet.

She stuffed her computer into the bag, clearly trying to be away from me. "Something like that."

Was she really going out with someone? Why did I suddenly have the urge to stalk her dorm to see? I was not only selfish but I was sick, too. "Well, let me give you a ride so you don't make Prince Charming wait."

"No."

"Shay, come on. What'll it hurt to take a ride?"

She said nothing, just heaved her backpack onto her back.

"Maybe I should meet him."

With a scrunched face, she looked at me. "What?"

"You know, make sure his intentions are good. I'm just looking out for you."

She scoffed. "Ironic."

My insides twisted into an angry knot, resenting her response. When the hell was she gonna let go of her animosity toward me? A breath whooshed out of me as my thoughts reverted to Thayer's and Giselle's words, and I felt like shit for getting annoyed with her.

She looked to Professor Raymond and raised her voice. "Good night, Professor."

He pulled out his earbuds. "Oh, you two are leaving?"

"Yes, he's good for tonight," she explained to him.

"Good night," he said with an appreciative smile.

Shay turned and walked out of the room.

Knowing she wouldn't let me drive her home, I followed her out of the building. "I'm gonna make sure you get home okay."

"No need," she called without turning around.

"Peace of mind," I said without stopping.

Our footsteps were the only sound as we followed the path back to her dorm. Again, I wanted to plead my case. I wanted to do *anything* for her to forgive me. But I chickened out.

She reached her dorm and flashed her keycard. I stopped, watching as she pulled open the front door. I couldn't let her walk inside again without looking back. "Shay?"

I expected her to ignore me, but she paused, reluctantly turning to look at me.

"Be careful. It's not only me. All guys suck."

I expected a reaction—maybe even a grin—but she turned away from me and walked inside. Once the door slammed loudly behind her, I had a sinking feeling that she was never going to forgive me.

17

———

SHAY

Some people were incapable of sitting alone in a crowded room and tuning out all the noise. But, over the years, I'd gotten good at it. I could sit somewhere and just disappear into my thoughts. Sometimes that was a good thing, but other times, not so much. I picked away at my blueberry muffin, opting for breakfast as my lunch in the campus dining room closest to my next class.

"How'd your hot date go?"

Inwardly, I groaned. Besides study group, Kason had been good about leaving me alone. But the fact that he was approaching me outside study hall made me think he thought my threats were idle. I pulled in a calming breath before lifting my eyes and meeting his gaze. He looked ready to hit the mountain in dark snowboarding pants and a hoodie. "Excuse me?"

"Your date the other night. Did he treat you all right?"

"Fine," I said, knowing I didn't have a date the other night. He'd assumed it, and I didn't correct him. But the truth was, the only hot date I had that night was with a long hot shower.

"You going out with him again?"

I shrugged. "Never know."

He nodded, his hands playing with the takeout container in his hand. "I'm heading to snowboard."

"I can see that."

He nodded again as if stalling for some reason.

"Well, don't break anything," I said, trying to hurry him along.

His eyes widened. "Nothing like jinxing me, Little One."

The use of his nickname for me sent a small zinger to my chest. I hadn't felt much since the charity event. Everything that had happened—the lies, the manipulation, the embarrassment—dulled everything inside me. So, why the reaction to my nickname? I guess it brought me back to all those nights in the library. And, even when I hated him most, it still affected me.

"Well, I'll see you Monday," he said.

"Study the quizzes we made. I have a feeling he'll ask a bunch of those questions on the midterm."

He shot me a sad grin. "I will. Thanks." He turned and left the dining hall, leaving me sitting there wondering why he kept trying to make things right. Why he kept trying to earn my forgiveness. Why did he care? I was no one to him but someone who could get him what he needed. Was it possible that he truly felt remorse for what he did? Had what happened with us changed him?

*Kason*

I stood atop the mountain, breathing in the fresh Colorado air as I eyed the slopestyle course in front of me. As usual, the jumps were outlined in blue so they could be seen in the otherwise whiteout world surrounding them. I lived for these courses. The rush. The satisfaction of landing a trick. The silence that encompassed me as I left solid ground.

"Ready?" Jesse asked from behind me.

I nodded.

His GoPro camera sat at the end of a telescoping pole with a blue grip, ready to capture my ride from a few feet behind me.

I inhaled and dropped in, curving my turns sharp to gain momentum as I descended. With the necessary speed, I headed straight for the first jump. I needed to perfect my quad if I was gonna pull it off during the Games. Jesse followed me down, his camera capturing footage of me for social media. I usually posted tricks I'd done before, amping them up with music that made them more intense. He wouldn't show any new tricks since I needed to save those for run four at the Games.

I gained enough speed and hit the second jump. My board left the snow and nothing but quiet filled my ears as I flipped, inverting three times and pulling off a triple cork. I landed it without a hitch. I went right into my front double nine pulling a grab switch. I came down hard, landing unevenly and flipping over my board. I tumbled a couple of times before totally wiping out.

"Dude, you all right?" Jesse said as he moved to me, the camera no longer recording me.

I jumped up and brushed the snow off me. "Yeah. Just don't use that part."

"Yeah, it was a nasty spill."

I shrugged, unsnapping my boots from my board and carrying it toward the lift. "If at first you don't succeed..."

"Spill, spill again?" Jesse asked.

"Speak for yourself."

He laughed. "Someone's sore."

I shook off his busting, and we made our way to the ski lift, hopping on and taking it to the top.

"You sure you're alright?" Jesse asked.

"It's not like I've never fallen before."

"Not what I meant."

My eyes cut to his.

"You've been off lately."

What the fuck was up with all my friends? Did they all decide it was time to rag on Kason? I shrugged, not in the mood to hear him out. There was only so much 'you're a selfish prick' I could take.

"How's your friend from the Slopes event?"

*Seriously?*

"You two..." he started.

"We're barely even friends," I snapped.

I glanced across physics class Monday morning. It had been some time since I looked in Kason's direction, but I wanted to see if he looked overwhelmed at the sight of Professor Raymond's exam. I'd been right about the questions being like the ones in our quizzes. But, Kason looked calm as he wrote in his exam booklet.

I finished my exam before anyone else but checked my answers before approaching Professor Raymond at the front of the class with it. "Professor, I wanted to remind you I won't be holding study group on Wednesday night since I'll be heading home that afternoon for Thanksgiving."

"Big plans while at home?" he asked.

I shrugged. "I guess I'll see once I get there. See ya." I walked to the door and stepped into the empty hallway. Professor Raymond had no idea how awful being back home was likely to be.

Footsteps echoed down the hallway behind me. "Shay!"

I halted, knowing who the voice and the footsteps belonged to.

Kason rounded in front of me. "How'd you do?"

"The question is how did *you* do?"

"I totally blew those math questions, but I think I got all the definitions since they were on the quizzes we made. So, I think I might've passed."

I gave him a thumbs-up. "Good for you."

"If I passed, it was all you."

I rolled my eyes.

"I'm serious. Without you, I would've failed a long time ago."

"I'm glad I could help," I said.

"If I were you, I would've taught me all the wrong information. I would've deserved it."

"I wish I'd thought of that," I deadpanned.

He smiled, and when he showed all his straight teeth and his blue eyes dazzled, I wished I didn't hate him so much. "You headed home for Thanksgiving?"

"On Wednesday. So, no study group that night."

"Yeah, I'm outta here after my morning classes." He buried his hands in his pockets awkwardly, like he didn't know what else to say but he wasn't walking away.

I saved him the turmoil. "See ya." I stepped around him and hurried out of the building.

---

Kendall and I ate dinner the following night in the dining hall. We were about to get dessert when my phone pinged.

SNOWBOARD HOTTIE

How'd you do on the exam?

He must've seen that Professor Raymond posted our grades. I responded.

ME

A+ You?

SNOWBOARD HOTTIE

C+

The slightest bit of pride flooded my chest, knowing he never would've pulled off a C+ without my help.

"What are you smiling at?" Kendall asked.

My eyes lifted to hers. "I'm not smiling."

"Oh, you were definitely smiling. Who's texting you?"

"Kason."

Her eyebrows lifted. "Oh, yeah?"

"He passed his exam."

"*That's* what you were smiling at?" She sounded let down.

"*If* I was smiling, it was because I was happy to see all that time I wasted tutoring him actually helped."

"If you say so."

My phone pinged again. I glanced at the screen.

SNOWBOARD HOTTIE

Have a Happy Thanksgiving.

"It's such a shame that you two don't get along," Kendall said, pulling my attention to her.

"Why? He's an ass."

"He's a fine ass."

I rolled my eyes as I texted the ass back.

ME

U 2

## 19

## KASON

I knew my mom loved when I brought gifts home to her, so I loaded the last of my dirty laundry into my Jeep. I ran back inside and called to Thayer, "Catch you on Sunday night."

"Have a good Thanksgiving."

"You too. Say hi to your dad and his newest gold digger."

"Say hi to Giselle for me," he called.

"Fuck off, douchebag."

He laughed, which was a hell of a lot more than I'd gotten from him since I fessed up about blackmailing Shay. He hadn't looked at me the same since, and I couldn't blame him for being disappointed.

I headed outside toward my Jeep and hopped inside. I cranked up my eighties rock and waited for all the outgoing traffic to pass my house before even attempting to pull out of my driveway. Just like me, students were heading home for the holiday after their last classes of the day. When the last car passed, I spotted Shay in the backseat. I waved but she didn't even glance my way.

A sudden curiosity filled me, one I knew I wouldn't be able to quiet. So, I pulled out onto the road behind the car. I knew Shay lived in Colorado, but she never said anything more than that. And, since she was clearly in an Uber, it couldn't be that far.

The car turned onto the highway and I followed it. It couldn't be considered stalking if I was already going in that direction. Right?

Thirty minutes later, the Uber's blinker flashed. I'd never taken exit seventeen before, but a little detour couldn't hurt. I followed for a few miles before I really began to feel like a stalker. The roads became dirt and the houses became closer together, smaller, old, and rundown. Snow was piled up on cars that were clearly broken and nothing was shoveled.

The Uber pulled to a stop outside a trailer. I hit the brakes, staying far enough back that I could see but wouldn't be seen. The back door of the car opened and Shay stepped out, her backpack on her back and a large plastic storage container in her arms. She stared at the trailer as the car pulled away. She stood there for at least two minutes before she placed the large container on the ground and sat on it.

I looked to the door and noticed a tattered sheet of paper attached to it and flapping in the wind. Something wasn't right. Why wasn't she going inside? Wasn't someone waiting for her?

I shifted into park and killed my engine. This could go one of two ways. Bad or to shit. I opened my door and stepped out. I walked slowly toward the sad scene. The snow beneath my sneakers crunched softly, but the sound wasn't enough to draw Shay's attention to me. I approached her, stopping a couple of feet away. "Shay?"

Her head whipped over her shoulder, her eyes filled with tears. "What are you doing here?"

I buried my hands in my pockets. "I was heading home and noticed you take this exit." God, I sounded like a fucking stalker. "I thought I'd stop and wish you a happy Thanksgiving."

She turned away from me. "Liar."

She nailed it. I *was* a liar. One who hadn't been honest with her since the day we met.

"Please just leave me alone," she said softly, and something about the way she said it without conviction, told me she didn't really mean it.

I walked over and nudged her with my hip so she'd move over. She did without argument which told me my instincts had been spot on. I sat down beside her on the large container, hoping the lid didn't collapse under my weight.

I didn't dare speak. I had no idea what to say if I *did* speak. I knew she said her life had been tough, but now I saw the foreclosure sign on the door and a padlock keeping it locked. She had no home.

"Now I know," she whispered.

"What do you know?" I asked.

"Why he's been calling."

I felt like a fool. I had no idea who *he* was. All the time I'd spent with Shay—against her will—I hadn't asked a damn thing about her. My friends and sister had been right. I was a self-absorbed asshole. "Who?"

"My father."

"Do you know where he went?"

She shook her head.

"Jeez, Shay, I'm sorry."

"He wasn't going to get help if I stayed. I was enabling

him. I needed to leave so he had nothing left. He needed to hit rock bottom."

I didn't say anything, realizing for the first time how bad her childhood must've been.

"Do you think I'm a terrible person?" Shay asked.

"What? No." I wrapped my arm around her tiny shoulders and pulled her into me, surprised when she let me. "I think you're an incredible person, Shay. He needs to find his way just like you need to find your way. You're the kid for God's sake. Not the other way around."

Her soft sniffles nearly broke me. Shay didn't cry. Shay didn't break down. Shay didn't confide in me. But now she was doing all three.

"What am I gonna do?" she whispered. "I thought he'd be here."

"Come home with me," I said.

She jumped out away from me as if she just remembered we weren't in a great place. "I can't do that."

"Of course you can."

She shook her head, her eyes still glazed with unshed tears.

I stood up and walked over to her, placing my hands on her shoulders. She glanced up at me through her damp eyelashes. "Let someone take care of you for a change, Shay. I'd say it's been a long time since someone has."

I wished I could've read the look in her eyes, but given her current situation, I was her only option.

It was a thirty-minute car ride to my parents' house. Shay was quiet the entire way. I'd expected even a small reaction once I turned on eighties rock, but she showed none. So, I left her alone with her thoughts, knowing she'd have to talk once she got to my parents' home.

We pulled into the driveway of my childhood home.

"Well, we're here." The brick exterior gave the façade of money, but we'd always just been an average middle-class family.

Shay stared out at the house. "It's beautiful."

Regret formed in my gut, realizing this was so much nicer than where Shay had grown up. "Come on. Let's go meet my parents." I jumped out before she could change her mind.

She met me at the back of my Jeep. "Let me just grab some things from my container."

The sight of that stupid storage container made me realize she didn't even have a damn suitcase. "I've got extra luggage my sponsors keep giving me that I don't need."

"It's fine," she said as she stuffed some clothes she'd taken out of the container into her backpack.

"You good?" I asked, leaving my dirty laundry in my Jeep. I'd grab that later.

She nodded.

*Here goes nothing.* I led Shay toward the side door. When I opened it, the smell of my mom's pumpkin pie hit us. "I'm home!"

"Kason!" my mother cried as she rushed across the kitchen and wrapped her arms around me. She was a foot shorter than me so I rested my head on the top of her head as she held onto me. "I missed you."

"Aw, Mom. You're embarrassing me in front of my friend."

My mom released me and noticed Shay standing there. "Oh, hello." I could tell by the way she took Shay in that she was shocked I'd brought a girl home—especially without telling her—but she was too polite to ever let on.

"This is Shay," I said.

"Nice to meet you, Mrs. McCloud."

"Call me Tabitha."

Shay smiled awkwardly.

I didn't blame her. The whole situation was awkward.

"Is Kason home?" my dad asked as he entered the kitchen.

"Hey, Dad." I greeted him with a hug.

"Who's this?" he asked as he released me.

"This is my friend Shay. She's gonna be spending the holiday with us."

"If that's okay," Shay added.

"Of course, sweetie," my mother said with a smile. "It'll be nice to have another girl around here."

"Is superstar home?" Giselle asked as she entered the kitchen, her face lighting up when she spotted our guest. "Shay!" She rushed over and wrapped Shay in a hug. Shay didn't know what to do with her arms and left them at her side. It would've been funny if it wasn't so sad.

"Hi."

Giselle released her. "I'm so glad Kason smartened up."

"Oh, we're—" Shay began.

"Study buddies," I said.

Shay's eyes cut to mine.

"She's a hell of a tutor. Shay's gonna be a biochemist one day."

She stared at me, likely surprised I'd been paying attention when she'd told me.

"Wow. She's smart," my dad said. "That's definitely new for Kason."

The three of them laughed, and I knew I needed to get Shay out of there before they embarrassed me anymore.

"Can Shay stay in the guest room?" I asked.

"Well, she's certainly not staying in your room," my mom said.

I watched Shay swallow down hard.

"Obviously, Mom."

"Yes. The guest room has clean sheets," my mom explained.

I ticked my head toward the doorway. "Come on. Let me show you to your room."

"Have you two eaten?" my mom asked as we began to walk away.

I glanced to Shay, having no idea if she grabbed a bite to eat before leaving campus.

She shook her head. "No."

"Well, I have some leftover lasagna. Let me warm it up for you."

"Sounds good," I said.

Shay looked at my parents. "Thank you for having me."

"Of course," my mom said, having no idea that if she hadn't allowed Shay to stay, Shay would've had nowhere to go.

"Anytime," my dad added as Shay followed me down the hallway to the stairs.

As soon as we were out of the kitchen, I could hear them whispering. I did kind of blindside them with Shay. I could only imagine what they were saying—or thinking, for that matter.

Shay and I climbed the stairs, and I led her down the hallway. "This is my room," I said as I stepped inside and switched on the light.

Shay stood in the doorway as I dropped my bag onto my bed. Her eyes moved over the snowboarding posters that filled the walls and the medals hanging from the mirror on my dresser.

"The guest room is right across the hall," I explained, walking past her in the doorway and flicking on the light in the room across the hall. The beige walls were bare, but there was a full-sized bed with a navy comforter and a dresser on the opposite wall.

She walked inside and placed her backpack down on the bed, keeping her back to me as she looked around. "This is so nice." After a moment, she turned to face me. "Thank you."

I knew how much it must've taken for her to utter those words to me after everything I'd done to her. "Don't thank me yet. You haven't endured a McCloud family dinner."

The corners of her lips twitched.

"The bathroom is at the end of the hall," I said.

She nodded.

"I'll meet you downstairs whenever you're ready." I stepped out of the room to give her space, knowing this must've been overwhelming for her.

But, now that I had her under my roof with nowhere to go, I didn't want to do anything to upset her. Since the event, I'd been trying to get in Shay's good graces. There was no way I was going to do anything to mess that up now.

## 20

## SHAY

I fell back on the bed, so happy to have some alone time to think. Everything had happened so quickly. From finding the eviction notice and lock on the trailer door to Kason showing up out of nowhere to take me home with him, I hadn't had time to assess my current situation.

I no longer had a home.

And though I never truly considered it a home, it was a roof over my head.

If I'd only known—if I'd only answered the phone when my father called—I could have made other arrangements. I could have tagged along with Kendall. I could have tried to stay in the dorm. I could have figured *something* out.

But, I hadn't.

Because I didn't want to speak to him. I didn't want to give him the opportunity to suck me into his troubles. And, truthfully, I just had nothing left to say to him. When I'd left for school, I'd made a clean break. It was necessary in order to stay sane. To move on. To have the future I deserved. Being back at the trailer made me feel dirty. It reminded me where I came from and where I desperately needed to escape from.

I could hear Kason and his family laughing downstairs and a sense of warmth rushed through me. I didn't know being in a loving home could feel like that. I shook off the feeling, reminding myself it wasn't my home. It wasn't my life. I was a temporary guest who never should've been there to begin with. I wondered if I should've accepted Kason's offer. I knew I didn't belong in Kason's world, but when he wrapped his arm around me, I allowed myself to believe that he cared about me. Because before he arrived, I felt like I was all alone in this world.

---

A short time later, I crept downstairs to find Kason and his mom at the kitchen table. There was a plate of lasagna in front of Kason and another plate at the empty seat next to him. Mrs. McCloud drank from a mug and her face lit up when she saw me in the doorway.

Kason, catching her expression, glanced over his shoulder and smiled when he spotted me. I wished a smile didn't mean so much. "Are your lodgings up to par?" he asked.

I looked to his mom. "They're perfect."

"Come sit," she said, gesturing to the empty seat.

I sat down, eyeing the large portion of lasagna she'd warmed for me. "This looks delicious."

"I bet the dining halls don't cook like me," she teased.

I shook my head.

She looked to Kason. "Remind me what *you're* eating these days."

"No worries, Mom. I'm getting all the food groups."

"Pizza doesn't count," she said.

"Of course, it does. Cheese is dairy. Crust carbs. Pepperoni protein. Pineapple fruit. And tomato sauce vegetable."

"Actually," I said. "Tomatoes are fruit."

"Liar."

"Nope. Totally fruit."

"Keep hanging around with Shay," Mrs. McCloud said. "Maybe her brain will rub off on you."

His mouth opened into a wide O. "Did my own mom just call me stupid?"

"The word stupid never left these lips," she said with a grin.

"It didn't need to," he scowled.

Mrs. McCloud and I laughed as she stood from the table. The love flowing through the McCloud home was undeniable. And, their interactions were so heartwarming to watch.

"Your mom is so nice," I said once she stepped out of the room, leaving the two of us alone to eat.

"At least someone thinks so. Did she really just call me stupid?"

"If the shoe fits," I said before taking a bite of lasagna.

He balled up his napkin and threw it at my head. It pelted off my forehead.

"Seriously?" I asked.

He nodded.

I rolled my eyes, knowing that he'd found a way to crack through (what I thought to be) the impenetrable barrier I'd been keeping between us. Now, how long would I be able to keep it up? And, did I really want to?

21

———

SHAY

Laughter from downstairs had me stopping in my tracks as I braided my hair in the guest room the next day. The McCloud's had been so welcoming to me and so kind. I had no idea how I was ever going to repay Kason.

*Yes. The irony of that thought was not lost on me.*

There was a knock on the door as I used an elastic to finish off my braid.

"Come in," I called.

The door opened and Giselle poked her head in. "Happy Thanksgiving."

"Happy Thanksgiving." The smile slipped from my face as she opened the door the rest of the way and stepped inside wearing a pretty floral dress. I glanced down at my jeans and T-shirt. "I'm underdressed."

"You look fine. But, I have lots of dresses if you'd like to wear one."

"I couldn't ask you for that."

She rolled her eyes. "Be right back."

I stripped out of my clothes so she wouldn't need to wait

before I tried on the dresses she was kind enough to offer. Almost immediately, there was a tap on the door. The door cracked open and a navy dress on a hanger was thrust through the opening. I moved to the door. Before I could get it, the door opened and Kason stepped inside. Since I was in nothing but a bra and panties, I ripped the dress out of his hand and covered myself with it.

Unfazed by my embarrassment, he crossed his arms and stood there looking at me. "Oh, you don't want to change in front of me?" he asked with a coy smile.

"Not really."

His eyes dropped to my feet, and it was then a wave of fear washed over my body. I wasn't wearing my boots. He realized the same thing and his eyes widened as they took in my legs. "Shay," he said with dread in his voice. "What happened to your legs?"

"Nothing," I snapped.

"That's not nothing. What happened to you?"

I dragged in a long breath knowing I couldn't hide the scars now that he'd seen them. "They're burns."

I could see the sympathy in his eyes as they drifted over the small circular scars speckling my shins and calves.

"My father was an angry drunk," I said, knowing he was waiting for an explanation.

His eyes lifted to mine.

"Don't," I threatened.

Indecision flashed in his eyes. Kason was a fixer. I could tell he wanted to fix it, but the damage had been done. "Get dressed. I'll be right back." He ducked out of the room.

I stood there for a moment, wondering what he thought of the information I just divulged. Would he start treating me differently or pretend he never saw my scars?

I slipped the dress over my head. Giselle was a little bigger than me, but the dress still worked.

"Shay?" Kason asked from outside the door. "Are you decent?"

"Would it stop you if I said no?"

"No." He chuckled before pushing the door open. His eyes latched onto the dress I now wore. "You look great."

"Thanks."

"Do you mind sitting on the edge of the bed for a second?" he asked.

It was then that I noticed something clasped in his hand. I had no idea what he was up to, but since he'd been so good to invite me into his home, I did as he asked.

He lowered to his knees in front of me and examined the scars on my legs. I almost jumped up, but then he opened his hand, revealing a tube of concealer that was probably Giselle's. He dabbed at the tube and a dollop of skin-colored makeup covered his fingertip. He held his finger to my leg before looking to me to make sure it was okay.

I nodded.

He pressed his finger to the biggest scar on my shin, dabbing it a few times until he covered it with the makeup. For the next few minutes, he was quiet, focusing on covering each scar with the makeup. I watched as he continued to dab the makeup on my skin, wondering why he felt the need to do this for me. "Do they hurt?" he asked, his eyes on the job at hand.

"Not anymore."

"I'm sorry, Shay."

"You didn't do it."

"No one should've done it."

I agreed with him one-hundred percent. I'd endured

things no child should have to. But at the time, I thought I was holding things together. My mother died and I only had a father. And I told myself, an angry drunk of a father was better than no father. Because if I had no father, I had no one.

Over the years, I told myself if I could just withstand his anger that he'd take out on me—if I could just stay out of his way when he was drunk—I'd be okay. But he began to be drunk more than he wasn't. Staying out of his way became nearly impossible. College would be my escape. That's why I threw everything I had into school. If I could just get scholarships to pay for college, I could leave, and he'd have no other option than to get help. But, now, I had no idea if that's what happened. He could be dead in some gutter and I wouldn't know. And the fact that I wasn't upset by the notion, scared the hell out of me. I was a good person. A good person who had just had enough. A good person who realized she couldn't fix someone who didn't want to be fixed.

My need to be a biochemist to discover a cure for addiction—was bred out of a place of necessity. And living through what I'd lived through, made me determined to help those who couldn't help themselves—*and* their victims.

"Looks like I got all of them," Kason said, glancing up at me. "That is all of them, isn't it?"

I tilted my head, not needing to explain there were others elsewhere.

His eyes lowered and he nodded his understanding.

I stood up, causing him to back up. I walked to the full-length mirror on the closet door and looked at myself. I couldn't see a single scar. And for once, I liked what I saw.

"I bet Giselle has some heels you could wear."

I glanced at him in the mirror. "I might fall and break my neck."

"How about some flats? I know she's got a bunch of those."

I nodded, appreciating how kind he was being.

He disappeared into the hallway, and I finally could breathe again.

*Kason*

I hurried into Giselle's empty room and dropped down onto the edge of her bed. I was so stupid. *So* God damned stupid. The pajamas. The combat boots. How had I not realized she was hiding behind those things? How had I not considered why a college girl was wearing footie pajamas?

My mind reeled back to the night in my room. The now-*infamous* night in my room. How had I missed the scars? Sure, it had been dark and I'd been in a rush to set her up. But I should have seen them when I slipped off her boots. Self-absorbed Kason was a true douchebag. One who didn't deserve someone like Shay in his life.

But I'd be lying if I said I didn't well up when she saw her reflection in the mirror without those scars. It was as if she was seeing a whole new Shay. Like those scars had somehow defined her until that moment. I was surprised she hadn't thought of it before.

What the hell had she endured in that run-down trailer? I wished I knew the truth behind those scars. Because, they weren't given in one shot. They were given over time. And the vision of a terrified young Shay made me feel rage I didn't know I was capable of.

"What are you doing?" Giselle asked as she stepped into her room.

I stared at her, not having the words to convey what I was thinking.

"You saw them?" she asked.

I nodded.

"There's got to be a hell of a story to go with those marks," she said, her voice low and plagued with sadness.

"Do you have a pair of flats to match that dress?"

Her lips pulled up in the corners. "Of course. But will she wear them? They don't cover her legs."

"I took care of them."

"You did?"

"I guess I finally started paying attention."

Giselle's smile broadened before she ducked into her closet and came back out with a pair of nude-colored flats.

I nabbed them from her hand. "Thanks, sis."

"I'm glad," she said.

My brows pinched together. "What?"

"That you started paying attention."

I nodded before leaving her room. I hurried back to the guest room and tapped on the door, pushing it open and stepping inside.

Shay, seated on the bed, glanced up at me.

"How about these?" I handed them to her.

"They're perfect." She leaned down and slipped them on.

"Do they fit?"

"They're a little big, but they'll work just fine," she said.

"Are you ready to head down?"

She pushed herself to her feet. "Yes."

We headed downstairs just as my mom was placing the turkey on the center of the dining room table. She glanced up at us, doing a double-take of Shay with a smile. "You look beautiful, Shay."

I didn't need to look at Shay to know she was blushing.

"You can sit right there," my mom said, pointing to the chair beside my usual seat.

Shay sat and I sat down beside her.

My dad walked into the room, noticing Shay and I were already seated. "Thanks for waiting for me," he teased as he took his seat at the head of the table.

"It's not like we ate anything," I said.

Giselle entered next, her eyes on Shay and me, her brows bouncing when Shay wasn't looking. She took her seat across from us. My mom placed the stuffing down and then took her seat across from my dad.

"Let's eat," I said, reaching for the stuffing.

My mom swatted my hand. "Let our guest make her plate first."

"Oh, no," Shay said, her eyes wild with embarrassment. "Please don't wait for me."

I looked to my mom, begging her to stop with my eyes.

She took the hint. "Well, if you insist. Why don't we start at the end and pass the sides around."

We did, filling our dishes with more food than anyone should ingest in a single day.

My dad lifted his glass before we dug in. "To my family. I don't know how I got to be such a lucky guy, but I am so thankful to have all of you." He looked to Shay. "And to new friends. Welcome to our crazy family. We're happy to have you here."

We lifted our water glasses and clinked them together before eating.

"So, how'd you two meet anyway?" my dad asked before sipping his drink.

I felt myself fidgeting, knowing the real story would not be a crowd-pleaser. Shay, likely sensing my predicament, reached under the table and did the unimaginable. She placed her hand lightly on my thigh. "You know me, Dad. Just pissing people off left and right. Shay was no exception."

My parents laughed and so did Shay as she removed her hand from my leg.

"Why don't I doubt that?" Dad said.

"Luckily, she came around and saw my charm," I teased.

Giselle made a deliberate choking sound. "Get me some crackers for the cheese he's spreading."

Everyone laughed.

We enjoyed the delicious meal and finished without any more questions that would make Shay uncomfortable. After leaving her alone last night, I'd warned my parents not to ask about her family.

My mom stood from the table, ready to clean up. Shay jumped up. "Let me help."

"Oh, honey. You're a guest."

"Please. I need to stand or that turkey is going to get stuck in my stomach."

My mother laughed as Shay picked up some dishes from the table and carried them in to the kitchen.

My dad and I moved to the living room to watch football. I could hear the girls in the kitchen talking and laughing. I was so happy to know that Shay had a family to spend the holiday with. Even more so because it turned out to be my family.

———

Just after ten, Shay excused herself and went upstairs to bed. I knew she probably had McCloud family overload, so I let her go.

"She's so nice, Kason," Mom said when the door to the guest room closed upstairs.

I didn't say anything, knowing Shay and I had our issues. However, after this weekend, I wondered if our issues would slowly become a thing of the past.

"She's different than the girls you're usually with," Dad said.

"You mean smart?" Giselle threw in.

They all laughed.

"Well, Shay and I aren't together," I explained. "Her coming here was a last-minute thing."

"Well, whatever brought her here with you, I'm happy it did," Mom said.

"She balances out your reckless side," Giselle said.

"Who's reckless?" I asked.

She cocked her head, knowing all too well I was a complete adrenaline junkie. "She's rational while you're not."

"Is that your way of supporting Mom's notion that Shay's smart and I'm dumb?"

They broke into laughter, confirming their thoughts.

With that vote of confidence, I jumped to my feet. "I'm going to bed."

"It's only ten," Giselle argued.

"Yeah, I'm hitting the mountain early in the morning."

"Is Shay going with you?"

"It's not really her scene." I walked over to my mom and leaned down and kissed her cheek. "Thanks for today. Everything was amazing." I moved to my dad and leaned down and gave him a hug. "Night, old man."

"Who are you calling old?" he asked.

I held out my fist to my sister to pound. "Night, Sis."

She rolled her eyes before reciprocating. "You're such a guy."

I climbed the stairs to the second floor. I stopped outside my room, pausing to listen for any noise in the guest room. I didn't hear anything, so I figured Shay had already gone to bed. I slipped inside my room and closed the door quietly. I changed out of my clothes, checked my phone for messages, then climbed into bed. I hadn't realized how tired I was until my head hit the pillow.

On the verge of dozing off a little while later, I heard the creak of my door opening. I lay there with my back to the door and my eyes closed, listening.

Soft footfalls padded across my room. I could tell it was Shay, so I waited her out. She sat down on the edge of my bed, the light weight of her not even dipping my mattress.

"Kason?" Shay whispered. "Are you up?"

"You can't come creeping in here unannounced, Little One. You might've caught me in the act."

As if electrocuted, she jumped off my bed. "Oh my God!"

I laughed, rolling over to face her and resting my cheek in my palm. "I'm joking."

Her shoulders relaxed, and I could see, even in the darkness, that she wore her footie pajamas.

"What's up?"

She moved back to the bed and sat down on the edge. "I just wanted to thank you."

"Thank me? What'd you have in mind?" I teased.

"Do you really want to remind me how much I hate you?"

"It was a joke."

She shook her head, amused I hoped. "I wanted to *say* thank you. Today was the most amazing holiday I've ever had."

I cocked my head, knowing it was the truth *and* it probably took a lot for her to come into my room to admit that. "Yeah?"

She nodded. "I can't remember a holiday where I didn't have to cook. And, it was usually just for me since my dad would end up passing out on the sofa before we even ate."

"Shay?"

She shook her head, not looking for my sympathy. "And forget Christmas. When I was six—just after my mom passed away, Santa didn't even show up. I told myself that maybe he just missed my trailer. But then when I was seven, and he still didn't leave presents, I knew something was up because the kids in the trailer next door got presents."

"Shay, I'm so sorry."

She shook her head, still not needing my pity. "I didn't come in here to lay my sob story on you." She moved to stand up, but I grabbed her wrist to keep her there.

"I wanna know more about you, Shay. You keep too much bottled inside. I'm here. Whatever you need."

She closed her eyes, seemingly pained by my words. "It's like you're these two different guys. And, I don't know which one you really are."

"There's only one of me."

"But you can't be the lying deceitful jerk who I swore to hate forever. And then be this incredibly thoughtful guy who comes to my rescue. Because let's be clear. I don't need rescuing."

I chuckled. "That's *abundantly* clear."

"I'm serious, Kason."

"So am I. I know you don't need rescuing. And, I also

know you need to decide how you feel about me. But just know, I'm clear on how I feel about you."

She was quiet for a long time. Then she stood. "Good night." She turned to leave my room.

"Hey."

She twisted back to look at me.

"Wanna come to the mountain with me in the morning?"

"Why?"

"Because it could be fun."

"To laugh at me?" she asked.

"I wouldn't think of it."

"Stop by my room before you go. If I'm up, I'll consider it." She moved to the door and walked out of my room.

She'd consider it? I'd never had to beg a girl to spend time with me before. What was it about Shay Miller that made me want to?

## 22

## SHAY

"Remind me again why I agreed to this?" I asked as I balanced on a snowboard, gripping Kason's hands, and moving along with him as he showed me what to do on his own board.

"Shay, we're on the bunny slope."

A kid who couldn't have been more than five years old sped by us on skis.

I growled, hating how uncoordinated I was when the little kid could move so effortlessly. At least I was warm in the winter gear Giselle had let me borrow.

Kason laughed. He was so carefree and lighter away from school. Lighter around his family. It looked good on him. "Come on. Just hold steady."

"Steady? This is the least steady I've ever been. How is it you flip and fly in the ski?"

"Fly in the ski?"

"You know what I mean," I said as I focused on keeping my knees bent as the board slid over the snow beneath me.

"You really need to brush up on your snowboarding lingo."

"Why?"

"So you can come cheer me on at the Games."

I didn't respond because I wasn't sure what January would bring. Things with Kason were always so unpredictable. You just never knew.

"Once you've had enough, I'll hit the slopestyle and show you some of my moves."

"I've had enough," I assured him.

"Oh, no. I need you doing this on your own before we quit."

Ugh.

———

We hit the lodge an hour later so I could thaw out. Kason grabbed me a hot chocolate then led me to a spot by the floor-to-ceiling window overlooking the mountain. From that vantage point, I could see the slopestyle course.

"Don't be too impressed," Kason said before taking off for the course.

"I'll try to control myself," I said as I pulled off Giselle's jacket and hat and sat down in a chair. I spent the next few minutes people-watching in the crowded lodge. Kids with flushed cheeks wearing snowsuits chased each other around as parents chatted with friends and warmed themselves with hot beverages near brick fireplaces. Snowboarders strutted through, checking out the pretty girls who seemed to be doing the same. The lodge was definitely a lively place to be.

A short time later, my phone buzzed with a text from Kason letting me know he'd be dropping in—which I learned meant he was about to come down the mountain. Since he wore an ugly hot pink Slopes helmet, he'd be difficult to miss. I stood from my chair, squinting as I attempted to spot the pink helmet. I saw it! Kason came down the mountain in a zigzag pattern, before flipping and making jumps like I'd seen him do in the video he showed me. And, though I'd never admit it to him, it was even more exciting to see him snowboarding in person. His talent was undeniable.

A kid in the lodge stepped up beside me, staring out the window at the course. "He's amazing, huh?" he said.

"Seems it," I said.

"Someday I want to snowboard like him."

"Do you practice?" I asked.

"Every weekend."

"Well, I bet if you stick with it, you can do all those cool jumps."

"Yeah," he said.

A woman who appeared to be his mother stepped up beside him. "Whatcha doing?"

"Just watching Kason snowboard," he told her.

"Don't blame you." She looked at me. "He's definitely something to watch."

A tinge of unwarranted jealousy balled up in my chest.

Kason sprayed snow at the bottom of the mountain. He turned to look at me through the window and waved his gloved hand.

The little boy beside me waved to him. I didn't wave back so the boy would think that Kason was waving to him.

Even with big goggles covering most of Kason's face, his smile still heightened unfamiliar feelings building inside me. I'd been honest when I told him he was two different guys. The one who thought he could do what he wanted and to hell with everyone else. But then he was this thoughtful guy who took me home when I had nowhere to go and was teaching me to snowboard despite my lack of coordination. Talk about infuriating.

"Looks like that wave wasn't for my son," the woman beside me whispered.

An uncomfortable laugh escaped me. "We're just friends," I assured her.

"I'd like to be friends with a guy who looked like that," she said before walking away.

I wondered if she knew what he was really like? Behind the good looks and snowboarding skills, did anyone really know Kason McCloud? Because I sure as hell didn't.

————

Giselle poked her head in the guest room that night when she returned from the boutique. "Did you have fun at the mountain?"

"Not sure fun is the word for it. But thanks for letting me borrow your stuff."

She laughed. "It's not like I ever wear it anymore. I'm glad it was put to good use."

"Yeah, well, most of my day consisted of watching your brother from the lodge."

She laughed. "Yeah, I always enjoyed hanging in the lodge too. Lots of hot guys stroll through there."

I smiled, thinking back to the woman checking out Kason.

She closed the door and sat down on the bed. "Can I ask you something?"

"Uh oh," I said.

"No, it's nothing to worry about. I'm just being nosey. Is there something going on with you and my brother?"

"What do you mean by something?" I asked.

"Well, first he brings you to the event. Then, he tells me it didn't go so well. Now you're here. I just can't figure it out."

I didn't say anything because, in all honesty, I didn't know what to say.

"I'm out of line," she said, taking my silence for annoyance.

"Oh, no. You've been so wonderful to me. It's just...I don't really know what's going on. He annoys me like no one I've ever met before. Not to mention, he's done some pretty crummy stuff to me."

"I'll kill him."

I laughed. "But then, there's something there that's redeeming. I just wonder if he knows it's there. Does that make sense?"

"I've known him all my life, and I still can't figure him out."

I smiled, appreciating that she let me off the hook.

She went to stand. "Did Thayer meet you guys today?"

I shook my head. "No, I think I heard Kason say he was with his dad and his dad's new girlfriend."

An unfamiliar expression flashed across her face for a split second before it disappeared. "Hey, if you're bored with my brother, I could always use some help at the boutique tomorrow."

"That sounds fun. He probably needs a break from me anyway."

"Don't be so sure," she said with a genuine smile that made me truly wish this was my family. "He's different with you."

"How'd working with my sister go?" Kason asked from the driver's seat of his Jeep.

"She actually paid me. I didn't want to accept it, but she wouldn't let me leave without it."

"Yeah, Giselle's pretty stubborn like that."

"How was snowboarding?" I asked, noting his red cheeks since he'd come right from the mountain to pick me up from her shop since she was staying late to do some paperwork.

"Good."

"You think you'll be ready for the Games?"

"Obviously."

I laughed. "Are you always so confident?"

"No reason not to be. No one else will do it for me."

As much as I hated arrogant people, he had a point. If you weren't your own biggest fan, you couldn't expect someone else to fill that job for you.

"You wanna come to a party tonight?" he asked.

"I don't think so. The last party I went to turned out pretty bad."

I meant for it to be a joke, but his jaw pulsed as his eyes stayed on the road.

"I'm actually pretty tired," I explained, not wanting to piss him off. "And, I won't know anyone."

He looked at me. "You'll know me."

"Go have fun with your friends. If I go, you'll be worried about me the whole time."

"I can stay home," he offered.

"Kason, you didn't bring me home as a date. I'm a tag along. I'm not spoiling plans you had with your friends before I crashed. I'm fine staying at your house with your family."

He didn't respond, and his silence was becoming more and more alarming.

Before long we pulled into his driveway. We hopped out, but while I headed for the house, Kason unpacked his snowboarding gear from the back of his Jeep.

"How'd it go?" Mrs. McCloud asked as I stepped inside the kitchen.

"Giselle does an amazing job with the boutique."

"She's always been a go-getter. Both my kids have been."

"What have both your kids been?" Kason asked as he stepped inside the kitchen.

"Go-getters," she explained.

"Shay's a go-getter too," he said, as he tugged off his hoodie. The T-shirt underneath lifted enough to catch a glimpse of his abs before he righted it.

My thoughts wandered back to the first night I'd met Kason, all bare-chested in only his boxers. I'd been affected by him that night—before he opened his mouth. And, I was currently being affected by him. *Dammit.* "I'm gonna go shower," I said, needing to get out of there before I started to focus on other parts of his body.

"We're having dinner at six," Mrs. McCloud said.

"Okay." I spun away and hurried upstairs. My sudden awareness of Kason *and* my comfort in his home had me questioning myself. If I could've left, I would've. But, Kason knew I had no home. And, picking up and leaving after they'd been so welcoming to me seemed like an odd thing to do. Not to mention, I really didn't want to leave, which made things a hundred times more complicated.

I showered and joined everyone for pasta and meatballs at six. Most of dinner was spent with Mr. McCloud recounting all the times Kason had screwed up as a kid. Kason sat there both pouting and laughing at the stories. I didn't have any fun stories of being a kid. Nor did I have anyone to recount them with if I did. The only memories I had with my father were bad ones. It was the ones with my mom that brought me true happiness. Like I told Kendall, those memories were mostly of her braiding my hair because that's when we'd have our daily girl talk. She'd tell me things about school and friends and boys. I remember groaning when she brought up boys because at six boys were gross. But, looking back, I realized she knew she was dying and wanted to instill her knowledge in me the only way she knew how. I wished I remembered everything she'd said. But, I liked to believe all the good in me came from her.

Kason left for his party a little after nine. I was happy he didn't stay home on my account. I was honest when I said I didn't want to spoil his plans. If he'd stayed home, I would've felt guilty. Mr. and Mrs. McCloud invited me to watch a movie with them, but they both fell asleep a few minutes in, so I ducked away to go work on some homework in the guest room.

Somewhere around midnight, I climbed under the covers and closed my eyes, feeling oddly content despite the reason I was at the McCloud's house in the first place. I drifted off almost immediately.

I was pulled out of a deep sleep at the sound of the guest door opening. I lay still, listening for whoever it was.

"Shay?" Kason whispered louder than he should've given his parents' room was just down the hall.

"Yeah?" I whispered.

"You awake?" he slurred.

Uh oh. "I am now."

He dropped down on the bed beside me, and I moved over as he kicked his feet up and took half of my pillow. The smell of alcohol emanated from his body, but it couldn't mask the arctic scent that always rolled in waves off him. "I'm drunk," he said.

I laughed. "Did you have fun with your friends?"

"Yeah. It was like old times. Except, now the girls who dissed me in high school actually wanted to be near me."

That same tinge of jealousy from earlier formed in my stomach. "Did you let them get near you?"

"Hell yeah." He chuckled. "So, I could diss them."

My lips twitched, liking his answer more than I should.

"Shay?"

"Yes?"

"I wish you came to the party."

"Why's that?"

"Because I like hanging out with you a lot more than those people."

My heart sped up and I didn't know how to stop it. I didn't want him saying things like that to me. It was too confusing given everything that had happened before this weekend. "You're only saying that because you're drunk."

He shook his head. "I'll tell you again in the morning so you know I'm telling the truth."

"I'm holding you to that," I teased.

"Scout's honor."

"You weren't a scout."

"But I could've been."

I shook my head, wishing I had *this* on video. It was quite amusing.

"Shay?"

"Yes, Kason?"

"I don't want to share you."

My brows shot up, confused by his words. "Share me with who?"

"Anyone."

I laughed.

"Shay?"

"Mmm?"

"Can I kiss you?"

"No."

"Why not?"

"Because you don't want to kiss me. You're drunk and horny, and I'm the only girl in the room."

"Not true. I wanted to kiss you at the event on the ski lift."

"I would've punched you."

"Exactly why I didn't."

Had he really wanted to kiss me at the event? I knew he was giving me that look that guys gave girls before they went in for a kiss, but I thought it was the darkness playing tricks on me.

It was quiet for a long time. I wondered if he'd fallen

asleep and if I should try to wake him so his mom didn't find him in there with me.

"Shay?"

I laughed to myself. "Kason?"

"Can I kiss you tomorrow?"

Even though his question caused butterflies to flutter deep in my stomach, I answered honestly. "No."

"But if I did, you'd know I wasn't just drunk-asking."

I closed my eyes, wondering if I wanted him to ask again tomorrow. Or, if I was just lonely. Or, confused. Or, out of my freaking mind. "I guess we'll have to see what happens tomorrow."

I waited for his response. But the only response I got was his soft snores. It was probably a good thing. Because each time he asked if he could kiss me, I felt my resolve weakening, and that was not okay.

24

———

SHAY

The next morning, I woke up with Kason's arm draped over my stomach. My nerves buzzed to life. Would he remember what he'd said? Would he be shocked to see he slept in here all night? Would this be as bad as the morning I woke up in *his* bed?

I wasn't about to stick around to find out.

I held my breath and slowly moved away from him, careful not to make any quick movements. I inched out from under his arm a tiny bit at a time.

Kason moaned.

I froze and stared at him, hoping I hadn't woken him.

I hadn't.

I released a small breath and continued moving away from him and out from under his arm. My body teetered on the side of the bed, so I twisted slowly, letting his hand fall gently to the bed. I stopped and looked to him to be sure the movement hadn't jostled him, but he was still asleep. I released another breath as I climbed to my feet and tiptoed out of the room, closing the door quietly behind me.

"What are you doing?"

I spun around with wide eyes, caught in the act by Giselle. "Oh, I..."

Her eyes moved to Kason's open door and empty bedroom before jumping back to the closed door behind me. "Is my brother in there?" she asked.

"It's not what it looks like."

A smile swept across her face. "It never is." She turned and moved to the bathroom. "Breakfast is sure to be interesting," she said before closing the door behind her.

I dropped my head back against the door, suddenly worried about breakfast. The only good thing was I would get down there first.

"What time are you two heading back?" Mrs. McCloud asked as she set a cup of coffee down in front of me at the kitchen table a few minutes later.

"I'm not sure," I said, glad she hadn't made mention of the footie pajamas I hadn't been able to change out of before escaping downstairs. I sipped my coffee.

"Any idea what time Kason got home last night?"

I nearly choked on my coffee, clearing my throat so I didn't draw attention to myself. "Pretty late from what I could tell."

"That boy is gonna be the death of me, I swear. Between snowboarding accidents and him out in the world without checking in with me, I'm going to be all gray before I'm sixty."

"That's what they have hair dye for," Kason said as he stepped into the kitchen and moved to his mom, planting a kiss on her cheek.

I looked down, not sure what to do with myself.

"I was just asking Shay what time you got in?" Mrs. McCloud said.

My eyes lifted just as Kason's caught them in his gaze.

"Pretty late," he said, nothing in his features giving away what he did or did not remember from last night. One thing was for sure, he knew *where* he woke up.

"Did you have a nice time?" I asked, trying to sound nonchalant.

"It was all right," he drawled and something about the way he said it caused quivers in my belly. "How was *your* night?" he asked me.

I swallowed my sudden nerves. "Great. I watched a movie with your parents and then got a jump on some school work."

He stared at me, again, nothing giving away what he was thinking. "Sounds exciting."

His mother swatted him with a dish towel, pulling his attention to her. "Watch it. Your dad and I know how to have fun."

"Since when?" he asked.

She rolled her eyes.

Kason looked back at me. "You good to head back in about an hour?"

I nodded. "Sure."

"So soon?" Mrs. McCloud asked.

"You'll see me at Christmas," Kason assured her.

"I was talking about Shay."

I stifled a smile as he growled. "Not nice, Mom."

She giggled, and once again I found myself yearning to be part of a normal family. Part of *this* family.

25

———

SHAY

An hour later, Kason and I were in his Jeep and I was staring out the window at the snowy mountains in the distance. Their peaks were covered with clouds as the early afternoon sun cast an almost blinding glow over everything.

My mind drifted to the weekend with the McClouds. I'd never been around a happy family who sat together for meals and talked about nothing in particular. They laughed together and smiled at each other and truly enjoyed each other's company. It was a reality shock to my system. I thought television shows got it wrong when they depicted happy families. But the McClouds proved me wrong. Happy families did exist.

I thought about my time on the mountain with Kason. And, despite me being a lost cause, he didn't give up. Because despite our past issues, he'd always been stubborn when it came to me. I saw that same stubbornness in each of his family members over the long weekend, and now I saw it as an endearing quality. I hadn't been taken care of that way since my mom. But with Kason, I felt something I didn't quite understand. I was a scientist by nature. I didn't let my heart rule anything. It was always my head. I needed proof before I allowed myself to believe anything I couldn't see. But, trying to determine if Kason had changed, or if this weekend just gave me a glimpse of the real Kason—the one he didn't let others see—was driving me crazy.

"What are you thinking about?" Kason asked, breaking the silence.

Though his eyes remained on the road, I glanced at him. "Just what a nice time I had with your family."

"My family? Am I included in that?"

I shrugged, hating that he hadn't acknowledged what he'd said last night. Had he truly not remembered? Or, was he regretting it and pretending he'd forgotten to save face? And, why the *hell* did I want him to remember?

"We had a nice weekend, Shay. Please don't go back into your shell."

"My shell?"

"The one you hide inside. I wish you let other people know the Shay I've gotten to know."

"Oh, yeah? Why's that?"

"Because you're nothing like the girl who pounded on Cora's door demanding the music get turned down."

"Oh, I'm definitely that girl. I still hate ignorant assholes."

He tossed back his head and laughed, the sound burrowing its way into the tiny crevices of my heart.

If one thing positive came out of this weekend, it was that all that anger I'd been holding inside me—all the animosity directed toward Kason after the incident—had dissipated. I felt lighter. I felt ready to get back to school and have the freshman year I had planned to.

We eventually pulled through the stone pillars of the

campus entrance. A nagging feeling tugged at my heart, knowing the sense of family and fitting in I'd felt all weekend was over. Kason neared my dorm and neither of us said anything. He stopped behind an SUV parked in the unloading lane. I opened my door just as Kason did and we went to the back of his Jeep to grab my stuff.

"I've got it," I said as I reached for the luggage he'd given me, claiming to have extras his sponsor had given him.

He reached for it but I pulled it my way. "Shay?"

"I'm serious. I've got it." I didn't mean to sound like a bitch, but it was hard enough knowing that the weekend was over. I didn't need him being all chivalrous. I lowered the luggage to the ground and pulled the handle up so I could roll it.

He closed the back of his Jeep and buried his hands in his pockets like he planned to say something. I waited for a second but he didn't say anything.

"Well...I guess I'll see you in class tomorrow."

He nodded, still quiet.

"Okay, then. Thanks for...you know." I turned and moved to the dorm entrance that was propped open for returning students. Sadness crept inside of me with every step away from him I took.

I carried my luggage up the three flights of stairs and then rolled it down the hallway to my room. I punched in the code and opened the door. I expected Kendall to be back already, but our room was empty. I sat down on my bed.

Silence surrounded me.

That silence was suddenly crippling.

The McCloud house had been filled with laughter and love. I hadn't realized how desperately I longed for that. I needed a minute. I needed to remind myself that *this* was my life. School. Getting a good job. Finding a cure for addiction. The weekend had been someone else's life. But, at least I got a taste of normal—even if it was only for a brief time.

There was a knock on the door and I moved to it, expecting Kendall to need help with stuff she'd brought back from home. I pulled open the door.

Kason stood there, his hands braced on the door jamb and his eyes staring into mine. "Maybe you can pretend last night didn't happen, but I can't." He stepped forward, and I stepped back. My heartbeat raced as he stood in front of me, removing my glasses and placing them on the desk. I couldn't tear my eyes away from his. They were so mesmerizing in such close proximity. He cupped my cheeks as his eyes riveted between mine. I couldn't breathe. "I told you I wanted to kiss you today." Giving me no time to register what he was saying or doing, his lips crashed down on mine. I lost all concept of gravity. My legs became weightless as his mouth moved over mine. His tongue swept inside, tangling with mine in an urgent race. I tried to keep up, knowing never before and never again would a kiss feel this perfect.

Kason pulled away first, his eyes all wild as he stepped back from me and dragged his fingers through his hair. "Jesus Christ."

"What?" I asked, my chest heaving and my mind reeling.

"I did not expect you to kiss like that."

My eyes widened. Was it that bad?

"Goddammit, Shay. Why didn't we do that sooner?"

Sooner? All his indiscretions came barreling back at me. The answer to his question sitting at the ready. I tried pushing the thoughts away. I tried reminding myself that his kiss was the most amazing thing that had happened to me in a long freaking time. And, *God*, I wanted him to kiss me again. But, I was Shay Miller. I liked spending time with people who understood science. Kason didn't know anything about it. He wanted to hang ten—or whatever it was snowboarders did—on snow-covered mountains. He was gorgeous and I was painfully average. He was outgoing and I didn't interact with people well. We. Did. Not. Fit.

"Where'd you go, Shay? Don't go into that shell again."

"This was probably a mistake," I said.

"A mistake my ass." He stalked toward me.

I backpedaled until the wall hit my back.

He had me cornered. He stepped to me, lifting his arms and bracing his hands on the wall above my head. My breath came out ragged as my heart threatened to pound right out of my chest. Kason smirked. "You can't run from this, Shay. You know it and I know it."

I tried to think of something to say. Something to rationalize us kissing. Us doing *anything* together.

"Stop thinking so much." He lowered his mouth toward mine, his lips lingering only a few inches from mine. His breath tickled my lips, the ones still tingling with his last kiss. "Tell me you want me to kiss you."

"No."

He dragged his tongue across his bottom lip as a smile tugged at his lips. "Stop being so stubborn."

"Maybe."

He chuckled, the vibration rumbling against my chest. He lowered his hands from the wall and slipped them behind the small of my back, gently pulling me into him. Needing to hold onto something, I draped my arms over his shoulders. I couldn't say if it was him or me, but our lips met halfway. This time his lips were soft and slow, and he took his time as he sucked on my lips, rolling them between his. I could feel him everywhere, and I didn't know what to do but fade into the kiss. My fingers tunneled through the back of his hair as his tongue pushed its way in my mouth. I arched into him as our tongues tangled in a mess of desire.

Needing air, Kason pulled away first.

Our chests heaved in tandem as we stood inches from one another, our eyes locked.

"Am I moving too fast?" he asked.

"For who?"

He laughed, pulling me into his chest and wrapping me in his arms as if it was the most natural thing to do.

Regardless of the novelty of our interactions, I relaxed into him, feeling so warm and protected in his arms. But, I'd be lying if I said this one-eighty didn't scare me.

"I don't want to mess things up again," he said.

I opened my mouth to respond, but I was cut off by the door opening.

Kendall struggled to drag three suitcases into the room with her. Her face lit up when she spotted us so close together. "Well, hello."

"Hey," I said as I stepped away from Kason, trying to sound nonchalant while my cheeks likely blazed.

"I go away for a few days and miss everything," she said as she shoved all three suitcases into the corner of the room.

Kason grabbed my glasses off the desk and handed them to me. "I actually have to get going."

I slipped my glasses back on. He had to go? *Seriously?*

He smirked before moving to the door. "I'll call you later."

Disappointment flooded my chest as he opened the door.

"Later, Snowboard Hottie," Kendall called as he swept

out of our room laughing at the nickname he'd given himself on my phone.

Once the door closed behind him, I fell back on my bed, covering my face with my palms. What was this feeling overtaking my body? I felt like I wasn't even in my own skin. Had the entire weekend been a dream?

"Oh, no you don't," Kendall said, dropping onto the bed beside me. "What *happened* this weekend?"

"I don't even know where to start."

"I thought you hated him?"

I dropped my hands. "I thought so, too."

## 26

## SHAY

Kason's text came a few hours later when Kendall and I were walking out of the dining hall.

SNOWBOARD HOTTIE

B by to get u at 7.

"I'm so freaking jealous," Kendall said as she glanced over at my phone.

"There's nothing to be jealous about," I said, stifling a smile.

She dropped her head back and groaned. "You hate a guy and he wants everything to do with you. I like a guy and he thinks I'm too forward. I can't win."

"What guy?" I asked.

"Ugh. It doesn't matter."

I laughed as we approached the entrance to our dorm. "I think you're looking into this too much. We kissed. Big deal. Isn't that what college kids do? Hook up and move on?" Though, I said it nonchalantly, it would've hurt to think that's all this was.

"Yeah, it's what college kids do," she said as she scanned

her key card. "But it's not what *you* do. And Snowboard Hottie knows that. This means something to him." She pulled open the door and we walked inside the building.

I had no idea what to do with all the uncertain feelings rushing through me since he'd left my room. They were foreign to me, not to mention so damn distracting. But, it also felt so amazing.

"What are you gonna wear?" she asked as we climbed the three flights of stairs.

"Wear?" I glanced down at my T-shirt, jeans, and boots.

"Well, I guess he fell for you in those clothes. Why change now?"

I laughed, wondering if *fell for you* was what he'd actually done. We'd spent a lot of time together this past weekend, but is that all the time he needed to see me differently than he had all those nights studying? And, the same for me. Was seeing him at home with his family—or liking the way he treated me with no one else around—enough to make me see him in a different light?

———

There was a knock on our door a few minutes before seven. Kendall glanced to me, satisfied with her work. I'd let her apply a little blush and eye shadow to my face. The girl wouldn't take no for an answer. And it wasn't like it was overdone or even that noticeable under my glasses.

I opened the door. Kason stood there with a smirk that said I know something you don't know. And, I really wanted to know what he knew. "I'm looking for my tutor."

Butterflies swarmed in my belly. "She's off duty."

"Well, that sucks."

I tried to suppress the smile that was sure to overtake my face.

"You ready?" he asked.

I nodded before glancing back at Kendall. "See you later."

"I sure hope not," she called loud enough for Kason to hear before I closed the door behind us.

We walked down the three flights of stairs until we were outside. Kason's Jeep was parked at the sidewalk. He hurried to the passenger door and opened it for me. "Thanks," I said, climbing into the seat and watching him round the front. This was really happening.

He hopped in but didn't start the engine. He turned in his seat to face me. "Did you eat?"

I winced. "I'm sorry. I didn't know you wanted to get food."

"No. It's fine. We're going to my house. I just wanted to be sure you weren't hungry."

I shook my head, curious what he had planned at his house.

"Good." He started the engine then reached over and linked his hand into mine. The small gesture filled me with a sense of reassurance that this wasn't just a hookup and move on sort of thing for him.

We arrived at his house a couple of minutes later, and he cut the engine in the driveway. The house was dark. And, while I liked the idea of being alone with him, I was also terrified to be alone with him. I clearly wasn't experienced in the sex department, so if he expected that tonight, I was definitely not ready for it. "Is Thayer not back yet?"

"Nope. We've got the house to ourselves."

My stomach dipped, and I couldn't tell if I was more terrified or elated.

"Wait there." He jumped out and circled around to my door, pulling it open and taking my hand to help me out.

We walked to the house with our hands linked, the cool night air sending goosebumps rushing up my skin. Kason unlocked the door and switched on the foyer light. The entire downstairs lit up and ease filled my body. The house looked a lot less ominous with lights on. He led me to the stairs, and we headed up to his room. My heart sped up, my mind going to places I wasn't ready for. He opened his door and memories of the night of his party flooded my brain.

He must've noticed the unease on my face. "We need to make some new memories in here."

My eyes widened.

He burst out laughing. "Not like *that*."

A breath whooshed out of me. "I knew that."

I stepped inside his room first, looking around at the space that I'd been desperate to get out of the last time. The snowboards still stood against the walls, but now I noticed a photo of Kason with his parents and sister. He'd clearly just won the silver medal he held in the picture. I picked it up, loving that I now knew the wonderful people in the photo. The ones who shaped Kason into who he was today and who made me feel like I was home for the first time in a long time.

"That was last year in Aspen when I won the silver medal," he explained.

"I figured."

"Will you come this year?"

I placed the photo down and turned to him. "Would you like me to?"

He nodded, and a vulnerability I'd never seen before flashed across his face.

"Then I'll be there."

He smiled as he stalked across the room until he stopped in front of me. I was so ready to have his mouth on mine again. But he didn't kiss me. He wrapped his arms around me and lifted me right off the floor.

I giggled. "What are you doing?"

He carried me to the bed and lay me down. I expected him to follow me down. My body yearned for it as every nerve ending inside of me buzzed to life. But, he lay beside me so we were side by side looking up at the ceiling.

*O-kay.*

After a long stretch of silence, he asked, "Will you let me do something?"

I stilled, nervous to ask what that something was.

"Can we redo last night?" he continued.

"Redo last night?"

"If I hadn't been so drunk, I could've told you how I was feeling." He reached between us and linked our fingers. His grip was warm and strong, bringing me unspeakable calm. "I couldn't stop thinking about you at the party, Shay. Every girl there paled in comparison to you."

I swallowed hard, completely unprepared for his honesty—or how much I liked it.

"They may've been pretty on the outside, but that's where it stopped. They had nothing interesting to say. I realized how much more I wanted to be listening to you talk about science stuff that I didn't even understand than pretend to be interested in anything they had to say."

My heartbeat raced inside my chest like an out-of-control pinball.

"Everyone kept coming up to me telling me how sick I was at snowboarding. And, sure, it was awesome for a couple of minutes, but then I just wanted you to be there to tell me I could pull off better tricks."

I laughed. "I would say something like that, wouldn't I?"

He released my hand and turned onto his side, gazing at me. "I like who I am with you, Shay. I like him a hell of a lot."

I stared into his pretty blue eyes—the ones I never thought I'd enjoy looking at so much. "Is that the real you?"

His eyes lifted to the ceiling, his mouth pursed in contemplation. "I think so."

"How can you not be sure?"

"You don't understand." He looked back down at me. "I've got to be a different person for so many different people. It's easy to forget who I really am."

"I don't understand."

He sighed. "It's like...I need to be this gnarly snowboarder who pulls off sick tricks to impress the judges and nab medals at competitions to be at the top of my sport. I need to be a role model for kids who look up to me and think I'm this rad guy even if I'm not. I've got to be a walking advertisement for my sponsor who always wants more from me whether I like it or not. I've got to be a social media guru who posts videos of dope tricks or else people will start forgetting about me and move on to the next great snowboard sensation out there. I've gotta be this student on campus who hides his struggles so not to appear less than. But, school is *so* fucking hard for me."

My heart clenched. I'd never considered the roles he had to play. And, of all the things he'd said, the fact that he'd admitted how difficult school was for him tugged at my heart. "I'm sorry."

"I'm not looking for you to feel sorry for me. I'm looking for you to understand what goes on in my head on the daily."

I nodded, knowing he wasn't someone who needed my

pity but appreciating that he felt comfortable talking about it with me.

"But then," he continued. "When I was home this weekend, I realized I really liked *that* me. The one who loves his family and loves snowboarding when there's no pressure. I could be *that* guy with my family. And I could be *that* guy with you."

I could see how he could lose himself along the way when he had to play so many different roles. He'd always made it look so easy to be him. He walked around as if he didn't have a care in the world. But, of all people, I should've realized you never knew a person until you walked a mile in their shoes. I'd put on a façade for teachers and friends my entire life. Why would Kason be any different? "I like that you can be yourself with me."

He smiled a vulnerable smile that softened something inside me that I'd shut off a long time ago. He leaned down, lowering his lips until they were a mere breath away from mine. "Then let me." He pressed his lips to mine, kissing me slow and gently. The soft touch tingled my skin, sending sensations coursing all the way down to my toes. Kason rolled forward until half his body covered mine. Could he feel the thrashing of my heart?

I pulled back first, needing some air.

Kason gazed down at me. "I can't get enough of you, Shay Miller."

My eyes lowered, finding it difficult to hold his gaze—especially since his words were directed at me.

"Look at me, Shay."

My eyes lifted to his.

"I like you. And, I hope to God you being here means you like me too. I've fucked up, but I won't make that mistake again."

"What do you want from me?"

"That's a loaded question," he said and laughed. "But seriously? I've never wanted a girlfriend because I'm usually so busy traveling. But for the first time, I want someone to be here when I get back."

"Someone?"

"*You*, Shay. I want to come back to *you*."

I gnawed on my bottom lip, knowing a smile would have overtaken my whole face if I didn't.

"This is where you say something to boost my ego," he said.

"As if you need more ego-boosting."

He laughed as he tightened his arms around me and rolled onto his back, pulling me on top of him. "I'd learn a lot more physics like this. Any chance you'll still tutor me?"

"Are you doing all this as a ploy to get me to tutor you again?"

His brows furrowed. "I hadn't thought of that. Would it work?"

I shook my head.

"Will you at least sit with me in class?"

"No. You're too distracting."

"You mean my good looks?"

I laughed. "No. You make a lot of noise."

"Noise?"

"You always slam your books down or close your laptop when it's super quiet."

"For someone who was ignoring me, you paid a lot of attention."

I rolled my eyes, but he did have a point. Even when I was ignoring him, his presence was always there.

"Will you stay with me tonight?"

My stomach flipped. "I have a seven o'clock class."

He smiled. "I know. Remember?"

My lips curled at the bad memory of our first encounter.

"I'll have you back to your dorm whenever you want," he assured me.

"I don't have my pajamas."

I cocked my head. "Shay, you don't have to hide with me."

He was right. He'd already seen my ugly scars and hadn't run.

"Besides, I want you wearing one of my shirts."

"Why?"

"Because you're gonna make it look good."

I laughed.

"We're gonna be good together, you know?" he said.

"Why's that?" I asked.

"Because we balance each other out."

"Sounds boring," I said.

He chuckled. "I meant it as a compliment. You're smart and I struggle. You're calm and I'm hot-headed. You play it safe and I take risks."

"Yeah, right. Being here with you is one of the biggest risks I've ever taken," I admitted. "I'm trusting you not to hurt me. That is not easy for me to do."

His eyes cast down, hopefully grasping the depth of my words. "I understand."

"Do you?"

He nodded. "Giselle and my parents will kick my ass if I hurt you, so there's that, too."

I laughed before he lifted his head and captured my lips in a long kiss.

27

———

SHAY

I woke to Kason trailing soft kisses over the back of my neck and his strong arms wrapped around me from behind. I didn't open my eyes or move, because I didn't want him to stop the glorious torture. I wanted to capture it in my memory forever. The feelings. The calm. The safety I felt wrapped up in his arms all night long. It turned out that he wasn't rushing me and sleeping beside me was all he wanted when he asked me to stay the night. I'd always been so independent. But, Kason had given me a taste of what it felt like to be cherished and taken care of. I just wished I didn't like it so much.

"Morning," Kason said, his raspy morning voice so deep and sexy it sent a quiver rushing through me.

"Hi."

"I like having you in my bed."

"Why's that?"

"Because I can kiss you whenever I want to," Kason said. "But I know I need to get you home."

"What time is it?"

"Six."

"A couple more minutes."

He chuckled into the back of my hair. "I think I'm rubbing off on you."

I could feel his erection pressing against my ass, but I knew that wasn't what he was referring to. I opened my eyes and lay still, the feeling so unfamiliar yet intriguing. I had the sudden urge to push back and rub against him. To feel what all the talk was about. My thighs quivered and I knew I was in uncharted territory.

"Shay?"

"Yes?"

"There's no rush. We have time."

"Oh...I..." Thankfully, he couldn't see my face because heat pulsed in my cheeks.

"Have you never been in bed with a guy like this before?" he asked, and I could hear the wonder in his voice.

I shook my head.

He tightened his arms around me. "That just makes this even better." He kissed the top of my head and then rolled away from me, leaving me alone in his bed.

I exhaled heavily and tried to slow my erratic heartbeat before slipping out of bed. I was wearing only Kason's T-shirt and my thong. I slipped on my glasses from his night-stand and grabbed my clothes from the top of his dresser. Before I pulled off his shirt, I glanced over my shoulder at him in the corner of the room. He'd stopped getting dressed and his eyes were on me. A boldness I didn't know I possessed came over me and I slipped off the shirt. I heard his breath hitch, surprised by my confidence—and the fact that I was only in a thong that left very little to the imagina-tion. And, while I knew he'd probably seen plenty of naked girls before, I'd never undressed in front of a guy.

"Shay," he whispered.

I froze. *My back.*

I felt Kason step up behind me, and I was so glad I couldn't see the look on his face. His fingertips drifted over the long diagonal scar on my back. I closed my eyes, knowing he must've had so many questions, but I didn't want to ruin what had been amazing up until that point. "We're gonna have to talk about this when you're ready."

I nodded, before hurrying to slip on my bra and T-shirt. I tugged on my jeans and boots.

Once I was dressed, Kason wrapped his arms around me from behind and rested his chin on my shoulder. "I don't want to bring you home."

"Why not?"

"I've gotten so used to having you around. I might need to have you with me all the time."

"I'm not a babysitter."

He spun me around, tugging me against his chest.

I tipped my head back and met his eyes, happy he wasn't looking at me differently now that he saw my back.

"You're definitely not a babysitter. Unless you're the type of babysitter horny boys daydream about."

My nose wrinkled as I pushed at his chest. "Ewww."

He laughed before planting a closed-mouth kiss on my lips. I appreciated the gesture since neither of us had brushed our teeth yet.

Kason dropped me off at my dorm with just enough time that I could shower before calculus. Then, he met me outside the physics building before our class and held my hand, bringing the sense of security I felt every time he did it. I didn't know if it was because he made me feel safe *or* if it proved he wasn't embarrassed to be seen with me. Either way, I liked it.

We entered the classroom and eyed our respective tables. Our table mates already sat at our tables. "Looks like this is where we go our separate ways," I said.

"Let me ask her to move," he said.

"I think an hour apart will be okay. And, like I told you, you're kind of distracting."

He laughed before lifting our joined hands and kissing the back of mine. "Fine." He released my hand and walked to his seat as I walked to mine, feeling like I was walking on cloud nine.

"Lucky," my table mate whispered.

I stifled a smile and slipped out my laptop.

My phone vibrated on the table beside my laptop a few minutes into Professor Raymond's lecture. I glanced at it.

SNOWBOARD HOTTIE

Can I take you out tonight?

Trying to be nonchalant, I slipped the phone off the table and into my lap. I texted back.

ME

Where?

SNOWBOARD HOTTIE

Does it matter?

I smiled.

ME

Fine. But pay attention.

SNOWBOARD HOTTIE

I am. You're pretty cute.

I laughed to myself as I tucked my phone into my backpack so he could see that I wasn't going to let him distract me anymore. Boy, what a difference a week made.

After class, he walked over to my table and waited as I packed up.

"So where are we going?"

"So impatient," he teased.

"Well, do I need a snowsuit or a dress?"

He considered my question as I began to slip my arms through my backpack straps. He grabbed my backpack before I could get it on and threw it over his shoulder. "Let's say no snowsuit."

"Thank God."

He laughed as we made our way to the door. "I'll make you a snowboarder yet."

"Good luck with that."

He slipped his hand into mine as we made our way out of the classroom and outside the building. Once we hit the top of the steps, he hesitated.

I glanced over at him. His eyes were locked on someone in the distance. I followed his gaze and saw Cora with a group of girls, and she was glaring at us. I wondered why that would bother Kason. He was the one to bring me to the event to make her angry. I thought he'd love rubbing us in her face. But instead, he pulled me away from Cora and her friends.

"So, tonight," he began as if nothing had happened. "Wear whatever makes you comfortable."

I tried to ignore his reaction to seeing Cora—and the tinge of disappointment I felt that he didn't want to be open with her about us yet.

But, something about the way he paused unsettled me.

Why did he care what she thought?

———

I sat on the edge of my bed tying my boots.

"Meet me at our spot in the library?" Kendall said, repeating Kason's text that I'd received earlier.

"That's what his text said."

"But I thought he wanted to take you out?" she asked.

"Me too." I tried not to sound disappointed, but when I'd received his text, I felt let down that we wouldn't be going out. Since the Slopes event didn't count, I wanted this date to be special. Something I'd always remember. I wasn't high maintenance, but I'd be lying if I said I didn't want our real first date to be romantic.

"Well, look at it this way. It's not like he's trying to hide the fact that you two are hanging out," Kendall said.

But was he? He'd avoided Cora. Now he was hiding me in the back corner of the library for our first date. Maybe today on campus made him realize we were total opposites, and I didn't fit into his world.

Feeling foolish for borrowing one of Kendall's sweaters, I grabbed my backpack and headed to the door.

"What are you doing?" Kendall asked.

"It's ten of seven. I'm gonna be late."

"No. Your backpack. This is a date."

"Yeah, but I've got a feeling it's a study date."

She sighed, probably catching the disappointment in my voice. "Call me if you need me."

I nodded before taking off for the library. I crossed campus in record time, probably because it was freaking cold outside and I needed the warmth of the library. I hurried inside to warm up then took the stairs to the third floor which was oddly deserted. I made my way through the stacks toward the corner of the library, stopping when I reached our spot. My eyes widened.

Oh. My. God.

A black tablecloth covered our normal table and tiny candles were placed all around it twinkling under the dim lights. Kason stood there smiling as "Something About You" by Bad Company played from his phone.

Kason McCloud *did* give me a romantic first date.

"Do you like it?" he asked.

"I think you might set off the fire alarm."

He laughed as he walked over to me. It was then I noticed his T-shirt. *Never trust an atom...they make up everything.*

I laughed. "Nice shirt."

"You like?" he asked, glancing down at the geeky science shirt he'd undoubtedly purchased for our date.

The trepidation about this not being a *real* first date released from my body.

"Why do you have your backpack?" he asked with confusion coloring his tone.

"Oh, I..."

He slipped it off my back and placed it on a chair. "We won't be needing that tonight."

Of course we wouldn't. I was seriously going to self-sabotage this thing between us if I always expected the worst. I needed to trust Kason. He'd proven to me that I could now.

He wrapped his arms around me and pulled me into his chest, his warmth encompassing me.

I tipped my head back to meet his gaze. "Thank you."

"I wanted to do something special for you. But everything about us has been so backward. I figured changing some bad memories into good ones would be the best start for us."

"Like last night's redo?"

"Exactly." He stepped forward, causing me to step back until my butt leaned on the edge of the table. He lifted me off my feet and sat me on the table with my legs dangling. "Stay right there." "Something About You" ended and Tesla's "What You Give" began to play as Kason pulled out a chair and sat in front of me.

Laughter burst out of me, understanding what he was doing. "I'm not spreading my legs."

He rested his hands on my thighs, brushing his thumbs over them. "I don't want any other girl sitting in front of me. That's what tonight's about. I just want us to be us."

"I think this is a perfect date..." I glanced around. "As long as you brought food."

He nodded. "Lasagna, since I know how much you liked my mom's."

I smiled, loving that we had already created some good memories of our own. I hadn't even realized it. And now, we were working on making all the bad memories disappear. "So, a library picnic."

"Only the best for you," he said. "Oh, I almost forgot." He stood and circled around to a chair. He picked up a rectangular gift bag the size of a pillow. He handed it to me. "For you."

"My birthday's not until March." I took the handle, skeptically eyeing the heavy bag.

He smiled. "It's not a birthday gift. Just open it."

I chewed on my bottom lip, curious what the bag contained. I hadn't received a gift from anyone in a long time, and I felt uncomfortable accepting it, let alone opening it in front of him.

"Just think of it as a thank you for all your help with physics."

"You haven't passed yet."

"Gee, thanks for the vote of confidence."

I laughed as I reached both hands inside the bag and pulled out a shoebox. I glanced to Kason but his eyes were eagerly on the box. I placed it on my lap and lifted the cover. A pair of glittery pink combat boots sat inside. My eyes flashed to his.

"I saw them in one of Giselle's boutique catalogs and asked her to get a pair. Do you like them?"

"I don't know what to say." I looked back down at the boots. I probably wouldn't have chosen them for myself, but they were kind of cute and quite a contrast to my worn black ones. I looked at him. His eyes were hopeful and his cheeks a little flushed as if nervous for my response. "I do. You didn't need to get me anything."

"I know that. I just saw them and thought of you. Besides, black doesn't match everything. You need options."

I laughed. "Did you really just say that?"

"I did." He grabbed one of the boots from the box and kneeled in front of me. He slipped my black boot off my foot and slipped the pink one on.

I laughed to myself. If I didn't feel like Cinderella at that moment, I didn't know when I ever would.

The boots would take getting used to, but I could already see they'd wear on me. He slipped off my other boot, and I handed him the pink one left in the box. He slipped that one on. "What do you think?"

I moved the empty box off my lap and scooted off the

edge of the table. I walked around in a small circle. "I like them."

He smiled, pleased with my response to his gift.

"Thank you."

He shrugged like it wasn't a big deal, but it was. Where I came from, gifts were few and far between. He grabbed my hand and sat down, pulling me onto his lap. "Let me spoil you, Shay."

"I don't need to be spoiled."

"Doesn't mean I can't."

My stomach dipped, and I knew that if this thing between us went south, it would hurt.

"So, I know it's sort of bad timing, but I'm heading to Salt Lake City Thursday night."

I pulled back so I could see his face. "Snowboarding?"

"Yeah. I'm hitting the mountains with some of my boys. We're gonna get a little pre-Aspen practice in and film some footage."

"Sounds fun."

"Who're you kidding? You think it sounds awful."

I smiled. "Only because I can't snowboard. But you love it, so it sounds fun for you."

"You gonna miss me?"

I pursed my lips, pretending to consider his question. "Well, I won't have to help you with physics, so there's that."

"I'm your only student, so I can't be that bad."

I cocked my head. "Only because you paid off that other kid not to show up."

His guilty eyes widened. "How do you know that?"

"Word gets around."

"It got me alone with you, didn't it?"

"Did you really want to be alone with me then?"

His lips twisted in contemplation. "I think I did."

My belly dipped again, and I knew Kason was going to be the death of my poor heart.

"And I really want to be alone with you now."

I stifled a smile, knowing—despite all his flaws and failed attempts to make things right with me—I was beginning to fall for Kason McCloud. And there wasn't a thing in this world I could do to stop it.

I turned the shower off, reached out of the stall for my towel, and dried myself before reaching for my glasses. I felt around for them, but couldn't find them. I pulled open the curtain and couldn't see them next to my shower caddy where I'd left them. I bent down to check the floor and under the other stall, thinking they must've slipped off the ledge. But they weren't there. Had I not worn them into the bathroom? I could've sworn I had. But, then again, with Kason on my mind lately, I'd been distracted.

I picked up my caddy and headed out. Before I reached my room, I spotted—albeit a little blurry—my glasses up ahead on the hallway floor. *How'd they end up there?* I couldn't have dropped them if I was wearing them. Had I grabbed them and not put them on? I bent down and picked them up, huffing when I noticed both lenses cracked. *Dammit.*

I walked into my room staring at the remains of my glass.

"What happened?" Kendall asked, still in bed.

"I must've dropped them."

"Do you have a backup pair?" she asked.

I shook my head, knowing glasses cost money I didn't have.

"There's an eye doctor at health services. You can get new ones there."

"Really?"

She laughed at my surprise. "You pay tuition, right?"

"Well, not technically."

She laughed again. "Well, I'm sure your scholarship covers it."

————

"Hi, Thayer," I said once he opened the front door.

"Hey." His eyes narrowed as if he knew something was different about me, but he couldn't quite figure out what it was. "He's upstairs," he said, stepping back so I could enter.

I moved inside, climbing the stairs and walking into Kason's room. He was on his bed intently watching something on his phone. "Hey."

He glanced up, his eyes widening when he saw me at the end of his bed. "Where are your glasses?"

"I got contacts." Kendall had been right about the campus eye doctor. It turned out the prescription I'd been wearing for years had changed. And, since glasses would've taken longer to come in, the doctor urged me to try contacts that were covered under my tuition. *And*, he had a bunch of free samples I could have right then. So, I relented. It took some practice touching my finger to my eyeball, but I was able to get the contacts in after a few failed attempts and a lot of cringing.

"You look hot," Kason said as he crawled off his bed.

I rolled my eyes. "You've seen me without glasses."

He cupped my cheeks and stared into my eyes. "Yeah, but you're always squinting without them. Now, your eyes are so big and green."

I laughed, grateful to whoever stepped on my glasses because it was making Kason look at me like I was beautiful. "Everything's clearer now."

"Am I even better looking?" he asked.

I opened my mouth to respond, but his lips captured mine, cutting off anything I planned to say. I giggled as he kissed me, deepening the kiss as if he really liked what he saw. I wrapped my arms around his neck and arched into him, wanting him as much as he seemed to want me. He pulled apart first, leaving us both breathless. "I'm stopping," he said as an apology.

"I didn't say you needed to stop," I assured him.

He laughed, moving us to his bed. We both lay down so we shared his pillow. He grabbed my hand and linked our fingers. I lifted our joined hands so I could inspect the tattoos on his arm. From far away you couldn't see all the detail. But up close, you could see all the hidden images that blended together like a true piece of art.

"What are you doing?" he asked.

"Just checking out your tattoos."

"And?"

"And...I'm wondering what it all means?" I said.

"It means I'm a badass."

I laughed, wondering if his jokes were his way of avoiding talking about stuff that mattered. "When did you get your first one?"

"When I was sixteen," he said, twisting his arm so I could see the snowboard on his tricep.

"Did it hurt?"

He shrugged. "A little because I didn't know what to expect. And, I was in Austria so it was a little different."

"Austria?"

"Have you ever been?" he asked.

I shook my head. "I've never been out of Colorado."

He grew quiet, and I assumed he'd just realized how unlikely it was for me to have ever traveled given my financial situation.

"Which tattoo's your favorite?"

He considered it then held out his forearm. The word *family* was written in script.

I'd hoped he liked that one best. "What was the last one you got?"

He twisted his arm in the opposite direction, showing me his bicep. "The silver medal. But, I'll be adding the gold after Aspen."

I shook my head, never surprised by his arrogance. "Always so confident."

He lowered his arm, ending my perusal. He was silent for a moment, and I wondered what he was thinking about. "You know..." he began, his voice quiet. "A tattoo could cover your scar."

*That's* what he was thinking about. "I know my back's ugly."

He reached over and turned my chin so I was looking at him. "That's not what I said. I just meant you could cover the bad memories with something *you* choose to put there."

I'd never considered trying to cover the scars permanently.

"Think about it," he said. "I could go with you."

"I'll think about it."

"How long have they been there?" he asked, and I could tell he was treading lightly.

"Too long."

His teeth clenched together.

I turned attention to the ceiling swirls above his bed, not wanting to see the anger in his eyes over something he couldn't control. Hell, I couldn't control. "My mom died from cancer when I was six," I explained.

"Shay, I'm sorry."

"After that, I was the only one there for my father to take out his anger on. And he did. Every time he was sad about my mom. Or he lost a job. Or felt hungover. Or even when I didn't make dinner fast enough. I couldn't stay out of his way even when I tried."

"Jesus Christ, Shay. He should be in jail."

"He was all I had," I said, knowing how ridiculous it sounded now. I'd been a victim. An innocent victim. "If he was taken away, I had no one. That's what stopped me from telling anyone what was going on."

"And when he wasn't drinking?" Kason asked.

"He was normal. He'd ask about my day. Clean the house. Rake what little we had of a front lawn. But those days were few and far between as the years went on."

Kason rolled me away from him onto my side, wrapping his arms around me and holding me tightly as if he could somehow protect me from my past. I appreciated him trying. But all the hurt was over now. We lay like that for a long time. After he'd seen the scars on my back, I knew it was only a matter of time before he wanted me to talk about it. And, as much as I dreaded that conversation, I felt better now that the truth was out there.

"Flowers," he finally said.

"What about flowers?" I asked.

"I think some colorful flowers would look nice on your back."

"Not something more personal?"

"Like what?"

"I don't know...your face?" I asked, trying to lighten the mood.

He chuckled, the vibration rumbling against my back. "Definitely not my face."

I smiled. "Well, I expect you to get mine on your arm."

"Oh, yeah?"

I laughed, knowing that was not something I'd want to see on his arm.

And, just like that, the somber mood disappeared. And though Kason couldn't protect me from the pain I'd once felt, he was making sure I felt safe in his arms now.

Within minutes, I fell asleep in Kason's arms knowing there was no safer place for me to be.

## KASON

I screwed down the mountain, taking the first jump like a man on a mission. I flew off the jump, rotating and landing my Switchback twelve with a force that couldn't take me down. After what Shay had revealed last night, I needed to release all the anger raging inside me. I couldn't shake the images from my brain. I couldn't *not* see my girl being hurt by the man who was supposed to love her and care for her. What kind of monster created those scars? I took the next jump, reaching down and grabbing my board as I rotated off-axis four times. I landed a backside 1440 hard but kept my balance. I curved my turn and stopped at the bottom of the mountain.

I lifted my goggles onto the top of my helmet and unsnapped my boots. I carried my board over to the outside patio outside the lodge. "Hey," I called.

Shay, bundled up in my spare jacket, gloves, and hat, glanced up from her laptop at one of the tables with a smile on her face.

I really wanted to keep that smile on her face, especially after last night. "Give it to me."

"Define joule."

"Easy. The standard unit of measure."

"For what?" she prompted.

"Energy and work."

She smiled. "Got it. How about kinetic energy?"

"Energy an object has due to its motion."

Pride shone in her eyes as she smiled again. "You're like eight for eight."

"Actually, ten for ten." I leaned down and kissed her before taking off for the ski lift.

"See you in ten minutes," she called, knowing the drill.

I lifted my board in the air to acknowledge her, loving that we could mix tutoring and practice—not to mention I could release all the anger I'd been feeling.


### Shay


That night, I lay snuggled into Kason's side watching a movie on his bed. I would've liked to say I knew the name of the movie. Or, what it was about. But, I'd never been alone in a dark room nestled under the arm of a hot guy who I was starting to have some strong feelings for.

I couldn't seem *not* to inhale his cool arctic scent with every breath I took. His steady heartbeat thumped beneath my ear capturing all my attention. My body buzzed with something unfamiliar to me, and I wanted to literally crawl out of my skin. I wasn't someone who thought about sex. And, it wasn't like I was ready to give up the V card tonight. But, my mind was on getting closer to Kason. I suddenly wanted him touching me. And kissing me. And wanting me.

"Shay, what the hell are you doing?" he asked.

"What?"

"You haven't paid one bit of attention to the movie."

"How do you know?"

"Because I can almost hear the wheels grinding in your head. What's up?"

What was I supposed to say? This was all new for me. Maybe I didn't need to *say* anything.

I reached up and entwined my hand around to the back of his head, urging his mouth down to mine. He willingly acquiesced with a cocky smirk. Our kiss started off slow and gentle. But, I had a feeling his thoughts were pretty much where mine were because he deepened the kiss. As his tongue competed with mine for control, he rolled me onto my back and took the lead. His hard chest pressed me into the bed, holding me in place. His heartbeat suddenly mirrored mine, pounding against his chest. I couldn't get close enough. The kiss couldn't get deep enough.

Kason was the one to pull away first, his chest heaving as he dragged a hand through his hair. "Sorry. I'm stopping."

"Why?"

"Because we're taking it slow. Shay, this means a lot to me. You forgiving me. You wanting to be here with me. You've held off for a reason. I'm not gonna screw it up by moving too fast."

What? No. "But maybe..."

His brows shot up, intrigued by my words. "Maybe what?"

I didn't know how to verbalize all these feelings I was having. Feeling anything other than heartbreak was new for me. I clutched the front of his shirt, pulling him back down to me and kissing him with everything I had.

Kason pulled away. "Jesus, Shay. You're really testing my resolve."

"I want you to..." My voice drifted away as I struggled to

verbalize what I wanted because I'd never done any of this before.

His eyes were wide, almost fearful. "You want me to what?"

I swallowed around the lump that was suddenly lodged in my throat. "Touch me."

Once the surprise in his eyes disappeared, a cocky grin slipped across his lips. "Oh, I can definitely do that." He leaned down and pressed kisses along my jawline, underneath my ear, and over my neck. I closed my eyes, letting every glorious feeling overtake me. He inched his way down my body, dragging his nose over my T-shirt but between my breasts. I held my breath, turned on beyond reason as he kept moving, inching his way down until he reached the top of my jeans. He reached for the button but looked to me for approval.

I met his eyes and nodded, my heart thrashing against the wall of my chest. Was I ready for this?

He unclasped the button and slipped my jeans down my legs as he made his way to my feet. He pulled them off and tossed them to the floor, leaving me very much exposed in a black thong. As if appreciating every exposed inch of me, his eyes swept from my feet to my thong and back again.

A shiver rushed through me. No one had ever looked at me, especially with my ugly scars exposed, with such hunger in their eyes.

Kason leaned down and pressed his lips gently to my legs, covering each ugly scar with a kiss. I tipped back my head and closed my eyes as tears began to prick them. Kason was unfazed by something that caused me such grief —such embarrassment. He just accepted them as part of me —even though they came from such an ugly place.

He abandoned the scars and continued kissing his way

up my thighs, each movement causing my heart to race more. He reached my thong and peppered light kisses across the thin material. Unprepared for what was happening between my thighs, I sucked in a sharp breath.

Kason's head shot up. "Is this okay?"

I met his eyes. "God, yes."

He didn't waste any time, his mouth returned, pressing kisses all over my thong. I had no idea something like that could elicit such sensations. He continued down a few inches until he neared the strip of fabric between my legs. He paused. I held my breath, and my body trembled with anticipation. He spread my legs a little bit and then his mouth descended, kissing a gentle path down the strip of material and then back up again. *Holy hell.* I waited for him to do it again, but his mouth moved away. I released the breath I'd been holding.

Kason's fingers slipped beneath the waistband and pulled my thong down my legs.

The fact that he hadn't asked permission told me his attempt to go slow had been thwarted by what I was allowing him to do. And, he was taking full advantage of the situation. Thank *God.*

I didn't open my eyes because I didn't want to see myself partially naked and sprawled out on his bed. But they certainly popped open the second his mouth returned and his tongue moved to where my underwear had been. I sucked in a sharp breath as he licked a path between my folds. I gripped the comforter at my sides, holding on for dear life. He continued his path, back and forth. I shamelessly began to pant. Then, he circled my clit. "Oh my God," tumbled out of my mouth, not even remotely sounding like me.

"I got you," he murmured against my wet skin.

His tongue circled and circled, the sensations beyond anything I'd ever felt before. Everything between my legs began to throb, building up until it had nowhere else to go.

"Ka-*son*," I gasped.

He didn't respond with words, lapping away at my clit and sucking on it until I was squirming from the intensity of all the feelings rushing through me. Within seconds, the spiral between my legs wound tight. Kason sucked hard. And, that's all it took.

My body quaked and tremors shot from inside out, emitting a buzz over my entire body. Kason stopped his torture, and my chest heaved as I lay there, a useless pile of goo unable to move. "Oh. My. God."

Kason chuckled as he moved beside me, pulling the comforter over me to cover me up. "That was unexpected."

My head fell to the side and I met his gaze. "You think?"

"Was it all right?"

"More than all right."

I thought he'd laugh, but indecision plagued his eyes. "I was serious about not rushing you."

"I know. That was all on me."

He gave me a crooked grin, knowing I really was the one to get things started. "You've really never done that before?"

I shook my head.

He brushed his knuckles over my flushed cheek. "Well, I'm glad I could be your first."

"You're my first for a lot of things."

"Damn straight I am." He laughed, and when he laughed like that, I knew—despite my initial reservations—that this thing between us was real.

I headed toward the bathroom wearing my robe and pink boots Friday morning. I was bummed that Kason had left for Utah, and I wouldn't see him until Sunday night—especially after what had transpired in his room. It had been a good stretch for us, spending time together each night. And, the more time we spent together, the more I got to know and like the real Kason. The one I was lucky enough to get to see.

I slipped inside an empty shower stall, placed my shower caddy down, and reached to turn on the water. A loud alarm sounded in the hallway and I jumped.

"Everyone outside!" our RA called in the hallway. "Fire alarm!" He banged on all the doors, including the bathroom. "Let's go!"

*Dammit.*

I switched off the water and hurried out of the bathroom, tightening my robe as I followed my sleepy dorm mates down the stairs.

Our RA ushered us like a herd of cattle out of the dorm to the front lawn. Since it was six in the morning and still dark outside, most had been awoken by the alarm. Luckily, everyone wore some type of pajamas, so I wasn't the only person out in the snow in a robe.

I found Kendall nearby with her comforter wrapped tightly around her body. When she saw me approach, she opened one arm and let me huddle under the comforter with her to keep warm. But, the temperature hadn't even hit thirty yet, so our attempt proved futile.

Fire trucks arrived with sirens blaring. Firemen jumped out and made their way into the building.

"I'm fr-ee-zzzz-ing," Kendall said through chattering teeth.

I glanced to the dining hall across the street. "Let's get warm."

We hurried over and stood in the doorway of the dining hall, waiting for the firemen to leave our dorm.

"Do you think it's a real fire?"

I shrugged, having no idea but hoping it had only been a hairdryer or something that caused sparks so I could shower and get to calculus.

Ten minutes later, they gave us the all-clear and we filed back into the dorm. I took off for the shower, in a hurry so I wouldn't be late for calculus at seven. I dried my hair in the bathroom so I didn't bother Kendall who'd gone back to bed.

As my hair began to dry, I stared at myself in the mirror. My eyes widened at what I saw. Oh. My. God. I dropped the hairdryer into the sink and grasped at my hair. Why was it turning orange? Why was it the color of a pumpkin? I grabbed my shampoo bottle and squeezed orange shampoo into my orange-stained hand. Oh, no. Oh, no.

The fire drill.

My shampoo.

Oh. My. God.

I grabbed my hairdryer, yanked the cord from the wall, and stuffed everything into my caddy. I would not cry. I would not give Cora the satisfaction because there wasn't a doubt in my mind that she had something to do with it.

I bent down, checking for feet under the stalls, but there were none. Was she waiting in the hall to see her work?

I grabbed my towel from the nearby sink and wrapped my hair up in it. No way was she going to see my hair. I moved to the door, pulled in a long breath, and steeled my features. If she was in the hallway, she was getting nothing from me.

Luckily, when I opened the door, she wasn't there. I bolted to my room and when I got there, I shook Kendall awake. "Wake up."

"What?" she grumbled.

"I need your help."

Her eyes snapped open.

I pulled the towel off my head, revealing my orange hair.

Her eyes widened. "What did you do?"

"I didn't do it. Someone poured something into my shampoo bottle. I'm guessing while we were outside."

"Cora?"

"Who else would do this?" Tears stung my eyes, but I blinked them away. I could handle this. I'd handled far worse.

"Okay. We need to get you to a salon."

A pit sat heavy in my stomach thinking about my orange hair. I didn't have money to pay for my hair to be fixed. "Can't we just get something at the store to fix it?"

"You need a professional. We could make it worse with store-bought stuff."

I stood from her bed and moved to the mirror. The color

was getting progressively brighter the more my hair dried. I grabbed a hairband from my desk and wrapped my hair into a knot on the top of my head.

"It's not as noticeable that way," Kendall said, though I could hear the lie in her voice. Hell, I could see the lie with my own eyes.

"Well, I'm not letting her win."

"Are you gonna call Kason?"

I shook my head. "It will only upset him."

"Then, what are you gonna do?"

"I'm going to class."

"You don't have to, Shay."

"Of course I do."

I thought she'd argue with me and try to convince me to stay in our room until we could figure out what to do. But instead, she smiled and I could see the pride her smile held. "I'll call salons once they open and see when they can fit you in."

"Not the high-end ones."

I watched realization turn to sadness in her eyes. "Go. Let Cora see you flaunt that orange hair."

I smiled as I left the room, but it faded as soon as I stepped into the hallway. Cora had purposely done this to embarrass me. To get revenge on me for dating Kason. But, if she wanted revenge on someone, why wasn't it Kason? He's the one who hurt her. Not me.

Regardless of her motives, I'd bounce back.

It's what I'd been doing my entire life.

31

────

SHAY

Because no salon could take me until Monday, I spent most of the weekend hiding out in my dorm room. Sure, it was the age of dyed hair and most girls could rock purple, blue, and pink hair. But, this dye job was *fluorescent* orange. Everyone but a clown steered clear of this shade.

I'd spoken to Kason multiple times while he was away, but I didn't mention my hair. I didn't want anything to ruin his trip. I knew how much he wanted to be out there preparing for the Games. This stupid prank—as malicious as it was—was not going to be the reason he lost focus.

"We can get takeout for dinner," Kendall offered on Sunday night.

"Nope. We're going to the dining hall."

"You sure?"

"Yup." We'd eaten cereal in our room all weekend, but I was done hiding, *and* I was hungry for real food.

We made our way across the street to the dining hall. I was in the mood for the salad bar, so I headed there while Kendall hit up the sandwich bar.

"A little late for Halloween," Cora said from somewhere behind me as I filled my salad plate.

Though my heartbeat sped up, I didn't turn around, continuing to pile tomatoes onto my plate of lettuce. "I think orange brings out my eyes."

Cora huffed, my calm reaction pissing her off. "Kason will definitely be rethinking being seen in public with white trash now."

Heat rushed through my veins. It wasn't like I hadn't been called names before. I had thick skin. But, did she really think he'd lose interest in me if she messed with my appearance? Did she really think he was that shallow? *And,* did she really think that I was just some toy to be messed with?

"He killed it in Utah," Cora continued. "You should've seen him crush his runs. I left before him, that's why I'm already back."

Even though my heartbeat had begun to pound in my ears, I tried to remain calm. She was just trying to get to me. There was no way she'd been in Utah and he hadn't mentioned it.

"*Ohhh.* You didn't know I was there?" she said as if she felt sorry for letting the cat out of the bag.

I lifted the ladle of French dressing and poured it in a zig-zag pattern over my salad, trying to harness all the emotions flooding through me.

"Maybe if you had your glasses, you'd be able to see things clearly. Like the fact that he doesn't really like you."

My glasses? *She'd* broken them. Why hadn't I considered that?

"Turn around. You know you want to say something." She shoved me, and I stumbled forward against the salad bar. The dressing splashed all over my shirt, seeping through and causing the fabric to stick to my skin.

I took some deep breaths and stood upright. I pivoted to look at her, a smile on my face. Despite all the horrible things she'd done and said to me, I would not allow her to break me.

I was stronger than that.

Now that she got the full view of me with orange hair and salad dressing drenching my shirt, she laughed out loud. "All you need is the red nose."

The combination of all she'd done came to a head. A ball of uncontrollable rage swelled in my chest. I tried to harness it. Tried to shove it somewhere else like I had while growing up. But, I just couldn't do it. I lowered my dish to the salad bar, begging myself to ignore her. But I couldn't do that either. I twisted back to face her with my hand tightened into a fist at my side.

She smiled, so impressed by her work.

That's all it took.

I pulled back my elbow and released my fist with everything I had, punching her in the face.

She gasped as she lost her footing, landing on her ass. She immediately covered her face, whimpering into her palms.

I cradled my throbbing fist in my other hand. *That freaking hurt.*

Kendall rushed over to me and moved me away from Cora and toward the exit. I wasn't sure if she thought I'd attack Cora again or if she was keeping me from getting into trouble, but it didn't matter. I'd done what I needed to do. I thought silence would be the best way to deal with what Cora had done to me. But she wouldn't quit. I'd never had the urge to hit someone the way I had the urge to hit her. And, it felt so damn good.

People rushed over to help Cora as Kendall and I rushed outside the building.

"That was awesome!" she said as we broke into laughter and hurried across the street to our dorm. "I am *so* proud of you. How do you feel?"

"So good."

———

That night, I lay on my bed watching Netflix, an ice bag on my hand. They don't show you the aftermath of a punch in the movies. But, my knuckles were so swollen my fingers looked like sausages. And, now, after all that anger, I was feeling regret. I wasn't my father. I didn't hit people. I ignored people like Cora, and my life was better for it. But, she just wouldn't stop. And, I realized in that moment that I had a breaking point. I wondered if it had more to do with jealousy than anything else. Because since I'd returned from the dining hall, the thought of her being in Utah—and Kason not telling me—plagued my every thought.

There was a knock on the door.

Kendall looked to me from her bed. "Kason?"

I shook my head. "He won't be back until later." I hadn't texted him about the run-in with Cora—or her claims. I knew we'd talk about everything when he got home. And, truthfully, I wanted to see his reaction when I asked about her being in Utah.

Kendall crawled off her bed and moved to the door. "Who is it?" she asked.

"Campus police."

She glanced at me with wide eyes. She motioned for me to tuck the ice bag away.

I tucked it under my pillow and sat up as she opened the door.

"Are you Shay Miller?" the uniformed officer asked her.

I jumped to my feet and moved to the door. "I'm Shay."

He looked at me, his eyes instantly going to the orange knot on my head. "Ms. Miller, we're here investigating an assault that happened this evening."

"Shay's innocent," Kendall pleaded. "That bitch dyed her hair orange." She pointed to my hair. "Look."

Ignoring Kendall's pleas, he continued. "Did you or did you not assault another student in the dining hall?"

I stepped back and sat on my bed. "I did."

"But only after Cora did that to Shay's hair and then taunted her about it," Kendall added, trying desperately to help.

He stepped inside the room and closed the door behind him. Had he not been wearing the uniform, he would've looked like any other college guy. "No matter what someone does to you, it's against the law to assault them," he explained to both of us.

"What do you call replacing her shampoo with orange hair dye?" Kendall continued. "I can't believe that's not some kind of assault."

His eyes shifted to mine. "If the victim did something to you—"

"The victim?" Kendall's voice raised.

He glared at her before continuing. "You needed to file a complaint. You never take matters into your own hands."

"I tried to ignore her," I said. "I didn't want her to think she broke me. But, she just wouldn't stop." I shrugged. "And, I snapped."

Kendall sat down beside me on the bed and wrapped her arm around my shoulders. "Cora's evil. You did nothing to deserve this."

"She broke the victim's nose," the officer said.

"Is this going on my record?"

He stared at me, his eyes holding regret. "Are you eighteen?"

I nodded.

"In Colorado, third-degree assault is a class one misdemeanor that carries a fine of up to five thousand dollars or—"

"Or what?" I asked.

"Or, a jail sentence of six to twenty-four months," he explained.

My stomach dropped and my mind spun as Kendall pleaded with the officer. "She'll do community service. Just make this go away."

"I need to take her to the station," he said.

Kendall jumped to her feet and stood in front of me with her arms crossed. "There is no way I'm allowing her to leave this room with you."

His head retracted. "*You're* not allowing it?"

"It's what Cora wants," Kendall explained. "We'll come in willingly once her ear isn't pressed to her door waiting for you to bring Shay in."

Dealing with Kendall as my bodyguard proved difficult for the young officer. He huffed. "Fine. But if you don't show—"

"Do I look like someone who's going to run?" I asked. "You'd spot my hair a mile away."

He almost laughed.

I wished I could laugh, but this was my life. And, up until this year, I'd had a well-established plan for my future.

But now, it was as if my world was crumbling around me and all I could do was grasp at sand that was slipping through my fingertips.

———

We left the campus police station after midnight. I stared out Kendall's passenger window into the darkness replaying the officer's words in my head. *Prison.* My heart sank at the thought that my future lay in the hands of Cora and her family. If they decided to press charges, I had no idea which punishment I'd receive. And, rationally, Cora hadn't worked this hard to destroy me not to press charges.

Tears stung my eyes. After everything I'd risen above to get to college—everything I'd done to give myself the future I deserved, it was all slipping away and there was nothing I could do to stop it. I was grasping at something I couldn't contain.

"You okay?" Kendall asked.

"I will be," I lied. "Can I ask you for one more favor?"

"Anything," she said.

"Will you take me to Kason's house?"

"Is he back?"

I shrugged. "I think so. I have a bunch of missed calls from him."

Within minutes, we were outside Kason's house. The lights inside lit up the main floor.

"I'll see you in the morning, then?" she said.

I shook my head feeling numb inside. "No. I'll be right out. Wait for me?"

Her brows furrowed. "You sure?"

I nodded as I opened the car door and stepped out. I

walked up the sidewalk in a daze. A daze I didn't know if I'd be able to get myself out of. My life was spiraling.

When I got to the front door, I knocked and heard footsteps inside. My heartbeat was a jackhammer in my chest. There was so much I needed to say to Kason. I suddenly felt overwhelmed by it.

The door swung open and Thayer stood there, his brows drawn in question. I didn't blame him. Last time he saw me I had brown hair.

"Is he here?" I asked.

He nodded. "He was pretty beat. He might be asleep."

I pushed past him and moved to the stairs. "That's fine." I climbed them to the second floor. Kason's door was closed, but I opened it. Thayer had been right. He was sound asleep in bed.

I knocked, announcing my presence.

Kason jolted upright in nothing but boxers. He looked totally confused for a moment but then focused on me standing in his doorway. "Shay?"

"I can see how you might not recognize me with orange hair."

His eyes zoned in on my hair. "That's a different look for you."

"Cora must've thought it'd be perfect when she replaced my shampoo with orange hair dye."

His mouth opened. "She didn't?"

"Oh, I assure you, she did."

He moved to stand.

I held up my palm. "Stop."

I watched the confusion flash across his eyes.

"Was she in Utah?"

He held my stare for a long time, and I watched the guilt pass over his features. He knew he should have told me. He knew, of all people, her being there would make me uncomfortable.

I closed my eyes. How had I been so stupid?

"It's not what you think. Her dad was there, and she just showed up."

I shrugged, not caring about anything at that point. "I'm shocked she didn't mention my hair. She's quite proud of her work."

"Shay," he said, sounding like he wanted to console me.

"It's fine. She'll have a nose job and I'm sure it'll be even perkier than it was before I punched her."

"You hit her?"

I nodded. "I'm done playing her game."

"No one should hurt you like that, Shay."

"You mean like *you* did?" It may have been childish to throw the way we started back in his face, but he'd kept her being in Utah from me. And, my emotions were all out of whack knowing the punishment I was possibly facing.

I watched the sting of my words hit him.

"Well, my victory was short-lived," I continued. "She went to the police. I was brought in on assault charges."

I watched as his expression changed. "What?"

"Oh yeah. Go big or go home is clearly her motto."

"Shay, I'm so sorry." He went to stand.

"Stop!" I yelled, getting angrier because everything that had happened had been *his* fault. All of it. She never would've gone to these great lengths if it weren't for him. "Just stop! I could go to jail, Kason! *Jail. Me.*"

He opened his mouth to speak, but the words just wouldn't come. Because there was nothing he *could* say. It was all screwed up. All of it.

"Since I met you, everything in my life has gone from bad to worse—as if that was even possible. This all happened to me because of *you*! If you'd just left me alone. If you'd just been truthful with me. If you'd just not used me to hurt her. But you couldn't do that. You're selfish, Kason. And, I thought I could overlook it. I thought I could see the real you shining through and I liked who that person was. But there's too much that I can't ignore." Suddenly, his room felt too small and it became difficult for me to breathe. "I need to get out of here. I need space. I need to think about everything. And, I can't do that with you around. I need you to stay away from me."

He climbed to his feet, moving toward me. "You can't mean that."

I stepped back with my palms raised, scared he'd try to touch me. And at that moment, I couldn't even stand the sight of him.

I could see the hurt in his eyes. "You're just upset, Shay. And scared. Let me make this better."

I spun on the boots he'd bought me and rushed out of his room, passing Thayer who had clearly been eavesdropping in the hallway. But I didn't care. He needed to know the hell his roommate had created. I hurried downstairs and out of the house, and only then when the fresh air hit was I able to catch my breath.

I reached Kendall's car and once I was safely inside, I dropped my head against the headrest. It hadn't been easy to push him away, but the bad outweighed the good with us. And I just couldn't handle that in my life.

"Everything okay?"

I turned my head and stared out the window, trying to keep the tears glazing my eyes from falling. "I said what I needed to say."

"Do you feel better?" I could hear the confusion in her voice.

"I have orange hair, I might go to jail, and I just told the guy I was starting to fall for that I need him to stay away from me."

She was quiet for a moment, likely processing what I'd said. "So, that's a yes?"

I glanced at her.

She burst out laughing, knowing what a shitty weekend I'd had.

I laughed too because the alternative was breaking down, and Shay Miller did not break down. She held her head up and wore a brave face, no matter how much hurt she felt inside.

32

———

KASON

I felt sick to my stomach as I teetered on the edge of my bed, wringing my hands. What the fuck just happened? Shay's words played on a loop in my head, hitting me in the gut like the punch she'd landed on Cora. She could go to fucking jail. And, Jesus Christ, her hair. Her fucking *orange* hair. How had things gotten so out of control?

Thayer stepped into my doorway. I knew he'd heard what went down. Hell, he'd been the one to let Shay in. He had to see her hair. He had to hear her words. He had to see the anger I'd created. "Well, now you know."

"What?" I snapped.

"What the aftermath of your actions looks like," he explained.

My brows furrowed, not liking where he was going with this.

"Have you ever stopped to consider all the people you've used over the years to get what you wanted?"

"Dude, you need to watch yourself."

"I'm your best friend, Kason. If I can't say this to you, who can?"

Though it sucked to hear, I didn't know what else to do but hear him out. As much as Shay thought things were crumbling around her, I felt the same.

"Up until now, being selfish has worked for you," Thayer said. "But this year, you've gone too far. And now you've hurt someone who didn't deserve to be hurt. She's caught in the crossfire of something she didn't start. And, it isn't fair, bro. It just isn't fair."

Heat pulsed in my cheeks as I clenched my teeth together, grinding them so hard my jaw ticked. "Don't you think I fucking know that?" My anger didn't stem from him being out of line, it stemmed from him being right. Shay *wasn't* someone you took advantage of. Life had already done that to her. And, what did I do at the first chance? I fucking blackmailed her and then used her to piss off Cora. I should've known better, but all I saw was a way to get what *I* wanted. And, though things had turned around for Shay and me, because of what I'd done before, she was paying the price for it. Thayer was spot on. I was a piece of shit.

"I know it sucks to hear this," he continued. "And I don't even fault you for it because it worked for you up until now. But seriously, bro. How long were you gonna be able to get away with putting yourself before all others?"

"I wasn't doing that anymore. I was doing right by Shay."

"Did you tell her Cora showed up in Salt Lake City?"

"No."

"Then, you weren't doing right by her. You were keeping shit from her. And that never ends well."

"She would've been hurt or pissed or I don't fucking know. It seemed better not to mention it."

"Do you still think that? Because by the sounds of it, that didn't seem the case."

I tunneled my fingers through my hair. "Well, what do I do now?" I asked, trying to push away the knowledge that not only had I lost Shay, I'd fucked with her future—the one thing in this world she cared about. I jumped up and moved to my dresser, putting on a black hoodie and dark jeans.

"What are you doing?" he asked.

"I need to get over there."

"She said to leave her alone," he called as I rushed downstairs, knowing what I needed to do.

*Yeah. I got that.*

I hopped in my Jeep and made my way to Shay's dorm, blowing through stop signs since no one was around at one in the morning *and* I had a lot to say. I knew Shay didn't want to see me. I knew she thought I caused all of this.

I screeched to a stop in front of the dorm and threw my Jeep into park, not caring that I parked in a tow zone. That was the least of my problems. I hopped out, realizing I didn't have an access card which meant I wasn't getting in.

*Fuuuuuck.*

I moved to the window of a room on the first floor. The curtains were drawn and the lights were off, but I knocked anyway. I waited, looking around to be sure I didn't look like I was about to sneak in the window. Given it was one of those push-out windows, I wouldn't fit anyway. I knocked again, hoping the sound woke whoever lived there. Finally, the curtains flew open. A girl glared at me. My guess was I wasn't the first one to knock on her window to open the door in the middle of the night.

"Could you open the door for me?" I shot her the smile that normally got me what I wanted.

She stared at me, looking about ready to hurt me, but then rolled her eyes before disappearing.

What did that mean? Was she letting me in?

A couple of seconds later, I heard the exterior door open. I rushed to it. "Thank you," I said as she turned away from me and headed back to her room.

I climbed the stairs taking two at a time until I reached the third floor. I banged on the door and waited, my hands gripping the door frame. My pulse began to race as I waited. Then I heard footsteps. I held my breath, stopping all the emotions that whirled inside of me.

The lock clicked and the door cracked open. I pushed my way inside and closed the door behind me.

"What took you so long?" Cora asked with a bandage covering her nose and a whole lot of makeup trying to conceal the black underneath her eyes.

I skipped my Monday classes. Kendall's mom had paid for my hair to be restored to its natural color after hearing what happened. Normally, I would've rejected such an expensive handout, but desperate times called for desperate measures. And, as much as I liked proving I could rock orange hair, I didn't want to.

"Has he called?" Kendall asked as I moved to the hairdresser's chair after she'd rinsed the neutralizing toner out of my hair.

I checked my phone then shook my head.

"How's that make you feel?"

"He's doing what I asked, *and* I don't have to worry about my hair turning another shade of pumpkin."

The sadness in her eyes told me she thought I'd been wrong to push him away. "You're still going to see him in class. And, study group."

I shrugged, knowing I'd face that obstacle when I got to it.

I hadn't been lying when I said everything that

happened was because of him. If he'd never coerced me into tutoring him—and used me to make Cora mad, none of it would have happened. I wanted my normal life back. I wanted to fly under everyone's radar. I wanted to get my degree and do great things. I never signed up for a first semester of college plagued with drama. The only good thing to come out of my time at Cranmore was my friendship with Kendall and the brief taste of normal I got with Kason's family.

But now, I just needed quiet back in my life. But, with my future in Cora's hands, I couldn't even think about my future.

———

I slipped on my black boots, grabbed my backpack, and hurried out my door early Tuesday morning, wanting to walk to class amidst the silence. I wanted to slow down the whirlwind that had been swirling around me.

As soon as I stepped into the hallway, Cora's door opened. I stopped in my tracks, contemplating turning around so I didn't have to see her.

But, it wasn't her.

Kason stepped out of her room. "See you later," he called inside before closing the door.

My pulse began to pound and my feet wouldn't move. What was he doing there? Had he been there all night? I shook my head, having no right to be questioning it when I'd been the one to tell him to stay away.

Kason turned his head, noticing me standing there. *Dammit.*

I expected guilt to cross his face, but he looked at me as

if he didn't even know me. His emotionless eyes looked right through me.

Was he happy I'd seen him?

Was he just as angry with me as I was with him?

Was this payback?

Then, without a word, he turned and walked in the opposite direction, stealing the breath from my lungs and leaving a hollow space in my chest.

I must've stood there for at least two more minutes, unable to get my legs working beneath me. I was the one to tell Kason to stay away from me. I was the one to blame him for everything that happened to me. But, that last thing I expected to do was send him running back to my enemy. To the person who'd made me look like a clown. To the person who held my future in her hands.

Had they been working together all along?

Had this been payback for that first night?

Had everything up until this point been a lie?

Was *that* why she'd been in Utah and he hadn't told me. Had they been together this whole *time*?

Oh. My. God. My knees nearly buckled as the truth came barreling at me at warped speed.

This was *all* an elaborate lie. A lie meant to get back at me and embarrass me.

I wanted to go back into my room. I wanted to crawl up into a ball and cry. I wanted to believe the Kason I'd gotten to know and the one who just looked right through me were two different people. But, he'd just proven that I'd be wrong.

I pulled on my proverbial big girl panties and put one foot in front of the other until I was heading out of the building. I'd be seeing him again tomorrow for physics class, and there was no way I'd allow him to think he hurt me. If he and Cora were together—if he really didn't care what she'd done to me—he was more selfish than I'd ever imagined.

34

———

SHAY

The following morning, I stepped outside the dorm, surprised it hadn't warmed up despite the bright sun shining. I wrapped my arms around myself and took off toward calculus.

My phone rang as I crossed campus. I slipped it from my pocket but didn't recognize the number. "Hello?"

"I paid you because you worked for me," Giselle began. "You weren't supposed to leave the money in my nightstand."

I couldn't help but smile at the sound of her voice. "Like my note said, I wanted to *help*. Not take your money." And, that was the truth. She'd welcomed me into their home and made me feel like family. I didn't feel right taking money from her.

"Okay. Now for the second reason I'm calling," she said. "I heard what happened."

"What exactly did you hear?" I asked, not wanting to say too much. Though I knew she liked me, Kason was her brother.

"Cora pulled some nasty stunts."

"That about sums it up."

"Just so you know, my brother cares about you."

I scoffed. "I saw him coming out of Cora's room yesterday."

"I. Will. Kill. Him."

"It's fine."

"It's not fine. She hurt you. There is no good reason for him to be anywhere near her."

*Unless it was their plan all along to make me look like a fool.* He valued his sister's respect too much to tell her that.

"I'm sorry, Shay. I thought he'd changed. I thought *you* changed him."

I'd thought so too. That's what hurt the most.

"I heard you broke Cora's nose."

"Yeah. Did he tell you she may press charges?"

"He didn't tell me any of this. Thayer did."

"Oh. I didn't realize you talk to Thayer."

She didn't respond.

"I'm sorry. It's none of my business," I said.

"No, it's just, he's pissed at Kason. And he needed someone to vent to."

"Oh."

"Shay, my parents and I are here for you. Even if my stupid brother flaked on you, you still have us."

"He didn't flake. I told him to stay away. I just didn't specify where he should or should not do that."

"Yeah, well, the Kason I know wouldn't have let you push him away. He would've fought you tooth and nail until you forgave him. He's stubborn like that. So, I have no idea what fool has inhabited his body."

As much as it didn't fix my problem to have Giselle on my side, it felt nice to have someone care.

"You have my number now," she said. "You call me if you need anything."

"Thank you. That means a lot."

We ended the call just as I reached calculus. I thought hearing Giselle's voice, and her assurances that her brother was an idiot, would've made me feel better. But as I stepped inside the classroom, I just felt worse.

My eyes flicked to my phone more than they focused on my calculus equations. I was dreading going to physics class, but I knew it was important to show up and prove that Kason hadn't broken me. Once my calculus professor dismissed us, I made my way to the physics building next door. I'd gotten good at ignoring Kason prior to Thanksgiving. I hoped it would be just as easy now.

He wasn't in class when I arrived which made it easier to relax in my seat. I took out my laptop and kept my eyes on the screen. And, even though my focus was on my screen, the hair on the back of my neck prickled. I could see Kason through my peripheral as he entered the class and took his seat.

A pit formed in my stomach, and I hated that it did. My entire life had been plagued by disappointment and hurt. I'd worked so hard to never allow those emotions in again because I was so much stronger than that. But since I'd met Kason, those emotions had stirred to life inside me. Good, bad, hopeful, ugly...I'd felt them all. I'd let down my guard with him, and they'd all flooded in. He had no idea what he'd done to me. No idea at all. But, there was one thing I knew for sure. I wouldn't let it happen again.

Professor Raymond began his lecture and I lost myself in his words, not allowing any outside thoughts to invade my brain. I was there to learn. To get everything out of my free education as I could. I couldn't lose sight of that. Especially because of a guy. A guy who didn't even deserve me.

At the end of class, I passed Professor Raymond's desk.

"See you tonight for study group, Ms. Miller."

"You bet," I said, knowing I was going to hate every second of it.

As I stepped outside the building, I noticed a group of guys holding skateboards. Kason stood with them, laughing and talking like his future didn't hang in the balance like mine did.

I was about to avert my gaze when Cora bounced over to him and covered his eyes from behind. He spun around and smiled when he found her standing there. That was just about all I could stomach. I turned back inside the building before they could see me and made my way to the opposite end of the hallway, sneaking out the back exit. It may have been a weak move on my part, but self-preservation was a strong motivator that I'd mastered a long time ago.

If I needed *not* to see them together to coexist, then that is what I was going to do. I mean, he was doing what I'd asked and staying away from me. It was the fact that he was staying away from me with *her* that stung like a son-of-a-bitch.

———

I checked my phone too many times as I sat alone in the conference room. Seven o'clock had come and gone and no one had shown up for study group—not even Professor Raymond. With a sigh of relief, I packed my things into my backpack.

The conference room doorknob rattled. I swallowed

hard. Nothing in this world could've made me look at that door. My heart sped and my hands began to shake.

"Is he here?"

My eyes flashed up. The guy Kason had paid *not* to attend study group stood in the open doorway. "Nope. It's just you and me."

He closed the door behind him and sat down. We spent the next hour talking about science. It was refreshing to work with someone who could follow along as I explained physics. I could feel the old me coming to life when he grasped the material.

I returned to my dorm a little after eight. It had been a long day and I just needed to get in bed and sleep. Kendall had a pledge class event which meant I had the room to myself. I made my way up to my room, stopping at my door and punching in the door code.

"Shay?" Kason said.

I stilled.

"How are you?" he asked, his voice nearing me.

I tore my eyes away from my door to see him standing five feet away. "Great," I lied.

"Be honest, Shay."

"The way you were honest with me? How long were you and Cora planning it?"

His brows furrowed. "Planning what?"

"Oh, come on. You've got to give me more credit than that. Setting me up. She had to be laughing her head off when she saw us together. 'Pathetic Shay actually thought you were dating.'" I shook my head, getting angrier now that I'd said it out loud. I'd been so blind. "Never mind. It's not even worth it."

"Shay, you've got it all wrong," he said.

The handle on Cora's door rattled. Kason's eyes

widened and I could see the fear in them. He spun away from me and hurried to her door, blocking her from stepping out into the hallway.

"There you are," she said from inside her room. Her hand reached out of her door and she grabbed the front of his shirt. And without even a glance, he let her pull him into the room.

My stomach roiled at the sight of him going in there.

Flashes of what happened behind closed doors between the two of us played through my mind. Though we hadn't done everything, we'd done enough for me to know what it felt like to be on the receiving end of what Kason could do. And the thought of him doing the same thing—and more—with Cora was more than I could stomach.

Thankfully, I didn't have to hear the two of them through my wall that night. He was gracious enough to spare me that.

## 35

## KASON

"Oh my *God*. I so need a latte," Cora said as we walked across campus. "It's frickin' freezing."

"It's December in Colorado," I said, noting the snow covering everything but the shoveled sidewalks.

"Yeah, well, I need Daddy to send me some of his below zero gear or I'm gonna freeze my ass off this winter."

"Speaking of your dad, have you guys decided what you're gonna do yet?" I asked.

"About what, babe?" she asked, burrowing her body into me to keep warm as we walked through campus.

"Pressing charges."

"Daddy wants to sue the bitch for all she's got, but it turns out she's got nothing. She's even more white trash than I imagined. So, it's probably jail time for her."

"Listen, I know you're not her biggest fan," I began, treading lightly so not to send her off the handles. "But, you did kinda provoke her."

"She broke my nose," she snapped, moving away from me. "Whose side are you on?"

"Yours," I said, trying to calm her. "But do you really think she'll survive in prison?"

Cold laughter tumbled out of her. "It sure would be fun to find out."

My gut churned. Cora was one cold bitch. There was no doubt about that.

We came upon the café and she took off, running over to some friends who clearly hadn't seen her since her surgery. They all wrapped her in a big hug. You'd think she'd had some disease she'd just recovered from. She'd had a nose job because she provoked someone into punching her. Did they not know that?

"I'm heading to the mountain," I called to her.

"Okay, babe. See you tonight."

———

I heard the front door open as I lay on my bed after dinner. I listened for footsteps, figuring it was Thayer who currently wasn't speaking to me, but wishing like hell it was Shay. She clearly had a lot she needed to say to me before Cora interrupted us in the hallway. I considered calling her to let her know what was going on, but there was no way she'd even answer. I didn't even blame her. I'd done a complete one-eighty when it came to us—or at least that's what she assumed. But, I thought of all people, she knew me better than that. I thought she'd chew me out because at least that showed she still cared. But to not say anything—to just let me move on without a fight—made me question everything I thought we had.

A kitchen cabinet opened downstairs, telling me it was Thayer. I knew I'd disappointed him by trying to get out of my contract, but even more so for holding a fake video over

Shay's head. Shit hit the fan once he learned Cora had hurt Shay. Thayer was a better guy than I'd ever be and him snubbing me lately, told me he hated who I'd become. I just wished he saw the guy Shay once saw. The one who wanted to be better.

My phone vibrated. I snatched it from my nightstand.

> GISELLE
>
> Has my brother returned yet?

Unlike Thayer, she at least let me know exactly what she was thinking.

I tossed my phone down, not bothering with a response. She'd heard what happened to Shay. And she blamed me for it. The irony was *I* blamed me, too. If I'd never barged my way into Shay's life, Cora never would've targeted her.

My phone vibrated again. Being the glutton for punishment that I was, I checked the screen.

> GISELLE
>
> If I catch you with Cora, I cannot be held responsible for my actions. That goes for both of you.

Yeah, life pretty much sucked.

I checked the time, knowing I needed to get to Cora's before she began blowing up my phone, but it was taking everything in me to get off my bed. I knew what needed to be done, but it was crushing me to do it. It was crushing me to hurt Shay.

Again.

---

## 36

## KASON

Jesse and I took the ski lift to the top of the slopestyle course. The sun shined bright, and I lowered my goggles over my eyes to block out the glare from the red glow.

I needed to get some good runs in. Not only would Jesse be trailing me with his camera to capture some footage for social media, but I needed to secure what I'd be doing for my final run at the Games. Some guys liked to come out swinging, showing everything they had in their first run. I was not that guy. I liked to see what everyone else did and then pull something off none of them had even considered. Sure, I'd get the normal backside triple and switch back twelve. But I'd been studying footage of what Amos and Ousterman had pulled off in Austria in their latest competition. Neither of them steered clear of taking risks. They went out there to crush it every time. I wondered if I needed to change my game plan. Wondered if what had worked for me in the past would work for me on this big of a stage against this caliber of competition.

Jesse and I moved to the top of the mountain and waited

for the few amateurs in front of us to go down first. I remembered being like them and just snowboarding for fun. Not worrying about landing certain tricks or impressing judges, my competition, and the fans. And while it wasn't always about those things at the forefront of my mind, the pressure to deliver was certainly on—not just from sponsors, fans, and haters, but also from myself. I needed to deliver for *me*. I needed the gold medal for *me*. Or else, all the hard work I'd put in over the years and all the time I'd spent trying to perfect my craft would've been for nothing.

"Ready?" I looked at Jesse with his camera on the end of a pole beside me.

"Whenever you are."

I laughed before dropping in, moving to the right in a wide arc to gain more speed to give me peak height off the first jump. The rush of air in my face and the rumble of the snow beneath my board followed me up the first jump, disappearing as I reached down and grabbed the front of my board, flipping through the air as I did. I was a child summersaulting in midair as if nothing else in life mattered. The rumble returned once I landed my jump and made my way up the next ramp. This time I had the speed I needed to pull off a front quad 1800, grabbing the front of my board and flipping once...twice...three times...I just needed to make it around one more time. I gave it all I had, making the fourth rotation and landing on my board with the precision of a gold medal athlete. I punched the air as I raced down to the bottom of the hill, spraying snow as I slid to a stop.

"Dude! That was fucking amazing!" Jesse said as he switched off his camera.

"Don't post that," I said.

"Why the hell not?"

"I may use it in Aspen."

He nodded. "You'd be a fool not to."

I ticked my head toward the ski lift. "Come on. I wanna try something else."

We hopped on the lift and before long we took our spots at the top of the slopestyle course. If I could pull off the front quad 1800 like it was nothing, I wanted to try something else I could add to my run that would get everyone talking. I pulled in a breath, letting the early morning air fill my lungs before dropping in.

I sped down the mountain once again, the rumble of snow beneath my board the only sound I could hear as I purposely veered toward the left, avoiding a couple of the jumps so I could catch the rail with more speed. I used my arms and hips to propel me up onto the metal rail and board-slid across it until I was backward. I twisted off the end, silence encompassed me as my body flipped off-axis in the air...once...twice...three times. I rotated a quarter more so I touched down facing forward, but I came down too hard and unbalanced. I needed to right myself quickly, so I threw my arms out to my sides and squared my hips to steady me. I stabilized myself enough and curved to stop upright at the bottom of the mountain. That's when the silence was replaced with Jesse shouting from behind me.

"That was a backside double cork 1170!" he called as I came to a stop. "You killed that, bro!" He stopped beside me.

"I didn't land it good enough. Let's try again."

"Dude, slow down. We have all day."

"Let's go," I insisted, making my way to the ski lift.

The need to perfect every trick suddenly consumed me. Every other part of my life was fucked up. This was the one thing I could control. And, I'd be damned if anyone thought they'd stop me.

Time after time, I sped down the mountain, trying new tricks and pushing my body to the limit. I needed to be ready. I needed the gold medal. I needed something to go right in my life.

Around four, the sun began to set. I stood at the bottom of the mountain and stared up at the course.

"Bro, my camera's not even catching all the footage anymore. If we go again, it'll be dark by the time we're coming down."

"We're going," I said. I was a man on a fucking mission —a mission to prove to myself and the world that I didn't mess everything up in my life. Just the things that mattered.

We reached the top of the mountain and, like Jesse had warned, it was just about dark.

"It's now or never," he warned.

I dropped in as Jesse trailed me down the mountain, capturing my run. I pulled a backside five, a switch backside nine, and a backside triple fourteen-forty nose grab. I braced myself for the final landing, but the nose of my board caught something in the snow and my body flipped over my board at full speed too many times to count. The last thing I remembered was landing on my head. Then, everything went black.

## 37

## SHAY

Professor Raymond had invited me to assist in the lab on a project he and some other professors were working on. I was *finally* in the lab. I wasn't involved in their research, more like their garbage collector and errand-runner. My phone vibrated in my back pocket nonstop. But, since it was my first time assisting in the lab, I didn't want to appear bored or uncommitted, so I left it alone.

I felt at home in the lab with all the professors using scientific language. It made my heart soar. I could see myself doing the work they were doing. I could see myself amongst all the cool lab technology making life-changing discoveries.

"You can head out, Shay," Professor Raymond said as he washed his hands. "We're just about done here."

"You sure?" I asked, so happy to be lost in the world of science when the other part of my life was a mess.

"Yeah. You were a huge help," he assured me.

"Thanks for the opportunity." I gathered my things, slipping on my jacket and backpack. "Good night," I called to the professors as I walked out of the room. Once in the hallway, I checked my phone. I had four missed calls from Giselle.

I returned her call, lifting the phone to my ear as I walked outside the building. Darkness blanketed campus since I'd been assisting the professors for hours.

Giselle answered on the first ring. "Shay?"

"Hey. What's up? Are you okay?"

Her voice was rushed. "It's Kason. He was in an accident."

"What?"

"He was snowboarding and took a bad fall."

Part of me wanted to rush to him. While the other part of me—the bitter part—wanted to tell her to call Cora. "Is he okay?"

"We don't know," she explained. "He was knocked unconscious for a couple of minutes. They're checking for brain swelling right now. And, he's got a fractured wrist."

"I'm sorry to hear that," I said, not sure how to feel. This was Kason. The guy who'd hurt me multiple times. The guy who'd moved on within seconds of me telling him I needed space.

"I just thought you should know he's in the hospital," she said.

"Thanks for letting me know." Once she hung up, I sat down on a nearby bench, a mix of emotions swirling inside me. Of course, I didn't want his injury to be serious, but everything between us had been such a rollercoaster. A relationship between two people should never be that difficult. And, now, I was being forced to distinguish how I was feeling.

My phone rang in my hand and Kendall's name lit up my screen. "Hey," I said as I answered it.

"Did you hear?"

"About Kason's accident?"

"Yeah. It's all over social media."

"His sister called me."

"Well, is he gonna be okay?"

"I don't know."

There was a long stretch of silence on her end before she spoke. "Shay?"

"Kendall?"

"I know you two aren't speaking, but it's okay to care. No one will think you're weak."

I sat on the bench thinking about her words long after we hung up. Did I care? Did I hate myself for caring?

———

I lay on my bed that night reading over my calculus notes, but unable to concentrate at all. I checked social media to see if there was any update, but nothing had been posted yet. I could have called Giselle. But then it would have confirmed I was worried. Confirmed I cared. And, I wasn't ready to admit that.

One thing I did need to admit was the fact that *I* punched Cora. No one made me do it, especially not Kason. I'd done it all on my own. She may have provoked me, but it was my fist. Kason didn't deserve the entire blame. And, I think down deep, that knowledge had been weighing on me.

There was a knock on the door. Kendall was at a sorority function with her pledge class, so I climbed to my feet and opened the door. Thayer stood there with blood-shot eyes and disheveled hair. "Can I come in?"

I nodded, stepping back so he could enter. I had a

sudden feeling that he came bearing bad news. I closed the door and gestured toward my desk chair.

He moved to the chair but just leaned against it as I sat down on my bed.

"Is he okay?" I asked, knowing it's why he must've come by.

He nodded. "A concussion and a fractured wrist. He's undergoing surgery for his wrist tomorrow. He'll be getting a few pins in there."

I cringed. "Sounds awful."

He nodded, but he didn't say anything more.

"Did you visit him?"

He shook his head. "He and I have been on the outs since what happened with you."

I nodded, knowing Giselle had mentioned that to me.

"I got tired of sitting back and watching him do things that hurt other people. That wasn't the Kason I was friends with when we were kids."

I knew he was right. Kason had hurt other people. But, he'd also tried to change. At least, he seemed like he had for a little while.

"But now I have this tremendous guilt that I wasn't there when it happened. Like me being there could have somehow stopped his accident. Getting the gold is his dream, and he's so damn close. I just hope this doesn't spoil his chance. He deserves that medal."

"You can't think like that," I said. "He's a grown man who makes his own decisions. Good and bad."

"I never thought he'd ever care about anyone more than he cares about himself, but then you walked into his life. He really cares about you, Shay."

"How can you say that? He's back with Cora."

He cocked his head. "Come on, Shay. You can't be that oblivious."

My brows scrunched together. "What?"

"He's trying to get her to stop hurting you."

My eyes widened. "What?"

"You seriously didn't realize that?"

I shook my head, completely blindsided by the information.

"He clearly couldn't let her know that's why he was hanging with her again, but he needed to get close to her to make sure she didn't press charges against you."

"But she hasn't."

"Yeah. He's having a tough time convincing her, but maybe now that she thinks he's on his deathbed, she'll be more receptive to his requests."

*Holy. Crap.* I felt so stupid. How had I not realized he'd never get back with Cora? I was so hurt—and so sure everything between us had been a sham—that I couldn't see the truth. Did he really still care about me?

"He finally started putting other people first like I told him to do. And, while he should've told you what he was doing so he didn't look like the asshole you clearly thought he was, he's trying."

I sat there speechless, surprised, and confused all at the same time.

"I'm gonna head to the hospital," Thayer said. "You wanna come with me?"

"What about Cora? Will she be there?"

He shrugged. "If she is, I'll distract her and give you some time alone with him."

I considered what he was offering. Could I just forget what caused me to need space?

Something inside me tugged at my heart. He'd been

spending time with someone who was a terrible human being just so he could convince her not to destroy my life. He was making sure *I* was okay. That *my* name remained untarnished. That *my* future remained untouched.

"Okay," I said.

Thayer nodded, then turned toward the door.

"Thayer?"

He glanced back at me.

"Thank you."

He smiled. "No problem."

38

———

SHAY

y legs trembled beneath me as Thayer and I made our way down the dim hospital hallway. Even though it was after hours and the lights weren't as bright, my pink boots still stood out against the stark white floor. Even though I hadn't been wearing them recently, I knew I needed to wear them to see him.

Too many emotions filled my body as we neared Kason's room. Fear of running into Cora. Fear of what to say to Kason. Fear of what I might do when I saw him knowing what he'd been doing for me.

"I'll go in first to make sure she's not around," Thayer said as we came upon his room.

"Okay."

He nodded before continuing to the last room on the right. He peeked inside before looking back to me and ticking his head.

I pulled in a deep breath and walked toward the room, each of my steps steeped in invisible quicksand. When I finally reached the room, I stopped in the doorway. Kason lay asleep in the only bed in the room. A bandage covered the right side of his forehead and the hospital gown he wore created a stark contrast to his sleeve of tattoos wrapped around his arm. All the balloons and flowers everywhere made it look like a party was about to begin. However, the monitors attached to his body beeping in a monotonous pattern made it clear that an accident had brought him in and not a celebration.

Mrs. McCloud sat in a chair at his side. Her face lit up when she saw me standing there. She jumped to her feet and hurried over. "Hi, honey," she whispered as she wrapped me in a hug.

That familiar feeling of belonging to the McCloud family flooded me, and there was nothing I could do to stop it. "How is he?"

She pulled back and released me. "He'll be okay. He's on a lot of pain meds right now for the fractured wrist, so he's been fading in and out."

"Is Cora here?" Thayer asked from behind me.

"No. Thankfully, she left." Mrs. McCloud rolled her eyes. "Why was she even here?"

Thayer and I both shrugged even though we knew the answer to her question.

"Well, he'll be glad to know you two are here," she said. "Will you be here for a while? Because I was just going to head home, but I really didn't want to leave him alone."

I glanced to Thayer who nodded. "Sure. We'll hang around and keep him company."

She moved to her chair and grabbed her handbag. "I'll be back in the morning so I'm here before he goes into surgery." She hugged Thayer, then me. "Goodnight you two."

"Night," I said as she moved to the door.

"I'll walk you out," Thayer told her before they disappeared in the hallway.

I appreciated him giving me time alone with Kason. I walked over to the chair Mrs. McCloud had vacated and sat down. Nerves consumed me as I sat there. Kason and I hadn't been good in what felt like forever. Now, there I sat, wanting nothing more than for him to be okay.

"Shay?" Kason whispered.

I leaned forward, trying to meet his eyes that were only partially open. "Hi."

"Am I in heaven?"

I rolled my eyes, knowing he was aware that he was not. "How are you feeling?"

"Like I landed on my head and broke my wrist. It's a good thing I can still snowboard with a bum wrist."

Neither of us said anything for a while. I wondered if he'd even remember our conversation in the morning. Was it worth telling him what I was thinking? How I was feeling?

"Shay?" he whispered, his eyes now closed.

"Yeah?"

"Can I kiss you?"

Unexpected laughter burst out of me. "I feel like we've had this conversation before."

"I know you're not happy with me. So, thanks for coming to see me."

"Yeah, well, Thayer told me what you've been doing for me," I said.

"For someone so smart you're really dumb."

"What?"

"Was it that hard to believe I'd fight for you?"

I didn't respond because he was right. I hadn't believed

he'd fight for me—especially after I'd blamed him for what I'd done and then told him to stay away from me.

"I hope you believe it now," he said.

Though he couldn't see me with his eyes closed, I nodded subtly. "Thank you."

"Don't thank me yet. I'm still working on her."

"That better be all you're doing with her," I said.

His head fell toward me and his eyes cracked open. "Someone jealous?"

"Maybe."

"I'll take maybe." He closed his eyes again and it gave me a moment to just look at him. The guy who I now realized *would* fight for me.

Thayer tapped on the door as he entered the room. "Is he awake?"

I nodded.

Thayer stepped up beside me, looking down at Kason whose eyes were closed.

"Stop looking at me like I'm dead," Kason said.

Thayer and I laughed.

"Good to see you're still your charming self," Thayer said.

"Always," Kason said.

Thayer buried his hands in his pockets and teetered on his feet uncomfortably.

"Thanks for bringing my girl," Kason said to him.

I swallowed around the knot that shot to my throat. His girl? Was that how he still saw me? Was it only me who'd thought we were over before we ever really began?

Thayer glanced to me. "I knew she'd want to see you."

"That's debatable. But I'm still glad she's here," Kason said. "You too, bro."

"Rest," Thayer said, patting Kason's leg over the blanket. "You've got a big day tomorrow."

"Yeah, the sooner I get my wrist fixed, the sooner I can hit the mountains."

Thayer glanced at me, his eyes filled with worry. "Right."

"Do you need anything?" I asked Kason.

"Just you in that chair," he said.

I looked to Thayer, unsure what I was supposed to do.

"I can come get you in the morning," Thayer offered.

I nodded, relieved that I'd get more time with Kason.

Thayer shot me a small smile before looking back at Kason. "I'll be here tomorrow to wish you luck, bro."

"Who needs luck?" Kason asked.

Thayer chuckled as he walked out of the room.

Now that Kason and I were alone, the room didn't seem big enough for the two of us.

My eyes moved from his disheveled hair to his face. How had we gotten to this point? There were so many things that happened—good and bad—to get us to where we were. I just wished I knew where that was.

"Shay?" he whispered.

"I'm here."

"Come lay with me."

Between the small hospital bed and his size, there was no way I could fit.

"I'll make room," he said, reading my thoughts.

"I might hurt your hand."

"It's the other one," he assured me.

*Oh, hell.* I untied my boots and slipped them off. I moved to the side of his bed and sat down slowly, making sure I wasn't pulling on any wires or tubes that were connected to him. He stayed on his back but scooted over a tiny bit, giving me no more than an extra inch. I turned onto my side and fit myself up against him.

"I miss this," he said, his eyes on the ceiling. "Everything sucked without you."

Until that moment, I didn't realize how much I needed to hear those word from him. I lay there breathing in his cool arctic scent, realizing how much I missed being with him.

"And, I couldn't tell you what I was doing with Cora, but I hoped like hell you could figure it out on your own. But you didn't. You *really* thought I'd want to be with her after what she did to you?"

"I told you to stay away from me."

"Yeah, and I was giving you space. *While* trying to help you."

"I didn't know that."

His head fell my way leaving our faces inches from one another. "I'm yours, Shay."

My belly dipped and bees seemed to swarm inside me.

"I know you blame me for a lot of things—with good reason. But, I want to prove I'm good for you. Because you've been so damn good for me."

I lifted my hand and cupped his cheek, my fingertips trailing over the hard lines of his jaw.

"It would've sucked if I'd died without being able to tell you that."

I chuckled at his over-exaggeration. "You weren't going to die."

"You never know. My head could've exploded."

"We both know that's never going to happen to you."

The corners of his lips twitched. "Do you think we can get back to where we were before?" he asked.

"I'm trying," I said.

"I can see that."

"How? Your eyes are practically closed," I said.

"Smartass. I just need to wake up and you've forgotten everything except the good stuff."

"Like library picnics?"

He forced a smile.

"And redo nights?"

"Exactly."

I leaned forward and pressed my lips to his cheek. "Go to sleep, Kason. I'll be here when you wake up."

"Promise?"

"Promise."

39

SHAY

My legs bounced beneath the table as I waited in the hospital cafeteria with Giselle and Thayer. I appreciated them waiting with me since I'm sure they would've rather been in the waiting room so they'd be there as soon as Kason came out of surgery. But, Cora waited up there with Mr. and Mrs. McCloud. We'd narrowly escaped her finding me in Kason's bed when she'd shown up this morning. And, as much as I loathed the idea, Kason and I both agreed he should keep up the charade until we were sure she wouldn't be pressing charges against me. I obviously wasn't comfortable with him spending time with her. But, he assured me nothing would happen between the two of them. And, knowing that he had a concussion and would soon be in a cast, I hoped that would stop her from trying anything with him. Fingers crossed.

"So, the two of you worked things out?" Thayer asked as he scrolled through the newsfeed on his phone.

"Baby steps," I said.

"He may not be the easiest guy to deal with, but my

brother definitely has it bad for you," Giselle said as she scrolled the newsfeed on her phone.

Her words brought me comfort, seeing as though she knew him better than most people.

"Yeah, well, sometimes having feelings for someone isn't enough," Thayer chimed in.

Giselle and I both looked to him, wondering if he knew he wasn't exactly being supportive.

"You know," he continued, looking strangely at Giselle who swiftly returned to looking at her phone. "Circumstances can sometimes get in the way."

Our phones all pinged at the same time.

He's out.

We jumped to our feet and hurried to the elevator. None of us said a word as it took us to Kason's floor. When we stepped out, Thayer and Giselle hurried down the hallway to his room. I stopped halfway, knowing I couldn't go in if Cora was in there. They disappeared inside and I stood there, feeling completely and utterly helpless.

After last night, I'd had a lot of time to think. Time to consider what Kason had done for me and how I felt about it. No one had ever gone to such great lengths for me before. No one had put me before their own happiness. I didn't want to be alone anymore. I didn't want to hold on to the pain anymore. I didn't want to stay angry at Kason. I wanted to love him.

Thayer came out of his room. "She's in there."

My shoulders fell slack and I nodded, knowing that would likely be the case. "How is he?"

"He's pretty groggy. Why don't you go hang down in the cafeteria and I'll text you when she leaves."

"Okay."

He shot me a sad smile before returning to Kason's room.

My heart sank. I was the one who should've been there supporting him. Not her.


*Kason*


I was so damn tired and in pain. In a *lot* of fucking pain. A nurse had just come in and added more pain medication to my drip.

Everyone around me spoke, but I couldn't really make out what any of them were saying, so I just closed my eyes, letting them know I wasn't in any shape to talk. But I hadn't missed that Shay wasn't there. Fucking Cora was, and I hated that. I needed Shay there. She just somehow made everything better.

"Do you want us to go?" Giselle's voice resonated.

I cracked my eyes open. "Yeah. I'm good."

"I'm not leaving," Cora said.

*Fuck me.*

I was too weak to argue. Too weak to do much of anything because the pain meds kicked in again and warmth and drowsiness washed over my body until I could no longer hold on.

———

I awoke to total darkness. My hand throbbed and I needed more pain meds. I reached for the call button with my good hand and was distracted by the small figure tucked into a tiny ball on the chair beside my bed. And, despite the pain in my wrist, I almost smiled.

"Shay?" My voice didn't come out. "Shay?" I tried again.

She stirred in the chair, her head twisting toward me. Noticing I was awake, she tried to sit up but her feet were twisted beneath her and she nearly tumbled onto the floor. She burst out laughing and the sound burrowed its way right into my heart. "Hi," she said, sliding the chair up to the side of my bed.

"Hi," I whispered because it's all that would come out.

"How are you feeling?"

"Like I've been hit by a bus."

She cupped my cheek and gazed into my eyes. "I'm sorry."

I lay there, lost in her pretty green eyes knowing if she ever forgave me, I'd never do anything to lose her again.

"The doctor said the surgery went well," she said.

Surgery not going well had never been an option in my mind.

"Do you need anything?" she asked.

"Just you." It might've sounded cheesy but waking up to Cora in my room earlier that day solidified the fact that there was only one girl I wanted. And, there was no point not letting her know that.

"I'm serious," she said, thinking my words were just a line.

"So am I," I said, my voice growing stronger.

Her eyes flashed down, never one to accept the truth when it made her uncomfortable.

"I told you I wanted to wake up and you'd have forgiven me."

Her eyes lifted to mine. They were unreadable.

"I want you, Shay. Only you," I admitted. "Do you want me?" I asked, feeling more vulnerable than I'd ever felt. Because, never until that moment, had I *not* known the answer I'd receive.

"Which you?" she asked.

My lips twisted in contemplation. "I guess all of them."

She stared at me, a million thoughts running through her mind.

"I'd like to say I can be the one you want all the time, and believe me, I'll try. But, I'm bound to screw up. I've done a lot of that over the years. So, I'll need you to be patient and take all of them for now."

Still, she said nothing.

I'd been honest with her. I wouldn't make her false promises. But, like I'd told her before, I liked the one who came alive when I was with her. So, that's who I aimed to be. "What do you say, Shay? Can we put everything behind us once and for all?"

She stood from the chair and slid it back against the wall.

Had I pushed her too hard? Was my pleading exhausting her?

But instead of leaving my room, she moved to my bed and climbed up beside me, nestling in so we were face to face.

I was scared to say anything, knowing I didn't want to push her too far.

"Yes," she whispered.

"Yes?" I asked.

"Yes, we can put everything behind us."

Worried I'd say something to make her retract her words, I leaned forward and kissed her. And, nothing in life had ever felt as right as Shay beside me right where she belonged.

## 40

## KASON

"I think you'll be good to go home tonight," my doctor said as he stood at the foot of my hospital bed the next day.

"That's awesome," Cora said from the chair beside my bed where she'd planted her ass all fucking day. She'd missed Shay by a matter of minutes.

"How long will I be in this cast?" I asked, raising my arm to show the cast that stopped before my elbow and wrapped around my thumb, leaving my fingers moveable.

"The pins need to stay in for four to six weeks, so we'll take it off then to assess your recovery."

"Will I need to get another cast after that?"

"To speak frankly," he began, "It all depends on you. If you stay off the mountain, chances for a faster recovery time are greater."

Stay off the mountain? I had the Games in just over a month. How the hell was I going to stay off the mountain? I needed to practice. I needed to stay fresh.

"Your silence is not reassuring," my doctor said.

"He will," Cora assured him like she'd become my mouthpiece.

He looked back at me. "He better."

Yeah. We'd see about that.

"I'll be back to discharge you in a few hours," he said.

"Thanks, Doc."

He nodded before turning and walking out of the room.

The room had suddenly become void of air. A panic attack teetered at the ready. I couldn't miss the Games. I needed to get on the mountain.

"Babe, you okay?"

"I am not fucking okay," I said, my voice raised in aggravation.

Her eyes widened. "Okay. Tell me how to fix it."

"Leave."

Her head hitched back. "What?"

"I need to be alone."

"Oh, babe. Let me be here for you."

"That's the thing. I don't want you to be here for me. I want Shay, but you won't fucking agree not to press charges. And, I am trying like hell to get you to do that."

She gasped. "What?"

"You heard me. You and I are not together. We will never be back together. All I need from you is your assurance that you're not going to press charges and destroy Shay's life."

She jumped to her feet. "You have got to be kidding me."

"Nope. Not kidding."

She pursed her lips together as her chest heaved. "I hate you."

"I assure you, the feeling is mutual."

She ground her teeth together, the wheels in her head clearly spinning. I just hoped to God she wasn't headed for Shay. "Fuck you, Kason. You're not even a good snowboarder."

I scoffed. "Now I know you're lying."

She spun around and stormed out of my room.

Once she was gone, it was as if all the air had returned to the room. I reached for my cell phone, placing it in my lap so I could scroll through my contacts. Even with the cast on my arm, I could still use my fingers. I found who I was looking for and made the call on speaker.

"Hey, Kason. How are you feeling? Cora said you've got pins in your wrist."

"Yeah, but I'll be fine to compete in the Games."

"Oh, that's fantastic. I'm banking on my brand being front and center while you do."

"Of course. Listen, I really need to talk to you about something serious."

"I'm all ears," he said.

"This might seem like it's coming out of left field, and I did try to talk to Cora about this before reaching out to you, but she's not hearing me."

"What's wrong?"

"The girl who broke Cora's nose. Shay Miller. We're friends. Actually, we're more than friends. It's why Cora and Shay don't get along. That's why I needed to step in and do something about this. I need you to not press charges against Shay."

"She broke my daughter's nose," he said, his voice deep, and not as happy to be speaking to me as he'd initially been.

"I understand that. But Shay and I are close. And Cora doesn't like that, so she's been taking it out on Shay. Shay finally had enough."

There was silence on his end.

"She didn't mean to hurt Cora. I assure you. That's not Shay. She's going to be a biochemist one day. She's the smartest person I know and having this potential charge hanging over her head is killing her."

"What do you mean Cora took it out on her?" he asked.

"She did some bad stuff to her. When, in all honesty, her anger should have been directed at me and not Shay."

"If I don't press charges, what's in it for me?" he asked like the shrewd businessman he was.

"What do you want?"

"I want to retain full exclusive sponsorship over you for the next five years."

"Done." As much as I hated the idea since Kincaid was a much better deal, I didn't have to think twice about it. I would've done anything to save Shay. I only wish I reached out to him sooner. It would have saved us both a lot of unnecessary aggravation and time apart.

"I wasn't finished," he said. "Contingent upon *if* you win the gold at the Games."

"Done," I said even though I knew I couldn't make promises like that. But if it meant Shay wouldn't be hurt, I'd say and do whatever I needed to do.

"Well, then. Looks like we have ourselves a deal."

"Thank you so much," I said. "This means a lot to me."

"Don't thank me yet. Get that gold." With that he hung up, leaving me wondering what the hell I was going to do if I didn't get the gold medal.

---

## 41

## SHAY

I climbed the stairs in Kason's house, hurrying toward his room. He'd texted, asking me to come by so he could tell me some good news. I wondered if his cast would be coming off sooner than he thought. I stopped in his doorway.

Kason lay on top of his bed in a black T-shirt and basketball shorts scrolling on his phone. "I was wondering if you'd take the hospital gown home," I said as I stepped inside. "It seemed like you enjoyed flashing the nurses your butt."

He looked to me and smiled. "You don't think I got tired of them all coming in just to see it every time I went to the bathroom?"

I rolled my eyes. "I'm sure you loved it."

He laughed before patting the side of his bed and scooting over to make room for me. I sat down and twisted my body to face him. He reached behind my head and eased my lips closer to his. "I missed you."

"I saw you at the hospital yesterday."

He closed the distance between us and kissed me, his

minty tongue pushing its way inside my mouth in a welcome exchange. I expected him to release me, but he deepened the kiss as if starved for me. I knew it was his way of showing me he was so damn happy to have me back in his life. The feeling was mutual.

I pulled away first, needing to catch my breath. "Well, hello to you too."

He chuckled.

"How's it feel?" I asked.

"You're going to have to specify which *it* you're talking about right now. Because both are throbbing."

I pushed playfully at his chest. "*Ewww.*"

"You love it."

"Which *it* are you referring to?" I asked.

He laughed.

I shrugged. "I guess you're rubbing off on me."

"Oh, I assure you I'm not. But I will if you let me."

"*Ewww.* Seriously?"

"No idea what you're talking about," he said with twitching lips as he reached for my hand and linked our fingers. "I'm glad you're here."

"What'd you need to tell me?"

Excitement filled his eyes. "I'm done with Cora. I told her it was never happening with us."

"What?" Part of me was relieved while the other feared for her retaliation. We'd agreed he'd keep up the pretense that he wanted to be with her until she dropped the charges. "How do you know this won't send her over the edge?"

"I spoke to her dad."

"Her dad?"

He nodded. "We have an agreement that they won't be pressing charges."

My shoulders fell slack. It was as if a giant boulder had

lifted from my chest and I could finally breathe again. Was I really free?

"Believe it, Shay," he urged. "Everything's gonna be okay."

Tears pooled in my eyes. *Tears.* I didn't cry, but the news just obliterated all the fear bottled up inside me—all the anxiety and uncertainty that had plagued me since it happened.

He squeezed my hand. "Oh, baby. Don't cry."

I shook my head, wiping at my eyes to be sure no tears escaped. "I just didn't know."

"Know what?"

"That you cared this much about me."

He cocked his head. "*Shay.*" A smile pulled at his lips. "You do things for the people you care about. And, I can't think of anyone else in this world besides my family who I care about more."

I turned on his bed and climbed onto his lap, straddling his hips as I cupped his cheeks. I gazed into his pretty eyes and saw so much more than I did the first time we met. I thought I'd known him then. I thought he fit into a certain category. But it turns out, I was just as wrong about him as he was about me.

I pressed my lips to his. They were so soft and inviting. I controlled this kiss. Our tongues danced in a beautiful rhythm. I turned my head and deepened the kiss so I could feel it all the way down to the tips of my toes. His erection pressed against me through his basketball shorts and I shifted my hips as I kissed him. Feeling bold.

Something inside me ignited. All the happiness I felt fused with my desire for Kason. I pulled out of the kiss, leaving his chest heaving beneath me as I sat back. His eyes were hooded and filled with so much want. That was all the push I needed. I tugged my T-shirt over my head, exposing my red bra.

His eyes rounded and were trained on my chest before flashing up to my eyes. "Shay, we—"

I shook my head, cutting off whatever he planned to say to ruin the moment. "I want this. And, I want it with you."

"God, Shay. I want it with you too."

My belly dipped as if I'd plummeted on a rollercoaster.

"But you're gonna need to help me a little with my clothes," he said.

I laughed. Of course, this was going to be awkward. He had a cast on one arm, and I'd never done this before. I climbed off his lap so I knelt beside him. He sat up and pulled his T-shirt over his head, tossing it to the floor.

I'd seen him shirtless before but never like this. Never with me in a bra on the verge of giving up my virginity to him. I lifted my hands and pressed them gently to his chest, mesmerized by his smooth skin and the hard muscles beneath.

He looked down, watching as my fingertips drifted lightly over the chiseled surface of his chest and abs. "Can you feel my heart racing?" he asked.

I nodded, loving that I wasn't the only one affected by our proximity and what we were about to do.

He reached up and cupped my cheek with his good hand. I leaned into it. "Lay down, Shay."

"Right now?"

He nodded.

I lay back so my head hit his pillow. He reached for the button on my jeans, removing them and tossing them to the floor as he stood.

His eyes swept over me as I lay there sprawled out on his bed in a red bra and a matching thong. "You look like my very own present." He wasted no time, tugging down his shorts so he was fully naked.

My eyes swept over his perfect body, fascinated by the carved V in his hips and his erection standing tall against his stomach. I'd never seen a naked guy in person, and Kason was one to admire. He wore a smug grin as he walked to his nightstand. My eyes followed his movements as he reached into the drawer and grabbed a condom. He tossed it on the pillow beside my head before crawling on top of me from the foot of his bed, slowly kissing his way up my body. I trembled when he reached my thong, pulling it off while his lips continued kissing their way up my stomach and over my bra. "A little help," he said when he realized he might not be able to remove it with his cast all big and clunky.

I sat up and unclasped my bra, keeping it on as I lay back down.

His brows shot up as if he understood what I wanted. He reached down and tugged each strap down my shoulder, before pulling the bra off completely.

I sucked in a breath, trying to keep my nerves from faltering as I lay there completely exposed for the first time in my life.

"You're beautiful, Shay."

My eyes cast down.

"And, you're all fucking mine."

I laughed as he leaned down and sucked one of my sensitive nipples between his lips. I gasped, unprepared for the sting. But he swiped his tongue across it, tempering it with the swirl of his tongue.

My head dropped back against the pillow as he moved between both breasts, swirling his tongue around each nipple until I was squirming beneath him. My hips sought reprieve from the ache between my thighs, but the weight of his body kept me still.

He inched his way up until we were face to face and his erection pressed into my thigh. He dropped his lips to mine and kissed me like it was the last time, savoring every swipe of my tongue. When we were both breathless, he pulled away. He grabbed the condom packet and used his teeth to tear it open. I watched as he rolled it up the length of him. When I could sense him looking at me, my eyes jumped to his. I swallowed hard. We were doing this. We were really doing this.

Kason kept his eyes focused on mine as he covered me with his body. Being skin to skin with him was a feeling like no other. His warmth permeated through me and I just needed him closer.

"You ready for this?"

I nodded.

He planted a chaste kiss to my lips. "I never thought you'd trust me. Especially with something like this."

I bucked my hips, loving what he was saying, but needing him to show me. "I'm ready."

"Oh, I know you are." He leaned down and kissed me.

I slipped my arms around to his back, digging my fingertips into his skin as he shifted his hips, pressing his erection between my thighs. I closed my eyes as the contact sent zingers coursing through me. He did it again. *Holy wow.* Having never done this before, I wasn't sure if he was trying to push inside me yet, or just making sure I was ready. But, given the throbbing in my clit, I was totally ready. He did it a third time, but this time he wasn't testing me. This time he stretched me wide, pushing inside an inch at a time. I hissed through the stinging because I knew it would disappear. People wouldn't enjoy this so much if it didn't disappear.

"You good?" he asked.

My eyes opened and I nodded. Being eye to eye with Kason when he was inside me was as intimate as it got. And I knew with much certainty that I'd remember this moment for the rest of my life.

With our eyes locked, he pushed the rest of the way inside me. I gasped, the feeling foreign but manageable. He pulled out some and then thrust back in. He broke our eye contact to press his mouth to mine, kissing me as he continued to thrust into me setting a steady rhythm. He eventually tore his lips from mine and dropped them to my neck, sucking that sensitive spot where my shoulder met my neck as he moved inside of me. He reached down between us, grazing my clit with his thumb—definitely not an easy feat when the arm he was using for balance had a cast on it. My head pushed further back into the pillow, the familiar sensation starting to build as he continued to use his thumb.

"You feel amazing," he said as he assaulted my neck with open-mouthed kisses that sent my eyes rolling back into my head.

"Keep going," I breathed.

"Not going anywhere, baby."

His thumb circled my clit, around and around, until everything began to build. My body was a tightened coil ready to give way.

I knew I was near. "Kason?"

"Shay?"

"I'm ready."

He pinched my clit and the coil between my thighs released, the sensations shooting out to every part of me. My body quaked, a warm buzzing spreading over my sensitive skin as I rode out the orgasm.

Kason used both arms for balance and continued to

thrust, burying his face in my neck and grunting with each thrust. "Oh. My. Fucking. God," he groaned as he slowed his thrust, stopping inside me. His body fell slack and I bore the weight of him, feeling very much sated and exhausted, but so incredibly happy.

After we settled our breathing into a calm rhythm, Kason lifted his head and looked at me. "Thank you for trusting me."

"Thank you for playing your music so loud."

He chuckled.

"If you hadn't been such a jerk, we never would've done that."

"So, forget my personality, stellar skills on a board, and good looks, you only want me for sex?"

I smiled. "Maybe."

"Well, at least you want me." The vulnerability in his words punched the wind right out of my lungs. "Because I'd be kinda lost without you."

Those words knocked me off my axis and it finally hit me. As much as I questioned what Kason saw in nerdy ole me, he was the one who questioned what *I* saw in *him*. He was the one scared to lose me. He needed me to make his world complete. And, I kinda liked knowing he did.

## 42

## KASON

"Oh my God, Kason. How could you promise him something like that?" Giselle asked as I sat behind the counter of her boutique.

"I didn't know what else to do," I admitted as she hung clothes on the racks after closing time.

"Yeah, but Kase, that's gonna put a lot of pressure on you when you don't even know if you'll be able to compete."

"I'm competing. That's not even an option." I glanced down at the cast on my wrist that had now been signed by all my boys and Shay. She teased me saying she should probably write some physics formulas on there so I could pass the final exam, but in the end, she just signed her name with a heart. "I still have one good hand and that's all I need."

I could see the uncertainty in Giselle's eyes.

"Pins or no pins, I'll be in Aspen," I assured her. "And I'll win the mother-fucking gold."

She sighed. "I don't doubt you can win it. I'm just saying you don't need that unnecessary stress on top of the pressure of getting back out there after an injury."

"When have you known me to back down from a challenge?"

She shrugged. "Who knows? You're a stubborn ass."

I laughed.

"Are you gonna tell Shay?"

"God, no."

"She deserves to know what you did for her," she said, pegging me with her eyes.

"Once I win the gold, I'll let her know. Because we both know if I don't, she's gonna find out anyway."

Giselle's eyes cast down, understanding the ramifications of me *not* winning the gold. "Like father, like daughter. I hate those people so much."

"Cora had to get her evil streak somewhere."

"Despite you ever dating that bitch, I'm proud of you, little brother."

I rolled my eyes.

"I'm serious. Shay's changed you in the best possible way."

"You just called me a stubborn ass."

She laughed. "Yeah, well some things will never change."

"Real nice. Well, Shay likes my stubborn side."

"I've gotta have a talk with that girl."

"You'll have plenty of time. I'm not stupid enough to ever let her go."

A proud smile swept across Giselle's face. She loved Shay. And, she loved seeing me happy. And, there was no doubt, Shay made me a cheesy kind of happy. I was Kason-mother-fucking-McCloud. I could be cheesy if I fucking wanted to be.

43

———

SHAY

Kason held my hand as we approached the McCloud's home. Since he still had his cast, I carried the gift bags in my free hand. He and I hadn't exchanged Christmas gifts yet, and I'd be lying if I said I wasn't curious what he'd thought to get me. But, those gifts were still in his Jeep since he wanted us to open them when we were alone.

Christmas music greeted us as we stepped inside the kitchen. The room was hazy with steam and, just like on Thanksgiving, pots and pans filled the stovetop. Mrs. McCloud, wearing an elf apron, spun to see who'd come inside. Her face lit up when she found us standing there. "Merry Christmas, you two."

"Merry Christmas," we said as she hurried over and hugged us.

She stepped back and gave Kason the once-over. "Let me look at you."

"Mom, it's just my wrist. And, this stupid cast should be off soon."

I choked into my shoulder. "Liar."

He gave me a look. "Fine. I want it off soon, but chances are it'll still be on for the Games."

Mrs. McCloud huffed. "You're still planning on competing?"

"Absolutely," he said.

She looked at me. "He's such a stubborn ass."

I laughed as she pointed to the gifts in my hand.

"You can put those under the tree, sweetie."

I left Kason with his mom and walked into the living room to find Mr. McCloud and Giselle watching *A Christmas Story*. "Merry Christmas."

They both jumped to their feet and hugged me, wishing me a Merry Christmas. I wondered where Giselle's boyfriend was since Kason said he'd be flying in to spend Christmas with her.

I went to set the presents under the tree with the rest of the gift boxes and bags. There wasn't a free spot so I piled some of them on top of other gifts. I'd never seen anything like it. Unlike Thanksgiving, I *did* belong there. And, I was making new memories with people who cared about me. People *I* cared about as well.

My phone buzzed in my pocket. I slipped it out and an unfamiliar number lit up the screen. "I'll be right back," I told Giselle and Mr. McCloud as I hurried into the sitting room. "Hello?" I said as I answered the phone.

"Shay Miller?" the woman on the phone asked.

"Yes."

"Hi, this is Marybeth Snyder. I'm a representative from Crossroads."

"What's Crossroads?"

"We're a full drug and alcohol rehabilitation facility. Your father asked that I let you know he's here."

A cold chill rushed up my spine as I lowered myself down onto the edge of the decorative sofa.

"He's committed to a ninety-day stay with us."

"I'm not really sure why you're calling me," I said.

"He knew you wouldn't answer his call."

I scoffed.

"But he wanted you to know that he's committed to his rehabilitation and is staying this time."

"If that's true, Ms. Snyder, I'll take his call in ninety days. I hope you understand that he's let me down too many times to count and has failed at getting sober the same amount of times."

"Oh, honey. We understand. Maybe you'll consider attending some meetings here or even at local Al-Anon meetings if you'd prefer to do that."

"I'll think about it."

"I think it would be good for you to begin to heal. From what he's told us, you've been through a lot."

Something about his acknowledgment of what *I'd* been through gave me hope that maybe this time rehab would stick. But, for my own self-preservation, I wouldn't get my hopes up. I'd done that too many times before. "Happy Holidays, Ms. Snyder. Thanks for the call."

"Merry Christmas," she said before I disconnected the call.

A long breath whooshed out of me. I would not get my hopes up. I would not allow myself to believe he'd be fixed after rehab. I had a science brain and had done too much research on addiction to know there was so much more involved in quitting addiction than ninety days. But maybe after the help he received, he'd come out on the other end a better person. Because there were so many bad memories—

so many physical and emotional scars to know if I'd ever be able to forgive him.

"Here you are," Kason said, sitting on the sofa beside me. He noticed the phone in my hand. "You okay?"

I nodded. "My dad's in rehab."

"How do you know?"

"The facility just called to tell me."

"How does that make you feel?"

"I thought I'd feel nothing. There's so much hurt there, you know? But, I feel strangely...at peace knowing he finally sought help on his own."

He slipped his hand into mine, squeezing it gently.

"She said I could go there for meetings if I wanted to."

"What type of meetings?"

"Family of alcoholics."

"Will you go?"

I shrugged. "I don't know."

"I'm not sure I'll ever be able to forgive the man who hurt you, but I'll support whatever you decide to do. I can even go to meetings with you if you'd like."

"Thanks." I released a long breath, letting all the thoughts of my father leave my body so I could enjoy my time with Kason and his family. "Okay, let's go help your mom. I don't want anything spoiling today."

"You got it."

---

We ate dinner in the dining room, sitting at the table long after the dishes had been cleared and darkness replaced the sun.

Kason cleared his throat. "I have an announcement."

All eyes moved to him, curious for his unexpected news.

"You all know Shay tutored me in physics," he said.

"Poor soul," Mr. McCloud said.

Everyone laughed, even Kason.

"What I was trying to say..." he turned to look at me in the chair beside him. "I passed."

My eyes widened. "Are you serious?"

"I emailed Raymond last night. I wanted to wait until today to tell you."

I grabbed his good hand beneath the table and squeezed it. "I'm so proud of you. You worked so hard and deserve it."

He nodded, his eyes filled with appreciation and happiness.

We spent the rest of the time talking about Kason's recovery, the upcoming Games, and Giselle's business. She never once mentioned her boyfriend who had yet to show up. I wondered if Kason knew what happened. I'd only ever heard that he was this wealthy business owner in Florida who found it difficult to get away. But, this was Christmas. What businesses were open today that he couldn't get away from?

We relocated to the living room and Giselle sat on the floor in front of the tree, while Mr. and Mrs. McCloud shared the sofa and I sat on Kason's lap in the recliner chair —but only because he pulled me down in front of everyone and when I tried to get up, he wrapped his arms around me and wouldn't let me go. His parents exchanged a satisfied glance, and I knew they were thrilled we were together. So, I stayed put, which wasn't actually a hardship.

Giselle began handing out the gifts. The McCloud tradition was one person at a time opened all their gifts so everyone could see what they received. Giselle gave her parents their gifts first. They thanked both Kason and me for their restaurant gift cards, coffee mugs, and sound bar for their television. I felt funny taking credit for gifts Kason had paid for and added my name to. But, he knew I had minimal spending money, so I appreciated him doing that. It was bad enough I cut into emergency funds for Kason and Kendall's gifts, but Giselle had hired me to work during winter break. So, my money situation would get better.

Giselle separated her gifts into a pile. Then, passed Kason and me some gifts. I hadn't expected anyone to get me anything, but by the looks of the three bags with my name on them, they had.

Giselle opened hers first. Most were clothes, except for our gift for her, which was a round-trip airline ticket to be used whenever she wanted to see her boyfriend. The smile slipped off her face for the slightest second when she realized what it was before it returned and she looked at us. "Thank you. This was such a great idea." But, her words didn't match the look in her eyes and I hated not knowing what was going on with her.

Kason urged me to open my gifts next. I did, unwrapping socks and scarves from the McClouds, and some hair accessories from Giselle that were all sparkly and something so much nicer than I'd ever owned.

Kason opened his gifts next, most of which were snowboarding-related gifts. Once the wrapping paper mess was cleaned up in the living room, we moved back to the dining room for dessert. I could have sat and listened to the McClouds talk for hours. And, I found myself talking more now that they'd accepted me into their family. The laughter came so easily and the love just exuded from each of them. I just wanted to bask in it for as long as I could.

Somewhere around ten, Kason excused us from the table so we could go upstairs and exchange our gifts. "Thank you," I said to the three of them, making sure to make eye contact with them all. I just wished the sentiment didn't sound so insignificant for what they'd given me—both physically and emotionally.

"You're welcome, sweetie," Mrs. McCloud said as Kason and I stood from the table.

"Thank *you*," Mr. McCloud said. "Can't wait to use my new coffee mug."

I smiled at his excitement over the mug.

"Thanks, you two," Giselle said. "Can't wait to use my ticket." Again, her happiness didn't reach her eyes and I hated seeing her that way.

"Good night," Kason said as he placed his hand on the small of my back and led me up the stairs. Once we were alone in his room, he pushed me down on his bed. I landed with a bounce. "I finally get you alone." He crawled on top of me until I had no option but to lay back. He kissed me and I could feel the love all the way through my body. I didn't want to be disrespectful making out under the McCloud's roof after they'd been so welcoming to me, but I needed Kason as much as he needed me.

When he finally let me up, I was all flushed and breathless.

He moved to his closet and pulled out a stack of gift boxes.

"Where did those come from?" I asked as I sat up and got comfortable against his headboard. "They weren't in the Jeep."

He smirked as he placed them on his bed. "They were already here."

I cocked my head, feeling like I didn't get him enough. "*Kason.*"

"*Shay,*" he mimicked.

I pouted, feeling uncomfortable with what looked like a boatload of gifts for me.

"Stop pouting and open these gifts," he said as he sat down beside me.

I eyed the stack of boxes. "This is too much."

"Just open them."

I began to unwrap the top box, knowing Kason hadn't wrapped it since his wrist was out of commission, hence all our gift bags for his family. When it was unwrapped, I lifted the top of the box. I pulled out a massive pink winter jacket with a white, fur-lined hood.

"What do you think?" Kason asked eagerly.

"It'll definitely keep me warm."

"Now, you can come to all my events and not be cold," he said with excitement in his eyes. It was then I realized the gift was so much more than a jacket. It was an assurance that he wanted me around for the long haul. This wasn't temporary for him. And, I loved knowing that.

I opened the rest of the boxes, all of which contained outdoor gear: hats, socks, ski pants, and boots. He wasn't kidding. He expected me out there with him—and he expected me to be warm.

I looked over the stack of new items he'd bought for me. "Thank you for all of this. But, it's way too much."

"Wait. You're not done."

"What?"

He reached under his bed and pulled out a small gift bag. "Those gifts were selfish. They were for me. They were to make sure you had no reason not to be at my events with me."

I tipped my head, realizing that I'd been right. And, also realizing that this strong confident guy had a vulnerable, less-assured side, just like the rest of us.

He handed me the bag. "*This* is for you."

The bag was super light as I took it and placed it in my lap. I reached inside the tissue paper peeking out of the bag and grasped a flat box. My heartbeat began to speed up. My eyes sought his, but they were eagerly trained on my hand slipping the box out of the bag. I pulled in a breath before lifting the top off the small box. I gasped as I saw what lay inside. A silver bracelet. I lifted it and examined the single charm hanging from it: a boat. What was I missing? My eyes met his. "It's beautiful."

He burst out laughing. "Do you understand the boat?"

"Not exactly."

"We're taking a cruise for spring break."

My eyes rounded. "What?"

"We'll get you a charm to commemorate every place we go together. That's the first of many."

I stared at the bracelet, at a loss for words. These gifts were so over the top and expensive. "I don't know what to say."

"Say we can go. And, that you love it."

"It's just way too much."

He lifted his hand to my cheek and urged me to meet his eyes. "You're worth it, Shay. You missed out on the Christmas experience for too many years. I wanted this one to be perfect."

"I think I just need to process everything."

"I'm sorry. I know my family's a lot. And, this is all new for you. But, you're part of our family now."

Tears glazed my eyes. "You're not helping with comments like that." I tried to laugh, but my voice cracked with emotion. "Let me give you your gift."

"I already got her."

I rolled my eyes but knew, despite his cheesiness, he still

meant it. I climbed off the bed and hurried into the hallway. I returned with a box Giselle had wrapped for me and handed it to him. I sat beside him on the edge of the bed. He tore into the paper before opening the box. He laughed when he saw what it was.

"Take it out," I urged.

He lifted the signature ugly pink Slopes helmet that I'd somehow snuck out of his room. It now had tiger stripe decals all over it leaving minimal pink which I knew he hated. "This is awesome."

"It's not a cruise."

"Don't do that," he said. "You knew I hated that helmet and did something to make it better. Don't you see? It's what you've been doing for me since day one. In that case, you hated me and still helped to make *me* better."

"The real Kason's always been in there. You just had to want to see him and let him come out."

"Which *him* are we referring to here?" he asked, and we both laughed.

"Thanks for giving me my best Christmas ever, Kason."

A flicker of sadness flashed across his eyes.

I didn't want my words to make him sad. I wanted them to convey how much I appreciated him and all he'd done for me.

He forced a smile. "Merry Christmas, Little One."

## 44

## SHAY

JANUARY

Snow blanketed everything in Aspen and continued to fall right outside the window of our hotel room. It was the perfect day for the Games. Unfortunately, the gorgeous view overlooking the mountains didn't bring me the type of calm I'd hoped it would.

The water in the shower filled the silence for the past hour. Kason had been known to take long showers, but this bordered on him hiding in there. I'd expected him to be calm, cool, and collected like he normally was. But, from the moment he woke up, he barely spoke and didn't even want to eat. I tried to make him laugh and talk about anything but snowboarding, but I only earned a few small smiles. I had never been around him before a big competition before, so I had no idea if this was normal. I hoped it was and I hadn't done anything to make him this way.

The shower switched off and a pit formed in my stomach. I was trying to be strong and act like nothing was weird, but now, I was afraid to say anything.

The bathroom door opened and Kason stepped out with

a towel wrapped around his waist and steam billowing out behind him. Our eyes met across the room.

I waited him out. Waited for him to say *anything*. But he didn't.

"Jesus Christ, Kason. You're freaking me out!" I blurted.

He tilted his head and a sliver of the Kason I knew shined through. He walked toward me until he stood in front of me. He slipped his arms around me and pulled me into him, dropping his chin to the top of my head. "I'm sorry."

I relaxed into his embrace, hating that he felt like he needed to apologize to me. "As long as you're okay, there's nothing to apologize for." I pulled back and met his eyes. "You are okay, right?"

His lips twisted and his eyes got that far off look. "Just got a lot on my mind. I need to kill it out there."

"You will."

He scoffed, and his reaction scared me. I was so used to the overconfident Kason. I wasn't sure how to take this uncertain version of him. I knew he wanted the gold badly. So, if I had to endure another few hours of awkwardness, I'd do it.

———

We drove to the mountain in silence, and I didn't dare break it since I knew it's probably what Kason needed. But, it didn't make me feel any less helpless.

We stepped out of his Jeep and the bitter evening air hit us. I looked like an Eskimo in all the snow gear he'd bought me, but I'd stay warm. Kason grabbed all his gear and we made our way toward all the madness behind the lodge. As soon as people spotted him, a small crowd formed around us. Reporters, Games' coordinators, and his friends greeted him.

"You have anything big planned for us tonight, McCloud?" a reporter asked.

"The snowmobiles are ready to take you up," a man in Games gear told him.

"We'll stay at the back," Thayer assured him. "We can give you feedback when you come off the course."

"Dude, you got this," Jesse added.

Ignoring all the noise around him, Kason turned back to me and pressed a firm kiss to my lips. "Wait for me at the bottom." He pointed to an area at the foot of the mountain where a small crowd had already begun to gather behind a snow fence bearing sponsor signs. "I want to be able to see you when I come down."

My heart sped up, all the love and fear I had for him coming to a head. "Good luck."

He stared into my eyes long and hard as if no one else was even there. "Thanks." And, then he was gone.

I stood there completely alone in a crowd of people, feeling just as helpless as I'd felt all day.

I walked over to the slopestyle course, the snow beneath my boots crunching with each step. I stared up at all the jumps on the mountain Kason would be competing on. It still amazed me that he could flip and twist and land the tricks that he did, especially with a cast on his hand. He'd only been back out on the snow for a couple of weeks. He knew if he had any chance of competing, he needed to let the pins in his wrist heal before even attempting any tricks. If he had fallen again, it would've ensured another surgery and eliminated any possibility of competing. So, he did as he was told. It just didn't leave him much time to train.

Once darkness descended on the mountain, huge spotlights zig-zagged across the slopestyle course and loud music played through giant speakers nearby. Kason explained music was normal for the Games because it pumped up the snowboarders and fans. He was right. The whole display brought an air of excitement to the crowd gathered at the bottom.

"Most didn't believe McCloud would be back competing after his concussion and wrist surgery at the beginning of December," the snowboarder-turned-commentator standing nearby said into a camera. "But he proved them all wrong, showing up strong in the preliminary runs this week. But, will he be able to medal again this year after such an injury? That's the question on everyone's mind."

Kason *had* proven them all wrong. And, I was so damn proud of the effort he put into rehabbing his wrist. Sure, it was in a cast, but he didn't need his wrist to snowboard. As long as he could reach down and grab his board, he assured me he was good to go.

"Ousterman looked good in preliminaries," another commentator said. "But will it be enough for the gold again this year?"

"Are they almost ready to start?" Giselle asked, squeezing in beside me.

"I think so."

Colored flashing lights and strobe lights now illuminated the course and an announcer's voice came over the loudspeakers. "It's the event you've all been waiting for. Men's slopestyle!"

The crowd around me cheered. My heart began to race. I was excited to see Kason compete but so damn nervous for him.

"We have eight contestants vying for the coveted gold medal. The men will each have four runs. The scores from their best two runs will determine their final standing," the announcer explained.

"He said a fifty was the highest you can get?" I asked Giselle.

"I've never seen a fifty, but yeah. That's on a run. The top two scores are combined to get the final score that determines where they sit on the leaderboard," she explained. It was then I noticed the same type of uncertainty and fear in her eyes that I'd seen in Kason's all day.

The lights turned off and the course was lit up with white lights, illuminating the entire mountain for not only the snowboarders but also for the crowd to get a good view of the course.

"Hey, you two."

I glanced over my shoulder. Mr. and Mrs. McCloud squeezed their way through the crowd to get to us up front. "Hi."

We stood shoulder to shoulder as the slopestyle event began. My nerves kicked into overdrive, growing more intense as the first seven snowboarders flipped through the air, some landing flawlessly and some slipping a little at the end of their run. Despite their finish, the crowd cheered like each of them had won the event. Then, everyone turned to the nearby leaderboard to await the score. Ousterman, who was Kason's biggest competition, scored a forty-six on his first run. And, the other six were high thirties and low forties.

Knowing Kason was up next, I pulled in a deep breath and tried to relax for him since I knew it's what he needed. A new song began to reverberate off the mountain from the speakers. I broke into laughter.

"What's so funny?" Giselle asked.

"This is 'What You Give' by Tesla."

"So?"

"It's my favorite song," I explained.

"Well, I guess we know why he chose it," she said.

"And, now we have McCloud's first run of the night," the announcer said.

Everyone around me cheered as I squinted, even with my contacts in I could only see a tiny figure moving down the mountain. Knowing it was Kason—and he was snowboarding to *my* song—had my heart jumping out of my chest. I looked to the nearby screen to get a closer look at his run. I held my breath as he made his first jump, flipping and twisting through the air as if it was the easiest thing in the world to do. The crowd screamed and I released my breath as he landed the jump flawlessly. He continued to the next jump, disappearing behind the huge ramp, then reappearing when he was in the air, reaching down and grabbing his board with his good hand as he flipped several times. The crowd cheered and I released another breath as he landed that trick without falling. He was nearing his last jump. He disappeared behind the ramp once more before summersaulting through the air in what felt like slo-mo. He came down hard but managed to stay upright. He thrust his arms in the air and the crowd around me exploded into cheers. As he came to a stop at the bottom of the mountain with a huge smile on his face, a spray of snow kicked up all around him.

Thayer and Jesse waited for him inside the fencing, clapping him on the tiger-striped helmet for what I assumed to be a great first run.

Everyone, including Kason, looked to the leaderboard, waiting for his score to appear. After a long moment, a forty-six lit up the screen.

The crowd cheered, and Giselle turned to me and

hugged me so tightly I thought she'd cut off circulation. Once she released me, she yelled to Kason. "Nice job, little brother!"

I looked to Kason who nodded like he'd expected that. But knowing him, I knew he wanted more. Especially, if he was going to beat Ousterman for the gold.

He turned our way. And, though his snowboard goggles covered most of his face and I couldn't see his eyes, I had a feeling they were trained on me.

A rush of excitement pulsed through me. That was *my* man. And, he looked so damn good doing what he loved. He had no reason to be so worried. He had this.

Kason's next two runs were just as good as his first, but he couldn't get higher than forty-six which put him at a ninety-two. Fortunately, Ousterman hadn't either. So, as we awaited the final run, it was clear that either Kason or Ousterman would end up with the gold. It was just a matter of who pulled off the best tricks in their final run.

My phone vibrated in my pocket just as the first snowboarder dropped in. I pulled off my heavy gloves, unzipped my jacket a little, and reached inside my inner pocket. I checked the screen and Snowboard Hottie was calling. My stomach dropped, terrified as to why he'd be calling. I pushed my way through the noisy crowd and headed toward one of the lodge's inset-doorways as I answered. "What's wrong?"

He laughed. "Nothing's wrong. I just wanted to hear your voice."

I reached the doorway and could hear him much clearer. "You're crazy. You need to go."

"In a sec. How do you think I'm doing?"

"Oh my God, you're doing amazing!" I couldn't contain my pride, especially since he seemed so much happier than he'd been all day. "Do you have something good up your sleeve for this final run?"

"I sure hope so."

The next snowboarder was announced.

"Okay, go," I urged Kason. "You need to focus before your run."

"You help me focus, Shay. There's something about you that makes everything better."

My heart tripped over itself. "Are you seriously going to say something like that to me when you're a mountain away?"

"You want me to say it again when I get to the bottom?" he asked.

"Yes," I laughed. "But, only *after* you're holding the gold."

"Will you still want me if I don't get it?" He suddenly sounded serious again.

The crowd cheered as the snowboarder's score appeared on the board.

"Of course," I assured him.

"Promise?" he asked as the next snowboarder was announced and began his run.

"Yes! Now go!"

"See you soon," he said before finally hanging up.

I laughed to myself as I tucked my phone away and hurried back to the crowd, pushing my way through and apologizing as I did.

Once I got to the front, Giselle turned to me with concern on her face. "Where'd you go?"

"Your crazy brother just called me."

"Oh, thank God."

"What?" I asked, confused by her reaction.

The announcer's voice came over the speaker announcing Ousterman.

"He finally told you," Giselle explained.

I cocked my head. "Told me what?"

Her eyes grew wide. "Forget it."

*Forget it?* "Tell me."

Her eyes cast down. "He's going to kill me."

"Giselle. What's going on? He's been acting weird all day."

"He told Cora's dad he'd win the gold medal if they promised not to press charges against you."

My mouth fell open just as Ousterman came down the mountain. I could barely register what was happening. The events of the day came flooding back. Kason's nerves. His reluctance to talk or eat. His phone call. He was terrified that he wouldn't win the gold, and my future would be destroyed.

I could barely breathe. I thought Cora's family agreed not to press charges. Kason had assured me of that. Now, I learned my future hung in the balance—all reliant on his final run. *That* was the agreement? *Jesus. Christ.*

Ousterman reached the bottom, and his team jumped all over him. From what I could tell from the excitement of all the fans around me, he'd killed his final run. He'd upped his game, and I had no idea if Kason could up his. I turned to the screen with my heart lodged in my throat, waiting for Ousterman's score to appear on the board while my world felt like it was crumbling down around me again. The calm I'd felt since learning I wouldn't be punished was replaced by fear. The all-consuming, body-trembling, can't-think-straight fear.

A roar erupted all around before I could even process

the forty-eight that lit up the board bringing him to a ninety-four.

Giselle and the McClouds wore the same disappointed expressions on their faces, knowing beating a forty-eight was going to be nearly impossible given the judges had only awarded one of those all night.

"McCloud, waiting to drop in, will be our final competitor of the night," the announcer said as Kason's music started up. This time he'd opted for "Fly to the Angels" by Slaughter. I found the selection apropos since I once told him he *flew* when he snowboarded.

Giselle wrapped her arm through mine, sticking close to my side. We both knew what this run meant, and I could barely breathe. I looked to the screen with bated breath as Kason teetered on the top of the course. I sent up a silent prayer before he dropped in, zig-zagging down the mountain to gain speed. He hopped on the curved rail—something he hadn't done all night—and slid across it, flipping off the end of it. Everyone around me cheered, but my nerves kept me quiet. He ascended the first ramp, flipping and spinning through the air, though this time it looked like more flips than he'd done in his first three runs. The crowd roared as Giselle jumped up and down, taking me with her.

"That was a backside double cork 1170!" the announcer reported.

"Is that good?" I asked Giselle.

"*Yes!* If that was what he did for his first jump, it means he has something better planned for his next two."

He hit his next jump. I held my breath as he flew higher than he had all night, grabbing his board with his good hand and flipping himself around at least four times before he landed.

I released my breath as the crowd cheered, hoping to God the judges were seeing what we were seeing.

He approached his final jump. I almost couldn't watch. I knew he'd give this final jump everything he had left but worried it still wouldn't be enough to push him past Ousterman's forty-eight.

I watched as he sped up the ramp, coming over the top in what seemed like slow motion. I held my breath as he made four rotations and three flips.

"That was a switch backside triple cork 1620!" the announcer shouted as Kason landed.

He threw his arms in the air, spraying snow everywhere as he came to a stop at the bottom of the mountain. His friends jumped all over him.

I looked to Giselle with expectant eyes, knowing I hadn't seen anything like that all night. "That was good, right?"

She threw her arms around me and jumped up and down. "Amazing!"

"Was it enough?" I asked, almost scared to hear the answer.

"I hope so." She released me and we both turned to the leaderboard.

The seconds ticked by, and still no score appeared. My body trembled and I couldn't control it.

"What's taking so long?" I asked Giselle as I glanced to Kason who had removed his goggles and was now also staring at the leaderboard.

"No idea," she said.

"Sorry, for the delay," the announcer said.

I looked back to the board as a big fifty lit up the screen! Kason's name moved ahead of Ousterman's to the top of the leaderboard with ninety-six next to it!

Laughter tumbled out of me as relief washed over me. I turned to see Kason who thrust his snowboard up in the air. His smile mirrored the elation sweeping through my body. His friends lifted him up in the air as he searched for me. He pointed to me with his cast and shook his head, a mix of disbelief and relief playing across his features.

Giselle hugged me, pulling my attention away from Kason. Then, the McClouds were there hugging us both.

I had never felt the love I felt in that moment ever before in my life.

## 45

## KASON

I finished my interviews then searched the crowd for Shay and my family. People patted me on the back as I moved through the crowded space. When I spotted my family near the lodge, I made a beeline for them.

"Hey!"

My parents rushed to me and threw their arms around me. "Congratulations!"

I laughed as I stepped out of their arms. "Thanks. I'm pretty stoked." I looked around, searching for Shay. But my sister stepped in front of me, throwing her arms around me. "You killed it, baby brother." Her voice lowered so our parents didn't hear. "Thank *God*."

I laughed, knowing exactly what she meant. The stress of not getting the gold was a son-of-a-bitch. I stepped back from her and looked around. "Where's Shay?"

She pointed behind me.

I twisted around. Shay stood there looking like an adorable Eskimo. I stepped to her with opened arms, but she pressed her palms to my chest and shoved me backward.

"Whoa. What was that for?"

"Don't you *ever* do something like that for me again," she warned.

I glanced over her shoulder at a guilty Giselle who mouthed, "Sorry."

I smirked before moving back into Shay's space and wrapping my arms around her. Despite her feeble attempts to break loose from my hold, I tightened my arms and lowered my chin to the top of her head. "If I don't, who will?"

She said nothing.

"Let me love you, Shay Miller. Let me love you the way you deserved to be loved all those years."

She began to sniffle.

*Shit.* I pulled back to be sure she was okay. Tears pooled in her eyes and she didn't even bother swatting them away as they trailed down her cheeks. "Shay?"

"That was such a stupid thing you did."

I pulled off my glove and lifted my fingertips to her cheek, wiping her tears away. "I'd do it again if I had to. I love you."

Her eyes widened.

"Yes, I just said that," I assured her, knowing I'd just put it all out there. "And, I meant it."

She closed her eyes as if taking in my words—and hopefully *believing* my words.

"I told you from the top of that mountain," I continued. "And I'm telling you again now. There's something about *you*, Shay. Something that makes me want to be a better man." She opened her teary eyes and stared into mine. "You showed me who I could be, and I'm working every day to show you *that's* who I really am."

"I know," she said softly, her lips curving. "I love you too."

My head snapped back. I'd *hoped* she felt the same way I did, but I wasn't crazy enough to expect it. I leaned forward, my eyes riveting between hers. "Thank God you wanted that music turned down."

Laughter tumbled out of her. "Thank God. Now, let me see this medal."

It hung around my neck so I held it up for her to see.

"You did it," she said with pride coloring her tone.

"I did it."

"Was it worth it?" she asked, obviously aware of how much had been on the line.

I shrugged. "You're worth it." Not caring who was around, I lifted her right off the ground. Holding her with my arm in a cast wasn't easy, so she helped, wrapping her legs around my hips and draping her arms over my shoulders. "You've always been worth it."

Our lips collided. And, despite all my shortcomings and flaws, Shay loved me. The *real* me.

46

———

SHAY

I lay with my head on Kason's bare chest with him on the verge of falling asleep. We'd returned from Aspen earlier and finally had some alone time together after celebrating his gold medal win with his friends and family.

"Shay! Kendall's here!" Thayer called from downstairs.

I tipped my head back to meet Kason's tired eyes. "She probably wants to congratulate you."

He smirked, and I couldn't believe I once loathed such a butterfly-inducing look. "You mean, she wants to see my medal up close and personal?"

I rolled my eyes as I climbed off his bed, tugging one of his T-shirts over my head and pulling on my jeans. "Put some clothes on if you're coming downstairs," I said to him before hurrying downstairs.

When I got to the living room, Kendall smiled. "Welcome back."

Kason came downstairs wearing his boxers, dangling his medal in his good hand. "Hey, Kendall. Are you here to see my medal?"

"No," she said, shutting him right down. "But congrats." She held up her phone. "I have something I need you both to hear."

Kason and I exchanged a glance, having no idea what she'd need us to hear.

She tapped on her phone, and a recording began to play.

"Your turn, Cora," a girl on the recording said.

"Well..." Cora began. "I pulled the fire alarm in my dorm so I could clear the dorm and replace some bitch's shampoo with hair dye." Cora laughed. "Her hair turned *orange*."

The girls on the recording broke into a chorus of *oohs* and laughter.

Kendall switched off the recording.

After having such an amazing time at the Games and Kason telling me he loved me, I didn't like being reminded of something so terrible. Why did Kendall think I'd want to hear that? "I don't get it," I said.

"I told some of the sorority sisters what happened with you and Cora. They have friends at Cora's sorority who can't stand her. Apparently, they're ruthless and make their pledges spill every secret they've got before allowing them to become sisters. *And*, they record them."

"Yeah, but we know Cora did it," I said.

"Yes, but we didn't realize she pulled the fire alarm in order to do it."

I was unclear where she was going with this. She was right that we hadn't considered the fire alarm being a decoy while Cora replaced my shampoo. But, I still didn't understand why that was a good thing.

"Pulling a fire alarm is a misdemeanor," Thayer added

from the sofa where he'd been playing a video game. "Punishment's a thousand dollar fine or a year in jail."

Excitement flashed in Kendall's eyes. "Exactly."

"How do you know that?" Kason asked Thayer.

"My law class."

"You normally skip that class," Kason said.

"Not that day," he said. "Apparently, pulling an alarm holds such a steep punishment since first responders are taken away from real emergencies to deal with the false alarm. So, it's not only a crime but a real shitty thing to do."

Realization hit me and my eyes shot to Kason. "Oh my God."

"What?" he asked. "You want Cora to go to prison?"

I shook my head, not caring what happened to her. "If her dad knows we have that recording and could take it to the police at any time, he'll want to keep us quiet."

"Yeah," Kason said, but the tone of his voice and the confused look in his eyes told me he still wasn't completely getting it.

"He'll offer *anything* to keep us quiet," I explained.

His eyes widened. "Like letting me out of our sponsorship agreement."

I nodded.

"Holy shit," he said, before looking to Kendall. "I'd hug you right now if I didn't think my girl would hurt me."

Kendall and I laughed as Kason swept me up in his arms and spun me around. "Kincaid. Here I come!"

I laughed at his excitement and the realization that he'd no longer be stuck in a bad situation because of something *I* did.

"This is only the beginning, Shay," he assured me. "With Kincaid, we're gonna travel this world together and fill that bracelet."

"Promise?"

He pressed his lips to mine, and that was all the promise I needed.

# EPILOGUE
## KASON

hay lay topless on her stomach as Mack, the tattoo artist I'd used in the past, pressed the ink gun to her back. I'd arranged for Mack to give her ink since he was a burly older guy. There was no way I was letting any of the younger guys touch my girl. Shay had been a real trooper, laying in that spot in the tattoo parlor for over two hours. And, she hadn't cried. Not even once.

"How's it look?" she asked for the hundredth time.

From my seat beside her, I took in the scar on her back that was almost non-existent now that Mack had been working on it. Though it was a bitch to tattoo over a scar, Mack wasn't necessarily trying to conceal it. He used it as a stem, trailing delicate small flowers off of it. I wasn't a deep guy by any stretch of the imagination. But even I couldn't ignore the symbolism of it all. Something so ugly—and done from such an ugly place—was turning into something so beautiful. "It looks amazing. I can't wait for you to see it."

She smiled and warmth spread to my chest. She smiled more these days. She was lighter. Happier. And, with Cora transferring colleges, Shay had nothing else to be weary of.

Besides, she had me and my boys now. No one would ever mess with her again.

"You're gonna have to come back in for me to shade in all the flowers," Mack explained.

"Can you handle that?" I asked Shay.

"I think you're forgetting who you're talking to," she said.

"Never." I would have laughed if I wasn't staring at the remnants of the scar on her back. I knew she'd endured a lot. And, little by little, she'd revealed more about her time in that trailer. I never pushed her. I always let her tell me what she wanted to tell me. I also didn't push her to see her father when he called to check in from rehab. She'd hear him out, saying very little as she listened to whatever he said on his end. I could tell she planned to keep him at arm's length, despite his success in recovery. And, if that's what she needed to do in order to move on and live a healthy life, then I supported her wholeheartedly. Truthfully, I didn't trust myself not to knock the son-of-a-bitch out if I ever met him. So, hopefully that day never came. Besides, she had my family now, and they loved her like their own.

"You gonna chicken out of your tattoo?" she asked me from the tattoo chair.

"I think *you're* forgetting who you're talking to," I said.

"Never."

I chuckled as I held out my arm and twisted it until I showed her the last vacant space on my bicep. "I'm putting one of your flowers right here."

She smiled, and I knew it came from a place of contentment and security. She wasn't worried I'd up and leave her. She knew this thing between us was real. I tried to prove it to her with everything I said and everything I did—hence the matching flower on my arm I'd be getting when she was done. I enjoyed giving her stuff like that because I knew it meant so much to her.

But, what she didn't realize—what she'd probably never realize—was that her loving me was the best gift she could have ever given *me*. I was a self-centered asshole when we met and, somehow, she actually looked past all my indiscretions and gave me a shot. *Thank fuck.* So, if anyone were to ask what drew me to Shay in the first place, I'd tell them it was the other way around. What drew Shay to *me*? Then, I'd tell them it wasn't her feisty attitude or her nerdy glasses and braids that had me falling for her. I'd tell them what I told her at the Games. There was just something about her that made me a better man. Maybe it was everything she'd gone through and still came out on top. Maybe it was the way she put me in my place. Maybe it was the way she didn't back down from a challenge. Or, maybe...it was just the way I felt when she smiled at me.

Regardless of what brought us together, I knew with much certainty that there was nothing in this world I wouldn't do for Shay Miller.


If you enjoyed Kason and Shay's story, be sure to check out Thayer and Giselle's story, *Something About Her*.

# ACKNOWLEDGMENTS

Thank you so much for taking the time to read Kason and Shay's story. I hope you enjoyed it! I love reading opposite attract and enemies-to-lovers romances, so this was so incredibly fun to write!

To all the bloggers, bookstagrammers, booktokers, and readers who have continued to share my books. I say it every time, but it's the truth. I could never do this without all of you! Thank you so very much!

To my wonderful ARC team who read and reviewed *Something About You,* as well as my other books. I am so lucky to have such a extraordinary group of ladies on my team! Love all of you!

To my reader's group, *J. Nathan's Book Boyfriend Lovers.* Thank you for being such a wonderful group! We may be small, but it makes me feel as though I know all of you! Thank you so much for interacting and for loving my books!

To my wonderful beta readers: Dali, Renee, Kim, Megan, Maria, Jill, and Kerrie. Thank you for always suggesting things that I can tweak! Your feedback means the world to me—regardless of how minor you might think it is!

To my editor Stephanie Elliot. Thank you for always making me a priority and for always giving it to me straight. You know how much I appreciate you (don't roll your eyes like my characters) when I say it again. You're the best!

To my always wonderful proofreaders, Gemma, from

Gem's Precise Proofreading, and Peggy. Thank you so much for being my eyes before I put my books out for the world to read!! I always know I'm giving readers a flawless book after you two get a hold of it. Ha!

To my wonderful PA Renee. Thank you for your brutal honesty—whether I mean-face emoji you or not, I still appreciate it! You are always my gauge if a book is ready. So, thanks for loving Kason and Shay!

To Kate at Y'all. That Graphic for creating another beautiful cover and amazing teasers! I'm so happy you still agree to work with me after how difficult I can be. LOL!

To Michelle Lancaster for the amazing photo of the gorgeous Anthony Patamisi. Your work never ceases to amaze me!! Thank you so very much for being so wonderful to work with!!

A big thank you to Grey's PR for your assistance with this release! You are a breeze to work with and so organized! Thank you, Josette for the gorgeous graphics!!

And, last but never least, thank you to my family. I am so lucky to have your love and support!

ALSO BY J. NATHAN

For You Standalone Sports Series:

Book #1 *For Finlay*

Book #2 *For Forester*

Book #3 *For Crosby*

Book #4 *For Emery*

Savage Beasts Standalone Rock Star Series:

Book #1 *Kozart*

Book #2 *Treyton*

Standalones:

*The Trouble with Players*

*All Your Tomorrows*

*Seren*

*I Just Need You*

*You're the Reason*

*Until Alex*

*Before Hadley*

*Since Drew*